Also by Carole Spearin McCauley

Fiction

HAPPENTHING IN TRAVEL ON

SIX PORTRAITS: WILD BIRDS ON A WINTER MOUNTAIN

Nonfiction

COMPUTERS AND CREATIVITY

PREGNANCY AFTER 35

SURVIVING BREAST CANCER

THE HONESTY TREE

by
Carole Spearin McCauley

FROG IN THE WELL
430 Oakdale Road
East Palo Alto, CA 94303

1985

All of the characters in this book
are fictitious, and any resemblance
to actual persons, living or dead,
is coincidental.

Library of Congress Cataloging in Publication Data

McCauley, Carole Spearin
  The Honesty Tree

  I. Title
PS3563.C3375H6   1985   813'.54   84-25905
ISBN 0-9603628-6-X

2288560

ACKNOWLEDGEMENT

The author thanks Paula Estey, editor of MAENAD, Gloucester, Massachusetts, for her support and encouragement. Chapters 2, 18, 19, and 20 appeared originally in the premiere issue of MAENAD.

there is nothing higher and stronger and more wholesome and good for life than some good memory, especially a memory of childhood. . . . and if one has only one good memory left in one's heart, even that may some time be the means of saving us.

HONESTY—hardy biennial of the family Cruciferae (from the crosslike arrangement of the flower's four petals). It is an attractive everlasting plant, two to four feet high, that bears heart-shaped, coarsely toothed leaves and pink or lavender sweet-scented flowers that bloom in May.

Commercially, **HONESTY** is widely grown for its decorative seed pods, gathered when the seeds begin to lose their green color and marketed just before Christmas. The name **HONESTY** probably arose because the seeds are visible through the pods that resemble silver discs, no thicker than a dime. Also called Satinpod, Moonwort, Chinese money tree.

Many legends surround **HONESTY**. Medieval witches valued it to numb the senses and produce the feeling of flying. It is thought they smeared their broomsticks with it.

The similar but less ornamental perennial **HONESTY** with oblong pods is also cultivated in certain locations.

OUTLAND
The Sixties

Dear Jody,

I don't know what you're into out there now, but I have a proposition for you: How'd you like to share a $100,000+ yearly business?

Remember you said if you had to be propositioned, you'd prefer it by a woman than a man? It would be *different,* anyway. You haven't written for a while; I assume you're busy. Or creatively dropping out, you Eternal Ski Bum!

My father died about three months ago of a stroke. The towns-people here were most helpful—they can be understanding sometimes, visiting the hospital, bringing food, nursing him so I could get free enough to tend the phone and the business. You've never seen the greenhouses, the nursery, or my home, but I think it isn't too different from where you live outside Boulder. There's even a ski slope here but, of course, nothing to compare with all those big bumps you gaze at in Colorado. I miss Boulder sometimes and our life as roommates and sister skiers—although not all that artificial pressure for exams and grades. I rejoice that phase is forever over.

Briefly my proposition is this: my business grosses around $100,000 a year and could easily make more if I had someone *dependable* to assist things I do only halfway now ("half-ass" as you'd say)—more advertising, more personal deliveries of orders to customers (I want to replace my station wagon with a truck or van), repairing the back greenhouse for use, etc. Currently I have a student, Nathan, part time from the college in town, but he's so eternally stoned or late that I consider sacking him.

Obviously I want and prefer an adult and a woman, so I thought of you, Jody. How you used to preach Independence Forever from Everything in those philosophy classes we sat through. Theory of the Creative Dropout or how did you call it?

3

Let me know. A living and a house await you if you're interested. This is a partnership, of course, not just a job.

Love,
Eila

Boulder, Colorado
April 22

Dear Eila,
Greetings from the land of—you guessed it—the Eternal Ski Bum! Or: what would life be without a parka and a windburn?
Been raining here three weeks. Hell on the tulips, great for the dandelions. Haven't skied seriously all that much. Don't get away more than once a week, that mostly for job interviews in Salt Lake or Denver. Big cities not for me. Couple months ago stopped looking for another phys ed job. Wanted further break from school teaching and get a gymnasium or Y job someplace. Answered one today:
WOMEN'S GYM TEACHER
Exclusive spa needs experienced all-around gal.
Call Miss O'Casey.
Not more demeaning than all the rest?
Problem #X: only places offer decent money are in polluted cities.
Also (real reason): my mother is dying of lung cancer and it's heavy happening even with all of us, my father and brother, helping. My family always was a real family; we loved each other. Feel I can't leave now. You remember my mother. No way is she a hypochondriac but the bravest lady facing an impossible time.
But don't hire anybody else permanent, huh, for your nursery? Give me time.
Can you come see me? Talk further?

Love,
Jody

Endfield
April 24

Dear Jody,
Am sorry to hear all you're coping with. Of course, I remember your mother. She was one whizz at poker that night we all played. Keep me informed how she does.

If you're serious about wanting me to come, I'll certainly try. After spring (Easter/Mother's Day) rush on the nursery here would be best for me. Business has been good; 100 customers last Sunday from neighboring towns, plus tourists. As Nathan said, "They're coming like Indians over the hill." I know our old skeptic friends would attack it all—a few bandaids of azaleas won't save the private lawn, let alone the nuclear family. But I enjoy handling greens and blooms—less complicated than people! Or maybe I feel I'm lifting the curse put on this New England soil. "Stone's got a heavy mortgage on this land" is how they say it here.

I enjoy helping people in this specific, limited way where my skill is sure. I'm contemplating a sign for my desk: "I CAN'T SOLVE YOUR LIFE, JUST YOUR AZALEA." It would warn Nathan to whom I've become, much against my will, a mother figure. He's currently off drugs because he believes they're ruining his mind. I heartily concur.

If you're serious, I'll make a plane reservation via LaGuardia for beginning of July for a few days' stay. Will you meet me at Stapleton Airport?

Eila

Boulder

Dear Eila,
Can do. Send word. Love, J.

INLAND
The Seventies

1

Eila dear,

I'm leaving early in the truck so I'll reach the show before all the best deals in shrubs and equipment are gone. Otherwise, it's "buy dear and sell cheap," like you're always kidding me when you pay invoices!

About Tinker's mother: If she calls and complains again about "child labor" or connected rubbish, tell her we'll pay Tinker for office work until the second week of June or so. Spring and graduation rush over then. Maybe I can get her a job at the library.

You know more about this town than I do, but that woman strikes me as jealous and vicious. Or maybe just full of problems —justified? Who knows? She could harm us or our whole business we've built. Better avoid her. I know you've got used to Tinker in the office because she's intelligent and useful but we shouldn't risk it. How do you feel about it this morning?

Love,
Jody

2

TINKER'S ADULT SURVIVAL KIT
(Endfield Cripplers to Avoid)

- Nice girls don't.
- Bad girls do.
- If it feels good, it must be bad—not to mention sinful.
- If it feels bad, repress it, for dwelling on it is unladylike—not to mention useless.
- When all else fails, gossip, blame, offer it up to God who must be the most bored man in the Universe.

Dear World: There's *got* to be a better way!....Through loving a few other people, like Eila and Jody, and earning a living, I've found it—outside Endfield....

It got to be a recession time in the town with all the buckling down, knuckling under, and shredding apart that implies. Even the town's bricked and ivied college had managed to lose its endowment through overspending in the era of plenty. So the year I was twelve, Ferncliff College at least had mounted a fundraising campaign that my father was chairing so that they would notice, finally promote and tenure him. So my mother could stop complaining about money, dirt on the floor, her heart condition, her sister's heart attack, my father, and me in that order of declining importance.

In my grandmother's phrase, the town was "young enough to stay alive and old enough to know better, as the rest of us should be." By tradition, Endfield is a farming community although there are few working dairy or crop farms left. During Daniel Shays' whiskey rebellion, a few embattled farmers massed and hid bottles up on the Ledge overlooking the town to avoid paying Federal liquor taxes, George Washington's new government being merely a rerun of King George and taxation they thought they'd just defeated.

And that's about the most exciting event in the town since 1790 until "a few hooligans and that riffraff from the College" set fire to Green Acres Inn as part of V-E Day merrymaking in 1945. Or until Eila came back with Jody and started running Brandi's Florist/Nursery that Eila's father had left her.

Endfield is, of course, a solidly Republican community. It's still said that all the Endfield Democrats could hold their meetings in a phone booth, although everybody speculates on what Ted Kennedy may still do to change all that. In any case, city people, even those who own summer homes and form "the ski and racquet crowd" or flaunt their money in other delicious ways, are not much loved.

Other than the quarry, the one towrope ski slope (without a snow-maker), and the Main Street of small businesses, you might say the town's chief industry is education, with private Ferncliff College and its funny students helping bail out the new regional school. That school has eaten 75% of town revenues for years; I was a member of its first seventh grade class. You might even think townspeople liked children until you hear the claptrap about "too many frills nowdays," this being merely a recycled version of "too many mouths to feed" from my grandparents' time when families waxed while parental patience waned.

When in gear, all those mouths, besides eating too much, sought their other diversion—gossiping—preferably unchallenged by the current victim. To challenge publicly the rot said about you was "in poor taste," "something a Pole or an Italian but not a lady would do." That's another way Jody seemed different—mostly she did what she wanted without a hang what people thought.

I realize now that the best service the older generation performed on its sons and daughters was to gossip us half to death so we left the town at half an opportunity, fiercely hopeful of a saner life elsewhere, preferably sheltered in the anonymity of a city like the one where I now work. After all, if they made it too soft and welcoming for you back there, you'd never leave, would you? You wouldn't have to.

Once I asked Eila why she came back after college in Colorado. "My roots are here. The green hills of home." Eila turned dreamy and po-etic sometimes, and I thrilled to that. It was a change from invoices. "Besides, I sort of missed the place." A year later she attended a re-union out West and brought Jody back with her.

I do know that if I'd never found Jody and Eila nor worked at their nursery, I'd never have escaped Endfield at all, away from my mother especially. I'd never have needed to. You can't cut any cord until you figure where it's strangling—and find who will help you wield the knife.

Jody with her eager eyes, generous smile, spriggy hair, and bustling *energy* (Endfield's women had a power shortage long before the nation discovered its own) made a figure none of us kids could miss.

Dressed in jeans and an old hunting shirt, she hired a bunch of us including me and my best friend, Pammy, off and on to help with the nursery work. She showed us how to plant seeds in straight rows, water just enough to avoid drowning them, rip sheets and use the strings to tie tomato plants until our hands turned greenly acrid. Most of all, she taught us how to walk and talk around living things. Of the kids she hired for odd jobs and beginning fifty cents an hour, I was the only one who stuck, partly because I lived just a few houses down Laurel Street. The other kids turned to paper routes, caddying, or babysitting just as soon or however long it took for what Catholics call "the age of reason" to hit.

People seemed to forgive Jody her irregular appearance and ways (although they gossiped behind her back) because she worked hard, told jokes, and never waited for you to say hello first. And she was supposed to be from Colorado where people were funny, anyway. At least they talked funny.

Once in a while if a Western, or mid-Western, came on tv, Jody dropped her cowboy hat onto her forehead, slouched on her spine, slung her feet onto a chair, and did her Old Ranger imitation where "things" became "thengs" and "penny" became "pinny."

Eila and I loved it, laughed and laughed. To me, Jody was the only woman in Endfield who dared to be laughed at, could be different without being thought "crazy." At first the town, except for my mother and other prematurely dispirited souls, seemed to enjoy Jody and forgive her because, "Of course, you have to remember she's an outsider, one of them she-radicals," I heard Mrs. Black say. I was young and dumb enough then to confuse an ounce of toleration with a pound of acceptance.

When I childishly repeated this comment to Jody, she answered, "Tinker, I think it's *ski* radicals she meant."

"What's that?"

"Well, once I showed Mrs. Black the trophy I won at Aspen. It's on the mantelpiece in the livingroom. You've seen it."

"Were you really *good?*" Told often I was helpless, hopeless, and awkward by my parents, I was easily awed by adult skills.

"You bet!" Jody laughed. " 'Course the trophy's only plastic. Our ski club was the last of the small-time cheapies. . . . Eila, how come I can't get you to go skiing with me on that one-ass slope you got here?''

Eila gazed from the check ledger where she was paying bills. Her forehead crinkled. "Look, skiing's for tourists and teenagers. . . . How about helping me arrange flowers for the Sayvilles' wake? Bill is bringing the hearse by at five."

Eila was tall and thin with white skin and kind eyes. She had shining black hair that she held back with woven or wooden headbands. When she moved, her hair swung free like a curtain, all in one piece. Of the women in Endfield, she was the one I most yearned to resemble. Of course, I never would and still don't. What can a skinny, left-handed 12-year-old make of stringy carrot hair, no bust, no hips, and braces on her teeth?

I was named after the Catholic saint Theresa. Not the strong lady of Avila but the other one, Theresa of Lisieux, alias the Little Flower, "remarkable for her piety and for her patience in enduring suffering caused by pulmonary hemorrhages." I remember when I was about seven, one old nun who coughed a lot caught me after Mass for fooling around and giggling during it. She led me by the hand to the convent and in the piano lesson room, gave me a talk on disrespect plus a pamphlet on Theresa describing each hemorrhage in goriest detail. I was to "meditate on it," with the strong suggestion that life's reverses, not to mention God's punishment, awaited those who Disobeyed. In other words, just about what I was receiving at home with a couple celibate and devotional twinges added.

Obviously I was baptised Theresa because somebody hoped I would flower—with or without benefit of pulmonary hemorrhages. All I had managed by the age of twelve, however, was to grow like a weed and develop one thorn after another, first criminal, then sexual. In Endfield and for girls, the two were still equated.

I know now what the wrong brand of religious training achieved: It screwed people up by downplaying the good-joyful in favor of the dangerous-forbidden. In this vale of tears: *Thou shalt not enjoy!* Stolen fruits waxed overdelicious. And if even thoughts are sinful—well, I'd rather be hanged for a sheep than a lamb. Now whenever I hear, "Jesus died for our sins," I add, "Let's not disappoint him."

That year my mother was already nagging me about learning to bouffant and tease my hair in rollers the way she did. The two nights I rolled and sprayed my head before a Christmas party resembled sleeping on a bushel of potatoes left in an airplane glue factory.

"You want to look like the other girls, don't you?"

"Yuh, I guess so. But it comes out straight no matter what I do.

And I don't even have a date. So what difference does it make?''

"Why don't you join that history club again?''

"Because Mr. McKenna gave it up until next semester. And I'm working Tuesday afternoons now anyway.''

My mother took the books and folk LPs off the chair next to my study table and slid them onto the floor. She put her hand around my right wrist. Always a bad sign, in the same class with calling me Theresa instead of Tinker, usually in preface to another "Your father and I" talk. . . .

"Theresa, your father and I,'' she began. "Well, we wish you would stop working at the florist. I know, I know.'' She raised her hand an inch, then replaced it. "You earn your pocket money and bought your new shoes. Your father and I will give you pocket money for a while. At your age you should be. . . spending more time with girls your own age. We just want what's best for you, you know. Pammy isn't, well, from the best element but what about Ellen? You could see her more.''

"Ellen keeps getting sick. Her mother says excitement bothers the eczema. Besides, who wants to play with somebody who sits in bed and scratches when you go to see her?'' I took my wrist away.

As usual, my mother signed and stared into space.

"You're very *stubborn,* you know, Tinker. Just like your father. It's hard for me, Tinker. At your age you don't realize that. I—''

"But I like working at the nursery. Jody and Eila are. . . happy. Jody makes jokes and—''

"Jokes? Look, *some* people can afford to find life a big joke. They have good husbands or good children. Or they have a bank roll. Or they didn't get married at all.''

"Is that why you're mad at Jody?''

"I'm not mad at her or Eila. I just think you spend too much time with those older women. And too little time helping me here.'' Getting up, she stuck her hands across her hips and faced me. "Tinker, I'm expecting another baby. That is, I'm pregnant again after the miscarriages. I hope it'll be a little brother for you. Your father wants a son. You're old enough now to understand about these things. Maybe you'll help me take care of him. It will be in June when you get out of school.''

I squirmed in my chair, too confused to answer. So I just looked at her, said, "Maybe'' as pleasantly as I could manage. Right then I hated her for belittling me and Jody both and then expecting me to care about the baby. I know now I resented everything awry in our family— her dropping snotty comments against my father among a bunch of sweet stuff, acting sick whenever anybody needed her, but most of all for the mist she exuded that nobody else had the right to problems, especially shocking ones. Once I remember yelling at her she never thought a broken arm or flunking a test or stringy hair or acne were *real* problems.

That describes my enraged moods. In better times I made allowances, based on what she herself explained—that she'd never left Endfield, that my father, despite (or because of) his intellectual interests, was hardly the lively companion she desired, that she'd passed her life under Older Sister Nedda's watchful eye and thumb.

As to the news I was about to inherit a baby brother, I couldn't visualize anything we needed less. I already pitied the poor kid for being born in our house. But I was curious about why grownups who complained about everything—taxes, husbands, the price of pork chops, doctors, priests, schools, children they already had—felt impelled to bring more of them into the world. It didn't seem fair or necessary; it still doesn't.

That night instead of memorizing Civil War battles, I was watching an animal program about a New Mexico rattlesnake called Cotilus. When the tv quieted so everybody could follow the snake on his rounds against rats and mice, I heard my parents through the open door to the kitchen.

"Did you have a good talk with her?"

"No. She won't give up working there and she couldn't care less about the baby. All she cares about is herself."

". . . hard on her. You can't expect a girl that age to care about housework. She's a good kid." Although I resented the "kid," I relished any smidgen of my father's praise. It was rare, and I knew I'd need it later.

"Why aren't you ever here to help me deal with her?" My mother's voice had dropped; I thought she was crying. Now *I* was sighing.

"Because I work. Also I'm trying to raise money so that school can stay in business and not so incidentally, we can still eat. You know I can't get another job in this education market."

". . . mark my words. . . . no good. That Eila—she should have married Jim Donohugh after they went away to college together. And that . . . pig . . . she lives with. Never even wears a dress, just that filthy hunting shirt. You should see their house."

"Jane, we've discussed all this before. At least Tinker's away from the house now, not falling out of trees or shoplifting. She doesn't bother you all the time anymore. She's moody but not the discipline problem she used to be."

"I want her to stop working there. . . . . . says the nursery business has gone downhill every year since Eila's father died."

"That's not what I hear. The Chamber of Commerce just voted at the last lunch to let them join. They'll be the first women members."

"If the town is silly enough to let them in."

When the conversation switched to my aunt's heart attack and how my mother had to go every day to see her, I tuned back to the rattle-snakes. It seemed nice to watch something that, if it molested people, did so only from self-defense and always rattled ahead of time directly to the person concerned, not behind his back somewhere. I also envied the snake his private sunny cave with the thick walls and no need to share a bathroom.

I hated my parents' talking like that and tried to remember when I'd overheard them without Ma delivering a list of complaints, Daddy trying to calm her without really getting involved, and her smiling later to conceal the whole process. It wasn't so much that I always lost, no matter the topic in this contest of bitter whispers. It was more that I never could have won in any difference of opinion involving me.

It has taken me years to see that nobody else won either, least of all my mother. Recently I speed-read a book about biorhythms, conclud-ing that my optimum periods of "intellectual, emotional, and phys-ical zest" coincided with her lowpoints. Paradoxically, she liked me *best* when I ailed with a fever or cold, for then I could be ordered to bed, neutralized with aspirin, sleep, and orange juice, read to like a child again. She felt needed, plus receiving a fresh chance to consult Nedda. . . .

Hearing her insult Jody really burned me. Why didn't I rush into the kitchen and tell her off? *Ladies don't do that. You're not supposed to listen anyhow,* I knew. So, sweaty and flustered, I sat there. I realize now a whole town like that can really do a job on your mind.

I felt sorry for Ma, but chiefly she left me with this deadness, that people afflicted with terminal depression shouldn't marry, go around starting babies—nor finishing off babies. I've learned that people who can't walk straight on solid ground shouldn't hire out as trapeze artists.

The days of comfortable life I'd shared with Eila and Jody were already numbered.

3

Most Saturdays I worked with Eila in the office, answering the phone, writing up orders, mailing bills Eila had made out, filing letters, wrapping cut flowers into cones of green tissue and the bright blue Brandi Nursery paper. We tied everything with red string for the Christmas season and green for the rest of the year.

Usually I walked home to lunch. Occasionally, however, Eila made us sandwiches in the kitchen of her house that was attached to the nursery office. She also brewed coffee in her Chinese red enamel percolator, and we ate at the wooden kitchen table. It was one of those butcher blocks that she never covered with a plastic cloth or even place mats.

The best of eating with Eila was that she never cared if you crumbed up her floor or spilled milk across her table. Sometimes when I talked during those years, I'd wave my arms around. Twice I remember upsetting things, like a tumbler of milk or the whole coffee pot. That time I even got hot coffee on Eila's aqua wool suit, which mortified me because I knew it was one of her favorites. I felt horrible.

I expected her to scream at me, but all she did was get the mop and a rag, swab the coffee and grounds in various directions while I drained them from the butter and the pop-up toaster.

Still shaken, I mumbled apologies. "But what about your suit? I mean, I'll pay to have it cleaned."

She did give her blue, now brown lap a sad stare when we got our breath back from the mopping. All she said, though, was, "Tinker, try to do it better next time, huh? But I tell you what. I'll try spot remover this afternoon, and if the worst doesn't come out, you carry the skirt down to Frank and have him clean it. You can pay for it if you want to." Next she put her arm around me so I *knew* things were all right again. After she found a smock to cover the coffee stains, we returned to work. Eila couldn't remove the spots. I did pay for the suit at the cleaner the following Tuesday.

That was one of the exquisite gifts both Eila and Jody gave away gratisfree. With either of them, although in different ways, you always knew where you stood at any moment. They were people easy to love because they returned more than they took—or at least rarely seemed to begrudge what they had available to give. Nor did they harbor lady-like reservations about some dreadful flaw in your actions or personality (not to mention your soul) and stab you in the back with it six months later.

Once in a while I did make mistakes—misfiled accounts payable invoices into the accounts receivable drawer, left Jody's cutting shears out in the rain, confused Mrs. James Williams with Mrs. Arthur Williams on the phone so Jody delivered potted chrysanthemums to the wrong house and had to drive back when Mrs. Arthur called to report strange flowers on her porch.

Sometimes Eila or Jody did things I didn't like—pile dirty boxes and leaky crates on my office chair, rip an arm of my new sweater left on the cutting table so my mother had to mend it, drop insecticide on my English book so I smelled weird for two weeks. But somehow we always talked it out, made us up. I mean, it all worked.

Two Saturdays before Easter Eila announced, "Jody wants you to help her deliver in the truck today. There's a lot of corsages and spring flowers for Main Street and the country club."

"But what about Danny?"

"Oh, he's coming today, but he'll do wreaths and baskets in the greenhouse for the afternoon trip."

What's up? I wondered, as this was unusual, even for Easter rush. Danny Thomas was the football-type Saturday boy who usually accompanied Jody to help carry heavy pots, baskets, or vases into wherever they'd been ordered. The rest of the week, John, a silent loner from the College, cultivated, fertilized, and arranged in the greenhouse with Jody. He and Jody worked well together, but he'd stroll right by the office picture window without looking up or waving hello to me. My mother claimed I was beneath his dignity. She also called him a sissy intellectual who prostituted himself at the nursery because nobody else would hire him. He was never mean, just distant-different.

That Saturday everything seemed normal at first. After checking Eila's order pile in the office, Jody wrote the names, addresses, and items on her clipboard and walked back to Danny, who had his own sheet and was finishing some orchid or carnation corsages. Jody and I began to load the truck—the usual preholiday assortment of lilies and gladiolas, funeral baskets and sprays, potted hyacinths and African violets. Like Christmas poinsettias, these last required truly loving care—quick loading into either the front seat or the very back of the truck for first delivery to prevent those delicate ruddy leaves from taking cold, getting bashed, or dropping off. If a pot had a narrow base likely to tip, I wedged it between my legs on the front seat until we reached its recipient's house. Still, if you looked at it cross-eyed, those pink petals shrivelled.

I loved delivering wedding bouquets. They were made to be portable into the house, down the church aisle, out to the reception. And the houses of wedding people, right from the door, flowed with smiles, welcomes, jokes, perfume smells, piles of silver and white boxes, flashbulbs exploding. For eats, they offered you free wine, cake, homemade cookies, those tiny sandwich triangles with the crusts gone if they were Protestant and doughnuts if they were Catholic. I remember once asking Jody "What do Jewish wedding families eat?" She said there were a few in town during summer, but mostly they got married back in New York or Long Island. She didn't really know what they ate. I discovered Jody had lived and worked in New York during her college years.

Anyway, wedding people glad-handed you, ushered you right in to meet the bride who dropped whatever she was doing—despairing over her hair, donning her veil, trying lipsticks, crying onto her mother's shoulder (Mary Haggerty did that)—to admire her flowers. Then I'd give her a lesson on how and where to hold the bouquet, to detach the orchid later, so the baby's breath didn't get crushed and the ribbons fell right. Meanwhile Jody distributed red or white carnations to the men's buttonholes or helped the bridesmaids pin on their corsages. Jody's usual joke to, or about, the couple was, "Well, now they're gonna find out how the other half lives, huh?" Sometimes everybody hugged and kissed us goodbye, especially whatever uncles had already drunk more than a few in honor of the bride's health—or the groom's last moments of freedom.

In fact, wherever we drove about town, businessmen enjoyed Jody. I think the men, like Jake and his crew at the garage, favored Jody because she never made them feel guilty as their wives often did. They never had to hide their lit cigars, purify their language in her earshot, or even give her their seat on a milkbox. Within the demands of waiting on customers, they talked freely with her about cars, trucks, hunting trips, politics, weather, the state of the economy. I either tagged along or waited in the front seat of the truck if we were double-parked. That Saturday morning we dropped flowers and wreaths off and picked up checks and money from the Clerk at the Town Hall, Mr. Haggerty at the drug store, the janitor at the College, Mr. Sims at the funeral home.

About the best part of driving with Jody was that once in a while if we got to deliver something on the mountain road or down in Little Italy or out at the cemetery, we got a chance to talk and / or Jody let me try puffs on one of her cigarettes. She smoked them right down to the butt; Eila was always nagging her to quit so Jody could smell the flowers again. That April she'd tapered down to ten smokes a day and was hoping to quit altogether by Easter.

"How old were you when you started smoking?" I asked.

"Oh, just about your age."

"Why did you start?"

"I thought it was a grown-up thing to do. My older brother and my father and mother all smoked. My mother died of lung cancer, too." Jody bit her lips together.

"When was that?"

"About ten years ago. Just before I came here."

"How come you never got married? My mother thinks everybody should marry even if they're no good at it."

"I never wanted to. Guess I was too busy earning a living. Now Eila, she was engaged for a while back in college. Why don't you ask her? She's better at that kind of thing than I am."

"What thing?"

"Thinking about marriage and what it's supposed to be."

"I don't think *anybody* should get married. Weddings are fun, but after that, I mean, Jody, why bother? If all people do, when they've done it, is argue. My mother's expecting a baby, and she's being a real pain about it. It was my father's idea, anyway. No wonder she's mad."

"You know you shouldn't tell me private things like that, Tinker. You should try to settle them somehow between you and your mother. ...But not everybody who gets married lives arguing ever after, you know. Some people really dig each other."

"What is sleeping with a man like? I already asked my mother. All she did was give me some sanitary napkin pamphlet to read so I'd get hooked for life on 'Modess...because.' Took me two weeks to get enough nerve to ask, and then all I get is this crummy pamphlet. And, of course, *that* wasn't in it."

"Slow down, Tinker. Pamphlets are better than nothing at all. She did what she could. . . . About your first question: It depends on the man, what he's like." Jody took a big inhalation on her cigarette.

"You know I've already been. . . with a man." I hated myself for gossiping, but I yearned for her attention to one of my freakier episodes, to help me explain it.

She gave me a sharp glance.

"It was three years ago. Mr. O'Connell at the Five and Ten. He was always alone on Sunday and invited some of us kids, Pammy and me, in."

"And you went?"

"Yeah. He just touched us a little in a few places. Pammy got scared and stopped going, but I went for quite a while. Always on Sunday. My mother thought I was at the movies." Endfield had already taught me to fake a cheerful bravado I didn't feel. I tried it, hoping she wouldn't shut me off or out.

"I think you should have been. . . at the movies."

"He's not working anymore. I guess he retired."

Jody looked straight ahead, concentrating on the road. "No, Tinker. They fired him. It was quite. . . a thing."

"Why did they fire him?"

"Well, they thought he was. . . sick. A man with a wife and grown daughters fooling around with little girls, exposing himself. Especially on Sunday." Jody winked at me. "What a sad guy that man must be."

"Why? I mean, I enjoyed it." More vibrato-bravado, assumed nonchalance to avoid frightening people. Or was I already repressing everything just as Endfield dictated? If it had no name, it didn't exist. . . . I continued, "He had interesting hands, as if he played the violin. He had a music box in the back room and a cow he made water come out of."

"Tinker, they're not all as brave as you."

"You mean as foolhardy, don't you? That's what my mother calls me."

"Did you tell your mother about Bill O'Connell?"

"No. My mother isn't the kind you tell things to. Mostly she tells you. . . about all *her* troubles. Even if you had a trouble of your own, you couldn't get it in edgewise."

"Well, somebody got real scared and told her parents."

"*Really?* Who?"

"Oh, it doesn't matter. It's just gossip by this time. You know what you think of ladies who spend all their time blabbing on the phone."

"Yeah. They're old biddies."

"Yeah. . . . No. They're bored with their own lives. They feel trapped. You just have to feel sorry for them. So don't you gossip, huh?''

"You won't tell me who ratted on Mr. O'Connell."

"No."

"Oh well, you just can't keep a good man down."

"Tinker! That's *obscene* when you apply it to Bill O'Connell. You know what a lecher he was." Jody laughed.

"Obscene is when it's fun but everybody pretends it isn't?"

"Something like that. . . . Tinker, you're something else. How can a poor woman concentrate on driving with you in the car?"

"Aw, quit acting like my mother. I hate that." I wriggled, sweating into the red vinyl seat.

"Okay, I'm sorry. But no more talk about sex while I'm driving, huh?"

"If you fuck, don't drive?"

"*Tin*-ker!"

We both burst out laughing. Jody's face got so red she nearly missed the turnoff to the cemetery. We giggled the whole way along the still frozen road between the fields of tombstones and dirty snow up to the gravediggers' shack where we delivered plastic lily wreaths for Mr. and Mrs. Clark's crypt. The Clarks had thought ahead to get the very best— the built-up kind with stone and metal swinging doors, slate roof, and a dry space that covered both graves. You can't take it with you, but you can erect it around you. The diggers would hang the two wreaths from iron rings on the swinging doors. In life the Clarks had had a maid plus a kitchen with white cabinets and two white swinging doors mounted on all four sides with oblong glass pieces screwed on just where you put your hand.

When I arrived at college and took a poetry course, I found the couplet:

> The grave's a fine and private place,
> But none, I think, do there embrace.

And remembered Mr. and Mrs. Clark and how they were spending eternity pretty much as they'd spent life. Stretched out stiff behind swinging doors.

But at least I'd finally told *somebody,* however ineptly, about Mr. O'Connell and how he'd snared me (Tinker, you snared yourself), about the fascination and horror he'd aroused, then played so skillfully to quiet me. According to my mother even now, "Men only want one thing." However, had she never stressed it, at least I might have discovered it for myself somewhere beyond the mature age of nine. So much for (im)moral education.

This particular Saturday, pink hyacinths for Miss Stanner at the library seemed to be our last stop. Jody pulled into the parking lot behind the pile of cement pillars and granite that housed Endfield's books. When Jody moved neither to examine her clipboard nor open the door, I knew something was different. She breathed deeply and sat back behind the wheel.

"Are you okay?" I asked.

She ran her fingers through her thatch of blonde hair and began a few words. "Tinker, Eila and I have been wanting to talk with you about something."

A warning bell clanged in my head. *Theresa, your father and I. . .*

"Okay, but you can't call me Theresa, promise? That's the first mistake my mother always makes."

"Okay, I promise." Jody smiled, but I began to squirm all nervous again. "Well, Tinker, your mother doesn't seem to want you to work for us anymore. We don't like giving you up, but I don't know what else to do." She put her hand on my knee. "Look, I've been talking with Miss Stanner here at the library. She says she can use somebody at just what we pay you now—or maybe even a bit more—for the summer."

In the winter I remember Miss Stanner wore smelly wool dresses and had sausage roll hair; summers she wore scarves. "But what could I *do?* I mean I don't like books all that much now, and Miss Stanner spends most of her time yakking on the phone to all her friends. You can hear her all over the library. What would I do?"

"Well, she needs somebody to reshelve books when they come in, answer the phone, and file cards. That sort of thing—just about what you're doing for Eila now."

"But I don't *like* Miss Stanner. I mean, she's silly."

Jody smiled. "Yeah, I know what you mean. Well, what're we gonna do? If Eila and I keep you on much after Easter, your mother will have a fit and she'll—"

"What?"

"I don't know. But there's no point in enraging the woman any more than—"

"Oh, she's already enraged. I guess she was born that way."

"What does your father think about this, Tinker?"

"He doesn't care. He doesn't notice anything anyway. He's too tired from everything at the College. He just wants my mother to stop complaining. Maybe after she has the baby, she'll get all buried in him and then she won't care what I do. . . ."

"Look, why don't I try to talk with her, ask her again if I can stay?

I'll wait till she's in a human mood. She's usually good on Sundays after Mass if we're going out to dinner. I'll try tomorrow.'' Although I said this fast, I wasn't at all sure I had the nerve to face my mother again about the problem. However, I couldn't devise anything else to tell Jody.

"But will you come in and present yourself to Miss Stanner, anyway, just in case it doesn't work? We'll deliver the hyacinths together, okay?"

"Look, if I can get my mother to talk about this, will you come and help me? Maybe if we did it together, she'd listen better.''

Jody stiffened. "Eila and I were going hiking tomorrow.''

"Oh.'' I tried to say it calmly; I guess it sounded pretty disappointed.

"Tinker, I have an idea. Why don't you and your mother come to our house, oh maybe twelve noon? I'll try to get Eila to join us, but I can't guarantee it. She doesn't like...controversy. Well, we'll see what we can fix up.'' Jody gave me a sudden smile.

At that moment I was so happy I nearly cried. Somebody who cared enough to bother to help me with something. And on their day off, even. I put my arms around her shoulders; she hugged me back. Then she took my arms away.

We left the truck and walked Miss Stanner's pink pot through the storm door and the oak swinging doors with brass plates. The plates looked greenly in need of polishing, and I hoped that wasn't one of the junky jobs Miss Stanner already had lined up for me. When we entered, she looked up and waved but she was, as usual, on the phone.

4

Jody,

I'm out walking. I couldn't sleep.

Why did you have to invite them here? I think it's a mistake. I don't even want to go there. I just want to ignore the woman until she calms down and we can make sure the conversation stays on Tinker's work or future and not on us.

Please call her and make some excuse.

I know Tinker won't be happy at the library, but is that *our* fault? Maybe we can rehire her next fall after things have blown over. I don't want her mad at us, too. I agree that would be dangerous. . . .

Why do you do these things without consulting me?

You know what this town is like. The first thing you learn growing up here is to calculate—and never take on more than you can handle.

I'll be back around ten this morning.

Eila

5

By 8:30 that Sunday morning my mother was all out of control about everything but especially about, How dare I assume she'd go with me to the nursery at twelve or any other time? She hated to say it, but she didn't want to set foot in their house, Jody was a pig, etc. Nor was there anymore to be discussed. Easter vacation would be my final days of work; that was all there was to it.

My mother had been up since five a.m. with an upset stomach from the baby. My father had got up with her although he was now buried behind the Sunday paper. It was a bad scene, and I didn't know what to do or say. I put on my slinky black ski outfit and slammed out the front door. I knew I'd miss Mass and hoped they'd go without me.

Walking around clammy and sweaty up Laurel Street, I found myself wishing again for Mr. O'Connell and his warm back room. I was that desperate. So what if he was some kind of pervert? He always welcomed me with cocoa and candy and handled things at my speed, a little more each week, it's true. But he never touched or exposed more than I wanted at the time, never got angry and yelled I was hopeless, brainless, or had failed him. It was, as they say in my father's College papers, "a liberal education with a dedicated teacher and a willing student." I missed the friendly excitement, intellectual or whatever.

Not that I'd *really* sorted out what Mr. O'Connell did to or with me. What still confuses me about men and women in Endfield: Sex was (is) something that *happened to* a woman or girl, not something she did, so was responsible for. If men "only wanted one thing," then *they* were responsible. Yet women got blamed too—if somebody found out. It never made sense. May the new feminists end such absurdities. . . .

However, by comparison with that Sunday morning, Mr. O'Connell's back room looked at least welcoming. He and I never fought, anyway. We'd been too busy, affectionately discovering everything I wasn't supposed to know because nice girls didn't—or didn't name it afterward. I can't remember when I first linked "indecent exposure," "masturbation," "partial intercourse," "child molestation" with some of what Mr. O'Connell had done. And was horrified, as I should have been originally.

Next I began to long for Pammy but knew her mother wouldn't care to see the likes of me at nine on a Sunday morning. Since I'd started working at the nursery, Pammy and I had grown apart.

Something else had happened too, the previous summer. One night before a picnic, we slept over at my house in my bed. About midnight we got to whispering about Mr. O'Connell. I asked her what he'd said and done to her. I gathered it was what he'd said and done to me, only less complete, less exciting. Anyway, in the dark, snuggled up close together, she let me touch her, explore a bit at the top and bottom. I remember her breasts, like mine, were just getting started, but already hers were bigger because she tended toward shorter and fatter.

Despite the heat, I couldn't get her to remove her new pajamas. Nor could I entice her to do anything back to me. I put her hand on my face, my leg, my waist. I kissed her cheek. Nothing. She just lay there, staring off, looking dead in the shadows, clutching her chest.

I couldn't believe it—Pammy who used to be such fun, always ready for any dare or game. She wouldn't touch me although she'd happily arched her back, got all moist, and had the greatest time under my fingers.

We never mentioned nor did it again. Maybe her noncooperation shamed both of us. I concluded she was practicing for ladyhood, when you just lie there, eyes closed, and pretend It—all and whatever—isn't happening. But *I* wound up that night one helluva frustrated, angry eleven-year-old woman.

Small town life really was (is) limited. How can you turn into an adult, erotic female like in the perfume ads, snarling and twisting out of control on a leopard sofa for My Sin or Infini ("a beginning without an end"), if you can't get any supervised practice?

I seemed to be the only one my age who actually *did* anything about the problem. Everybody else giggled and pretended to things they'd done with boys or girls. If I questioned them, though, I discovered they'd learned only about enough to cover the first thirty seconds. After that, I found they didn't know what they were talking about, especially how to finish the job right.

For three months that year I tried my level best to get interested in boys, especially in Pammy's boyfriend, Eddie. Unfortunately they were all shorter than I and passionate only at baseball and skateboarding, which they pursued in male teams with such religious fervor that I finally ignored them in favor of doing something useful and money-earning at the nursery.

My mother explained how boys take longer to mature than girls; I should be patient, wait for them to notice me. Already I wondered (1) when it would hit them and (2) would it be worth it? I could see that Danny Thomas, at sixteen, was a bad case of acne and smelly feet—and no more interested in me than John, who was maybe twenty.

When I was about eight, I'd had a religious fervor phase myself, hoping to become a priest. A high school biology book showed me that girls lack the right hormones, not to mention the right equipment, ever to be ordained or speak to groups of Sunday people over mirco-phones. Since the nuns in my life were a spindly lot at the time, I gave up on religion, although not on God. I still expect he's the supreme being around here someplace if you can hack your way through all the stuff they hide him in, even for this so-called ''new Church.'' When I read of the old European one later in history class, I didn't see they'd changed it all that much. They may explain it differently, but the basic rules, especially for women, remain. Unselfish, cheerful obedience to your family's intimate needs so your kids won't get solitary, neurotic, or malnourished; the same years of pretending to like people you wouldn't stand if you weren't related by blood or work; and the last worst, no extra sex. . . .

As I wandered along Laurel Street, alone with about half this pack of morbid thoughts and with drifts of the last freak blizzard, I planned to climb the hill behind the school where I always got a high and total view of the whole town. All my frights, joys, sorrows could fall into place as I saw clear to the rim of the hill on the other side of town, imagining Albany or New York City beyond it.

Jody once promised to take me to Manhattan but we hadn't got to it yet. She reported that her old neighborhoods in Greenwich Village and the East Side had changed. Her friends were gone or married into the suburbs; she wasn't sure she wanted to see them again. I still wonder what sort of friendships other adults create if they see each other only once a year and never get too personal, I guess, for fear of getting stuck with somebody else's problems.

Continuing my route to reach the hill, I saw Eila's back disappear-ing up the long nursery driveway to her house. I yelled but she didn't hear. I scooted along the driveway behind her, but she reached the back door without turning or noticing me. I gathered she wasn't in the greatest mood. I slowed down, afraid now to ring the bell. I guessed what must have happened—Eila probably wasn't any more eager to meet my mother than my mother was to return the favor and everybody was mad at somebody about it. Jody said she'd have trouble getting Eila to cooperate.

I wondered whether it was Jody or me she was mad at. How could I find out? I dropped onto the back step before the storm door, puzzling what to do.

Next I heard loud voices from inside, not screams, more like crying. I peeked through the gauze curtain inside the door but couldn't pick up anybody in the living room or through to the kitchen. I realized they must be in the bedroom on the opposite side of the house.

I should apologize for what I did next. I'm not sneaky or mean, but have always been curious about people, how they run their lives, what *truly* makes it all worthwhile, as opposed to what they tell you when they hand you a line for work or other reasons.

Creeping along the cement foundation of the house, I got past the first door, around the sloping cellar door, reached the bedroom window. I peeked through a space between the heavy blue drapes. What I saw didn't surprise me too much—at first. Dressed in her green nylon raincoat, Eila was seated on the bed crying into her hands while Jody looked all startled and groggy up from the covers in her nightgown. Jody seemed to making "there, there, Eila" type movements and words, stroking Eila's hair, her shoulders, her rigid back. Then Jody hugged Eila, who suddenly relaxed and returned the hug.

When Eila stood up, I assumed everything was over; I should scram out of there before somebody caught me. Eila didn't leave the room, however. First she removed her raincoat, then her charcoal slacks and dancer kind of tights. She always had fantastic legs, the ones in bathing suit and Lady Schick ads. When she'd got down to a blue lace minislip, she smiled a bit at Jody, who was watching from the side. Then Jody made room in the double bed for Eila, who climbed in and sort of collapsed on the pillow in Jody's arms. They kissed each other, all very natural and easy and warm and human.

Of course, I was shocked, too. In the years I'd known Eila, Jody, other women, I'd never seen anything like this. Maybe a man and a woman doing something naked in a film but never two women—except for Pammy and me.

Unlike Pammy and me, however, they didn't rush, fumble, or quit. They blended to each other so even I could see they'd done it hundreds of times, that both enjoyed it as one relaxed part of what they needed or got from each other. They looked complete, happy; I loved both of them thoroughly, although I felt rather left out. Barred by the cold window and smelly asbestos shingles, I envied them the cozy bed, the old house, their greenhouse full of shrubs and flowers, their adult life that needed nobody to approve or notice.

I wondered what my Sunday school teacher, Miss Bossidy, or the priest (even the new one) would feel about such consoling, this kind of lovemaking. I know now the Church condemns it: If it feels good, it must be bad. Officialdom avoids serious consideration of, including real focus on, such topics by a neat trick of logic: Condemn something ahead of time; then when you meet it, it doesn't exist. Very simple; no reasons given or needed—apparently. But if it doesn't exist, why condemn it? Luckily it takes very little college reading of history to realize the Church, like other organizations, gets rid of problems by getting rid of the people considered problems. Or forces them to abase themselves in the category called "sinners." . . .

A car sped past. For a moment I panicked, assuming it was my parents back from church or out hunting me. I ducked away from the window and hid behind the slope of the cellar door. There the snow was melting; I got some soggy knees and shins in that corner between the house foundation and the platform holding the slanting door.

To be honest, I didn't know what to feel about what I'd seen. All I knew was that, compared to fighting a husband over money, sex, babies, or housework, it looked sane and natural what some women could be and do for each other. Or it was another way of happily doing for someone what you already knew you'd enjoy for yourself: maybe a swinging version of the Golden Rule. As I brooded over these complications, I found I couldn't even consider them all simultaneously, let alone choose one or two for Eila and Jody or me.

Well, I've read there's no paradise but paradise lost. Sure enough, I saw my mother streaming along Laurel Street, coat open, hair uncombed, her stomach, which now protruded, thrust out. She looked distinctly unhappy; I didn't have to "use my head for something besides a hat rack" to guess where she was headed. I flash froze into a smaller pile while my mind dug around for something to do about anything.

Then I stood up straight—and banged on the bedroom storm window. The next moment the drapes pulled far apart. Jody stood there, clutching parts of her nightgown around bulgy parts of herself where it didn't quite cover. I could see her eyes and mouth getting ready-set-go to be furious, but I ignored that. Through two layers of glass I began to point and talk, without shouting to all the neighborhood

beyond the side trees. "My mother! She's coming. *Do* something,"
I mouthed.

Jody did something. She dropped the drapes and slammed down a
venetian blind. Both closed promptly, four inches from my mittens.

Okay for you, I thought. I sank down again near the foundation,
wondering whether to pretend I wasn't there. Leaving Jody and Eila
to face my mother alone might serve them all right. Or I could head
her off before she climbed the driveway. Or I could let her enter the
house. If she entered, then I could stroll nonchalantly to the front or
back doors as if I were returning from a walk—after they'd already
started talking. Deciding on the third possibility, I began to rub my
cheeks and smear my boots with snow to pretend I'd been for the brisk-
est jaunt in the wilderness.

By this time, I could hear my mother assaulting the back door on
the other side of the house, plus some quick thumps from inside the
bedroom. If they were smart, they wouldn't let her in at all, but was
that door even locked?

6

Although my mother always considered herself as having cornered the market on headaches, after I'd crept to the road and begun sauntering along it, my right temple told me I had fixings for a first-class migraine. Such headaches were new to me that winter; they'd come with the onset of my periods and seemed equally useless. I wondered whether this one would coalesce into the array of bouncing black spots that had already blotted out the numbers during a fractions and decimals review. Somehow I'd gotten a B+ anyway, although math remained my bugaboo subject.

As I kicked lumps of melting snow along the road, I revised my judgment: If all the little dots danced themselves into one massive dot, it might be just the thing to blot out that whole morning, which so far hadn't shaped up splendidly. Not only was everybody mad at me, but they seemed about to scream some more at one another because of it.

At the beginning of Eila's driveway, I hesitated, dragging a foot, trying to decide whether to get involved. Maybe I should just retreat to Pizza Hut for a fifty-cent lunch (which would quiet both head and stomach) and return when all had Blown Over?

If I'd had half a brain in no matter what shape, I should have done the retreat.

Instead, I started up the driveway toward the back door. Somehow my mother must have got in. My final decision: If I didn't want any garbage said about me in my absence, I'd better get there, too. Fixing my eyes on the horizon beyond the greenhouses, I tried out different ploys:

Your Avon Lady calling...

My, I was just passing by and thought how lonely you all might get without me...

Will you spend 35¢ a day to save this orphan or will you turn the page?

32

After my mind had generated *Hi. I think I forgot a notebook in the truck yesterday. Can I look for it?*, I summoned enough guts to climb the back step and ring the bell.

I rang again.

Nothing happened. *Oh well, since they're not home....*

Suddenly Eila opened the back door and stared through the glass storm door. Her eyes looked wild, her face grim. However, she had all her clothes back on—at least, the charcoal slacks and pale blue blouse. One button over her breasts gaped undone, but otherwise she looked fairly normal. She opened the storm door and held it as usual, her arm along the glass above my shoulders.

Jody, too, looked normal on the dusty horsehair sofa. She was wearing her Sunday outfit, suede jacket and jeans. It wasn't until I looked down that I noticed both Eila and Jody were barefoot on the faded green carpet. Jody nodded at me.

Everyone sat silent. Maybe what I was interrupting hadn't occurred yet? My lost notebook speech would have sounded silly. I sat down in one cloud gray wing chair while Eila stood behind me.

It was my mother seated in the other wing chair opposite Jody who looked abnormal. Her right hand fidgeted around her collarbone; she stared at me. I feared a lashing about why I'd disappeared.

However, something was happening between her and Jody. "Well?" my mother said.

"Well, what?" Jody answered. "What's the problem, Mrs. Tharp? You burst in here without even waiting for Eila to get the door. What's *your* problem?"

Clever of Jody to make it my mother's problem! I tried to note that for future use.

"I want my daughter back. She ran away here this morning."

Jody glanced at Eila, then at me. When she spoke, it was with her collection voice—a tone polite but edged with exasperation, reserved for people who had promised a check or cash over the phone and "just don't have it" when we showed up to collect.

"You can have your daughter. We haven't stolen her. In fact, I've been trying to get her the library job. But we are tired of your phone calls. In fact, if you *cared* about your daughter, none of this—"

"Jody!" Sharp tone to Eila's voice.

Jody ignored her. "This wouldn't have happened. Children who like home don't come courting serious jobs when they're eight years old."

"What business is that of yours?" Was my mother agreeing with Jody's analysis?

"Eila and I hired her." The conversation was circling around to where it must have started. I grew confused and desperate.

"Ma, I *like* working here! Why can't you see that?"

"Because I want you home where you belong. I don't even want you at the library." Giving up on Jody, my mother turned to Eila, who was shifting behind me. "Eila, I never went to college the way you two (nod in Jody's direction) did. I got married right out of high school so I know my. . . viewpoint is different than yours. What I'm trying to say is, I haven't liked Tinker working here for some time. But it made her happy so I was willing to let it go on. But now I can use her at home—"

"Ma, I'm *here!* Will you stop talking about me like I'm not?"

"You want a built-in babysitter, huh?" Jody sneered.

My mother's face flushed. She surprised me by crumpling deeper into her wing chair. I rose, paced around. The right side of my head rebelled. Eila's face looked winter-white; I doubted any help from her direction.

The bedroom door stood ajar, revealing the sprawl of unmade bed, sticky breakfast tray, two nightgowns dropped and tangled into each other. Had my mother noticed it?

Right then what to do or say stumped me, but I clutched after something useful because the suspense was eating my already empty stomach. As when my parents "disagreed," I got the same urge to peacemake or, failing that, to shake them up, throw a tantrum, anything to break the tension. Pacing the room from china cupboard to stairway to wing chairs, I glared at the tight-lipped, steel-rimmed ancestors Eila kept hung on the wall. Why do those people never give you anything you can use—and then expect eternal gratitude for it?

"Tinker, sit down, huh?" Eila asked. She stretched her arms out toward me, then withdrew them.

"No. It's like all of us are. . . screwing this up. And you don't even know it. Why don't we talk about the *real* problem, what it is?"

From her wing chair my mother stared in alarm. Eila sighed. Jody crunched around on the horsehair.

I stabbed at some words. "You don't want me working here because you're afraid I'll. . . get too attached. And you think women shouldn't . . . love each other. You think, like I'll get corrupted."

My mother's eyebrows rose frantically. "Don't be silly. I *trust* my daughter. I always have—I—"

"Ma, I've been corrupted for, like, years. You never noticed. You were too goddamn busy with your headaches and everybody's heart attack!''

Jody snickered. My mother gasped, then glared at her and me simultaneously.

It wasn't going right. *As long as my mother and I had at each other, that let Jody and Eila off the hook.* Just like my parents, eternally with each other to protect or run to, while I remained the scapegoat nuisance. No skin off *their* psyches.

"Sit down, Tinker." Eila pulled me back onto the chair where I got reduced to twisting my legs and crushing a doily around my fist.

Again we sat/stood in silence, staring downward at uninteresting laps and rug tatters. It wasn't going right, not at all like a movie or one of those clever plays where some programmed actress delivers either the crushing insight or the stunning insult that solves everything—or at least ends the scene.

Then I realized *why* nobody spoke. Silence seemed simpler. It wasn't to anybody's advantage to do anything about me or That Other Problem, while it became to everybody's advantage to shut up and go away. I felt bleeped over—lured onto a branch to make a fool of myself, only to discover those gentle gutless wonders back there were sawing off my limb.

Besides the black spots, a wave of red hatred for everybody in that room surged through me. Four years of working at next-to-nonexistent pay at a place and nobody could care less—apparently. Once on tv, I'd seen a teenage soldier who'd been young and dumb enough to believe the "Okay, guys, go out there and get those little yellow bastards" pep talk only to discover himself stuck alone in Viet Nam, his buddies dying around him, the generals on their buns back at the bunker. How to fight when you can't decide which set of yellow bastards to attack?

I stared first to Jody, then around to Eila. Nobody would meet my eyes. I stood up, looking down at my mother. "Well, they sleep together. That's what you wanna know? That's what you're scared—they're different. . . . Ah, why is everybody sitting here like sticks!''

"Tinker!" Eila screamed at me.

It was a lucky thing for both front doors that they weren't locked because I stormed out and down the driveway. . . . *Go berzerk on Laurel Street, take off your clothes, run naked around the school roof.* At that instant I steamed enough to try anything—rolling in the grimy snowpiles, jumping into Greenwater Pond. But how *good* it felt to be moving. I sped down Laurel, not even glancing at my house, laughing at my poor father and the raging wreck of a wife soon to inundate him.

I jogged the length of Franklin but decelerated, out of breath, as I rounded the corner by the restaurant onto Main. It's never good to run on Main. Old ladies stare; everybody assumes you're still a child who doesn't Know Any Better. Discovering a big pain in one ankle, I limped and panted sedately along Main.

Margaret at the newspaper store had locked up already and, of course, the Five and Ten never opened on Sundays anymore. Mr. Romello hadn't opened the doors or the ticket booth for the movie matinee yet.

Without deciding, I found myself headed toward the College where at least the Union Building or the gym might be open.

7

Beyond the dorms and lawns the library loomed as the first lighted building I found. The man at the checkout counter recognized me as a returner of my father's overdue library books and let me pass. He even waved, which made me feel human for the first time that day.

The library had just opened. A few sleepy people, minus shoes, sipped coffee from paper cups, shuffled notecards, read newspapers. I plunked myself in the magazine section and pretended to leaf through the nearest bunch of pages, in order to gain some time to think.

My accident in magazines, however, couldn't have proved worse. I was holding a new *Ebony* for black people whose opening pages contained a bunch of letters protesting or applauding some previous article by a homosexual man. One letter was so awful I had to read it twice to understand it. Until then, I hadn't imagined a separate group of people called "homosexuals" or "homosexual men" who all loved each other or some of each other, whatever they could find. I thought it must resemble being black people in general: Endfield had none in winter but a few came as babysitters or maids for the summer people. But what about Eila and Jody? Were they included? And what about me who, loving both of them, now felt furious at both—and at myself for betraying them to my mother?

The letter read:

"SEX WITH THE ANGELS"

Your article about homosexuals and lesbians was sickening. God made male and female; homosexual is not a sex, just a delusion and it is abnormal. According to the Holy Bible, Sodom was destroyed because of homosexuals. They wanted to have sex with the angels who came to Lot's house (Gen. 19:5). The tribe of Benjamin was almost destroyed for the same reason (Judges 19:22). For those who are not sure about what God says about homosexuality, read Lev. 18:22, Lev. 20:13, 1 Cor. 6:9, Romans 1:17–32,

1 Tim. 1:10.

Although it puzzled me how anybody could have sex with a bodyless angel (maybe they did it with their head or mind or something?), I doubted the Bible would enlighten me. I rose and walked along an aisle of weighty reference books. I chose a black dictionary type that I could lift easily without dropping it or alarming everybody. Besides the letter, some pink and lavender signs on campus had taught me which words to look up.

Thumbing nervously to "homosexuality," I found "inversion. See lesbianism." Thumbing onward, I found "lesbianism" after "leprosy" and before "lesion." It read: "Perversion in which sexual desire of women is only for one of their own sex. It may be expressed physically or psychically."

At least they give you a choice. Maybe that's where the angels come in.

"See: sapphism, tribadism *urningism (urnism), uranism."

"Urningism" was the first one I could find; the news from there was no better:

> Lesbianism is a term applied only to the female sex. The op-
> posite sex has no interest for urnings, but seems to inhibit the
> normal sexual act. Passionate love and deification of the love
> object are common. Such perversion may be congenital. Sexual
> paresthesia is often present.

"Paresthesia" turned out to be some combo of Greek and Latin that means "abnormal sensation without objective cause, such as numbness, pricking, etc."

"Sapphism" was from "Sappho, the reputed instigator of Lesbianism."

I dumped the book back onto the shelf before anybody caught me. Retreating to my chair, I tried to hid behind yesterday's *Endfield News*. I felt lousy, but it was no exotic numbness or pricking. It was the daily variety of hunger in the stomach, headache across the total forehead, and confusion in the brain. It's a good thing I never believed textbooks except for undisputed facts like history dates or world capitals. They can really do a job on your head.

Slowly I regretted the whole morning. I should have stayed longer at the nursery, talked to Eila and Jody better. . . . But which of them was the "urning"? What about me, who'd given up on boys a whole year before? And was my mother "congenital"? I hoped so although, as usual, such musings left me low, dry, and nowhere.

Banging one foot against the chair wood, I tried to sort through my dazed emotions. In the beginning Eila and Jody must have fascinated me as the exciting older sisters I never had—exactly the competent people I hoped to become when I'd chuck my teeth braces, divide faster, write neater, and never miss saying The Right Thing. It must have been when I was nine that I began to love both, enjoying their contrasting personalities. Doing different work along with each, I rarely resented—or even noticed—what they must mean to each other as I'd just seen it through the window. I banged my knuckles on my head. How could I know when they'd never shown it publicly? Maybe that long afternoon before Christmas when Jody pulled a back muscle and Eila dropped work, undressed her onto the sofa, massaged and hot compressed while Jody groaned? Was this lust—or first aid?

For puzzling contrast: I resented my mother's and oldest sister Nedda's verbal and other intimacies, including enthusiastic hugs and kisses at comings and goings. I always suspected them of gossiping, sharing secret conclusions about my father and me, my life and prospects— before I had any. Of kissing in particular: Eila never did it publicly to anybody. Off to a plant show and sailing out the door, Jody would direct a two-armed flying wedge sort of affection equally to both Eila and me.

Between the library stacks I now wandered, torn with a further dilemma. How could, should, I help Jody and Eila, impress them with my loyalty, untangle the mess I'd made?

Digging through my ski jacket pockets, I found fifty-four cents, one dirty handkerchief, two pieces of lint. Again I imagined food; my mouth watered. Then I spotted John far across the room, settling his books down to study.

I walked near him. "Hi, John." He jumped and turned at me. I was getting ever more popular that day.

"What are you doing here?" he asked.

"Uh, John, I could use about fifty cents for a hamburger. I have fifty but I need more. Can you spare any change? I'll repay you next week."

"Why don't you ask your father? He's right outside. He's talking with some seniors."

"He *is?*"

"Sure. Didn't you come here with him?"

"Yuh, well, I could still use fifty cents. He's busy now. You know, I wouldn't want to bother him." I said this fast, hoping it would sound convincing. It must have, because John sighed, dug into his jeans, and found me two quarters.

"Thanks a lot. I'll pay it back." I walked away, which I guess was what he wanted. Before the front glass doors, I stopped and checked on my father. Not visible in any direction. Hoping he'd gone to his office, I crossed the lawn between the dorms, then the street, and entered the Union Building and the C-Shop. Dave, the manager, stood washing dishes at the sink between his refrigerator and grill. The grill sputtered with food already.

"Hi, Tinker. You want something else?"

This puzzled me but I answered, "A hamburger, medium, and a large Coke." I was sufficiently starved for an orgy of junk food. Pammy, worried about her skin, hated junk food, but I still indulged.

"You here to pick up your father's burger? He just ordered it."

Ye gods, oh crap, him again? "No, it's my burger. I mean, I want to order my own."

Dave raised his blond eyebrows.

"It's okay. I can pay. Here's a dollar." I laid my quarters on the counter.

"Okay. I'll stick on another one for your father."

"Yuh, just give it to me fast. I'll eat it outside."

Dave built the Coke and wrapped the burger.

Once upon a time the C-Shop had two glass doors, but to prevent candy-stealing and increase table space, Dave had blocked one. As I turned to leave via the other, my father opened it. He walked around the counter toward me. He was, unfortunately, alone.

"Tinker! Your mother's driving all over town looking for you. What's got into you?"

Ever since I could remember, my parents had believed firmly in what my mother called "united standards," which mostly meant Us Against Them, parents glued together in self-defense against their own kids. As a result, I never could tell when my father was merely "upholding" my mother and when he really belabored some problem himself. Since few domestic problems penetrated deep or long enough to grip him, or my mother grew ashamed to reveal some of her more stunning failures with me, I hoped he hadn't heard yet about this morning. With luck, it could become another thing explained away as, "Well, Tinker's so moody lately. I just don't know what's got into her."

"Sit down." He pulled out a chair for me, then one for himself at the nearest greasy formica table. His overcoat collar was twisted; his eyes looked puffy and tired. *Don't pity him*, I decided. *That's how you always lose.* So I worried about my burger going lukewarm and my Coke melting but decided it wouldn't look right to open it or wolf it down before his eyes. Stymied again. Its meaty odor tantalized my nose and brain.

"Tinker, I've been wanting to talk to you. Your mother's very worried about you. You must know that." When I didn't answer, he continued, "Well, she is. You don't seem to be growing up at all right. You don't do anything age-appro—appropriate to your age. Look at your clothes now. Your pockets are ripped. You've got mud down the legs of that new ski outfit. Your face and hands are dirty. You can see how much trouble you cause your mother." Then he stared away. I still felt he hadn't addressed me yet, only my ski suit. It was truly my day to be the Invisible Menace.

"It doesn't look all that bad," I mumbled. "I'll wash it off." I hoped the whole thing was over so I could scram out of there. Then I got an idea. If he was forcing me to talk, how about his answering some questions that had bugged me for years?

"Daddy, I'll fix the ski suit. I really will." *Anything to get off the ski suit.* "But, look, why is Ma, she, in such a . . . mood all the time? So tired and ugly? Nothing pleases her. It's like she decided a long time ago I'm no good."

Now he looked at me. "Your mother works very hard, Tinker. She tries to do her best by you and your aunt."

I admit I began to sulk—my ancient and only weapon against getting "poor Mommed" to death. Finally I dared, "That isn't what I asked you."

"Tinker, I've had enough this morning. We're going to walk home, and you're going to apologize to your mother."

"I'll walk home by myself." Now *I* stared at the floor. Just as Dave called, "Hey, Mr. Tharp, your burger's ready," I grabbed my paper bag and ran.

8

That week of school vacation before Easter dragged by in nightmare time.

On Monday and Tuesday I was quarantined, ordered to help my mother first with rug beating and curtains, then with spring window washing and scouring the cellar. Our dank basement lay full of old newspapers, broken dolls, boxes of mildewed clothes. It felt surprisingly good to rope them, lug them upstairs, and dump them out front for Kerry, the junkman.

Of course, I longed to call or see Eila and Jody, to discover how they were doing or what they thought of me and the whole thing. I made no move toward them, however, because I wasn't yet sure what I thought myself, how I could restore our good times.

I'd made that apology to my mother on Sunday. After running around in the car for two hours, she had accepted it and collapsed into bed, nursing my promises about housework. Sunday evening I was confined to my room with Civil War homework.

When my mother didn't refer again to that morning at the nursery, I assumed she was running true to form—if you don't mention things, they Go Away. Next day when she got up, she actually bustled as we attacked the various cleaning jobs.

At one point between the rug beating and the curtain orgy, she confessed, "You know, I think I've been selfish, too. I think now you only spent time with those terrible women because you didn't feel we love you. Or you never had enough to do here. Am I right? It's not too late, is it?"

"No. Yes. I don't know." That last was true; I didn't know what to answer. Certainly I had enough to do, and what difference could it make after all these years, anyway? The reprehensible truth was I didn't believe her repentence any more than I'd believed anything she'd ever stuck out for me to trip over. Angry and lacking trust, I feared she'd soon revert to the listless, exasperated mother who depressed me. Years later I discovered she'd lacked the identical faith in me—she feared I'd never change, never amount to anything useful. . . . That spring our family was big on despair.

"Tinker, I'm going to Confession before Easter. Will you come with me? Will you tell Father Henry. . .whatever you did with those women? And get it all cleaned up? Then we can go on and be happy like we used to be."

That we'd ever been happy was news to me, but I answered, "I didn't do anything with them. Just worked there."

"You know what I mean."

It now tortured me that I hadn't reached Eila or Jody. I longed for the exhausted mother of early pregnancy who'd spent half the day lying down. Then I might at least have sneaked in a two-minute phone call.

"Tinker, those women have got to be stopped. . .before they brainwash more young girls. That's one reason I called Father."

"That's silly. They didn't brainwash me. I loved it there."

"Don't use that word about them! They don't deserve that word. . . .It's over, Tinker. You're not to see them again. This summer we'll find a nice camp for you to attend with girls your own age."

She and I were over; how I wished that was the thing I'd never see again. That's what she couldn't see—the *nerve* of her assuming she could cajole me into mistaking her power to order me anywhere for real love or concern. I also realized why she hadn't protested four years sooner about my nursery work, why only now she was equating me with Patty Hearst and poor Eila and Jody with something about as charming as the Symbionese Liberation Army. Quite simply, the nursery had kept me busy, out of her hair, until the coming baby and her renewed flurry at housework became projects at which I should ideally assist her.

Between killing spiders and hauling junk that day, I did my best to puzzle out why I enjoyed so much working with and for Eila or Jody and why, by contrast, my mother and her needs repelled me. It wasn't that I'm naturally stubborn, distant, cruel. It was rather that my mother's way of working distinctly pained me, for she lacked the most elementary self-worth or self-belief. Jody disliked Endfield, too, but never belittled her work as boring or stupid duty like my mother in fits of anger or self-pity. Writing invoices or even shoveling manure somehow never degraded Jody or Eila. They never needed to pretend, as my mother tried constantly, to hide her disappointment with both my father and me behind a strained smile while she grumbled to or about her sister, the dirt, the dishes. Maybe if somebody had *paid* her for housewifing, either the house or I might have acquired more status in her eyes.

But what can you do with somebody who comes to you *pre-bio-degraded,* all geared for her portion of life's disappointment or drudgery? You leave them behind to drudge there in gray shades of suffocation while you move on to somewhere with freer air, brighter colors. . . .

By Monday night I still hadn't made it beyond the house, even to the store. My father handled my usual job of bread and milk run. That night I stayed awake, plotting, until after eleven when I heard my parents go to bed.

Then I snuck through the dark hall, down to the kitchen, brought the phone to the window, and dialed. I don't know which I feared more—that Jody or Eila would answer or that they wouldn't.

Well, they didn't.

After five rings I hung up and crept back to bed, avoiding the noisiest floorboards of our old house, still ignorant whether they, like my mother, were pretending yesterday's speakout never happened.

Tuesday: In between washing the car, vacuuming the sofa and radiators, and attacking the attic, I got tired and tried to remind my mother that a woman in her special condition shouldn't overtax herself with all this flurry. It didn't succeed. Not only did it fail as a method to stop the madness, but it totally backfired into the plea, "If you really care, you'll do more so I can lie down." Which left me feeling as if, stumbling along a plank over a pool of piranhas, I'd just found my ankles chained together.

At lunch on Tuesday I discovered what she really wanted before she'd dismiss the dustmops and detergents. It involved the impending visit to Father Henry. "Tinker, I want you to *help* me. Those women have to be stopped before they touch more young girls." She stirred her tea and crinkled her forehead. I liked her blue maternity outfit that day, but then it reminded me of Eila, who also favored blue. I got sad and looked away.

"Please look at me, Tinker. You're so distant sometimes when I try to reach you." She said the words softly, and her begging seemed sadder than her orders to me. All I could do was blush, for which I hated myself.

Finally I mumbled, "I'll go with you to Father Henry, but I won't say rotten things against Eila or Jody. They're just not true."

"Tinker, remember what you told everybody Sunday. You know their life is...sinful. And it takes somebody outside the situation to see that. You don't understand yet."

By this time, even the dusty radiators seemed a good alternative to that conversation; I attacked them with a strange vigor that pleased my mother while it confused the hell out of me. I began to see how a diet of constant insoluble problems—emotional dirt—created a woman like her and how by contrast or extension, housework—battling physical dirt—could begin to loom as a way out, the only place your efforts could hope to produce any results.

As they said in my father's educational papers: "The unexamined life is not worth living." After a few years in the town of Endfield, I was hardly likely to wind up with one of those.

Tuesday night my insomnia progressed to puzzling further over my mother and how she and I could survive without dying of mutual frustration. She wasn't a bad person, I repeated, just inadequate to face those parts of the modern world which the Church labeled "sin." What a shame her religion, which could have gladdened her, seemed to strengthen her only in suffering by providing ready-made encouragement to "offer it up" instead of dealing with "it" when and where it lay.

Sorrow, boredom, guilt, rage over the whole process consumed me that night.

By Wednesday morning I grew frantic at being six houses away from Eila and Jody but so housebound it might have been the moon. When I inquired about walking to the nursery "to find my notebook," I got the usual maternal outburst that I wasn't ever to see those women again, my work there was over, my father could pick up the notebook if I really needed it, etc.

When the phone rang, interrupting all this family bliss, I ran upstairs to my father's desk. The only thing in his stationery drawer that looked both nonvital and nonofficial was an old picture postcard of Mt. Washington. I scribbled a couple sentences on it, light and bright as I could manage, then dashed along Laurel to the nursery mailbox.

As I ran, my sentences ran with me in my head:

Dear Jody and Eila,
Am being held political prisoner—no ransom will save me.
Am really sorry about Sunday. As Eila said once, I talk too much
and nobody can concentrate.

Love,
Tinker

I hesitated over the "love" but decided four years of three lives deserved something along that line. I yearned to carry it right to the
nursery office but had to satisfy myself with the mailbox at the road.
I left the red flag down so the mail truck wouldn't steal my card away
to the post office. I had neither stamped nor addressed it.

As I dashed back, I began to have second thoughts about the card.
Had I apologized too much on it? Three days with my mother had
blotted out how mad I'd been at Jody and Eila also on Sunday. . . .

9

Somehow Holy Thursday arrived and somehow my mother and I survived a split-level confession with Father Henry at the rectory. My mother had requested him because by both appearance and job description, he functioned as "the middle priest." He gave shorter, cheerier Sunday sermons than rotund Father Ogle, yet his style was not quite the towering "Rah, team! Go out there and kill 'em, for Christ's sake" stuff you got from Father Riley, who coached the parochial basketball team. In addition, Father Henry supposedly was "sensible," "down to earth."

As I sat in the rectory hallway awaiting my mother, however, I wondered whether his earth and my earth could communicate in anywhere the same universe.

The oak door opened; my mother exited, frowning. "Tell him everything," she ordered into my ear.

Father Henry's room had a faded, bookish, stale pipe aura that I recognized from the offices of my father's male colleagues. To the right of his desk stood a red velvet-covered *prie dieu,* an iron rack of holy candles over it. I hoped I'd escape having to kneel there in broad daylight for the whole ceremony. Father Henry, a cleanshaven man in black suit and round collar, sat behind the oak desk. He motioned me to the armchair before his desk.

My mother had insisted I look "ladylike"—wear my new skirt, a multicolored mini, with my black sweater. As I sat down, I had to fiddle with the skirt to coax it to cover bits of my knees and thighs above the black kneesocks.

Father Henry waited patiently, watching me.

When I'd got it all together, he said, "Now, Theresa, what seems to be the problem?"

This threw me because I had assumed my mother was the lady with the problem(s). *Look him in the eye.*

"It's—it's my mother. She wants me to stop working at the nursery."

"Well, she tells me the work is upsetting you, that it's not a good influence on you at this particular time."

"No. It's upsetting *her*."

Father Henry stared and sighed.

"Theresa, would you like to make a good Confession now of anything you may have done or seen that is . . . against God's law? You know, God has given us laws to help us and let us help other people. Your mother tells me that you hold these women in high regard, and we should do whatever we can to help them lead the best lives God has in mind for them." *But Eila and Jody aren't even Catholic. . . .* "Will you make a good Confession now?"

"I haven't done anything!" Did he want to know, maybe, about Pammy and me? She *really* didn't do anything that night. I decided to ignore my memory of Pammy and me in bed. Let her fight it out with her own priest.

"Theresa, are you refusing to receive the sacrament of Penance? Are you refusing God's absolution?"

"No. I don't need to confess. I just want to say something!"

"What?"

"Eila and Jody aren't . . . terrible people. My mother gets ahold of one thing, and she blows it into a mess."

"Your mother is worried for your safety. . . . Tinker, in your years with these women, did you do or see anything that went . . . beyond the boundaries? Something must have happened because you're causing your mother some upset."

She's a pain about everything. . . . Well yes, Father, I saw them making love, and it's none of your damn business.

"No, Father. It's just . . . she's very upset about the baby coming."

"I see. And you're sure you've done nothing against God's law . . . in these matters?" Father Henry's forehead rose against me. "You're at a very sensitive age, Tinker. You must be watchful at all times. Now say a good Act of Contrition." He smiled. "And I'll send you on your way."

"Oh my God, I am heartily sorry," I began to mumble. *Oh my God. . . .* In between detesting my sins and knocking a few years off what I already knew would be a lengthy stay in Purgatory, I sneaked a look at Father Henry. He was reading an open magazine on his desk from which he unglued himself just in time to absolve me.

I laughed inside, guessing something else my mother probably hadn't noticed—that dealing with two semi-hysterical women on a busy day like Holy Thursday was no doubt the last thing Father Henry needed. Of course, I knew my mother's suspicion that priests, like doctors and other men, simply Did Not Care; they let your worst horrors "flow in one ear and out the other" without so much as a sympathy stop between. In this case, she was right, and I was glad.

I craned to see his magazine, wondering whether holy magazines had theological centerfolds—maybe the Martyr of the Month or something equally inspiring. Anyway, it was too small for *Playboy* and too big for *Reader's Digest*. I never learned the title.

Finally I gathered all my knees together and stumbled from his office. On the way out, I realized he hadn't mentioned "homosexual" or "lesbian" or "crime" or "sin against Nature"—any of the stuff from that letter that I knew now I'd been expecting. I'd got off light. Maybe the "new Church" was worth something after all. *O come to me, all ye who are heavy laden, for my burden is easy, my yoke is light.* . . . and my lace is lavender. Besides, even the Devil can misquote Scripture. . . .

On Good Friday I finally escaped the house—long enough to walk Main Street and make the Stations of the Cross at St. Mary's with my mother marching six pews behind me.

10

Well, great blobs of bleep next began to hit the fan—just when I'd dared to hope all had Blown Over and was anticipating a two-minute visit at the nursery.

On Easter Sunday my mother's sister, Nedda, phoned. Over the previous weeks she had recovered from her heart attack and had resumed her heavy and customary labor—minding other people's business for their own good.

It dawned in me that it was mainly during these last months of Nedda's illness that my mother had begun "our nice talks" with me about housework, babycraft, cooking, and all my father's faults. However, with Nedda's recovery, I noticed my mother's desire to talk with me (as opposed to about me) had decreased. On Easter, listening to Ma's excited chatter, I again suspected I'd been a temporary (and unsatisfactory) replacement while Nedda recuperated. Once when I asked my father why Ma spent so much time phoning somebody she saw nearly daily, he answered that my mother was very close to her family who always Helped Each Other Out.

I twiddled this realization around in my head with its corollary—my mother and I were condemned to act at frantic cross purposes, doubting each other's good will or strength unless. . . unless somehow we came to love and understand each other. Further thinking informed me that our previous talks had derailed because they had begun wrong. Either I, having crept behind one of her eightballs, apologized (or felt I should) for my latest egregious error. Or, she began wrong by detailing illness and my father's mistakes until I squirmed with claustrophobia. How to end this, divert us to something less deadly?

A funny *Endfield News* filler rippled through me: I have many flaws, but being wrong isn't one of them. Did everybody believe this, including me? No wonder so few people profit from knowing all the other people.

That bust-up Sunday at the nursery, I'd seen how right she considered herself, compared to anyone living differently, and what a public scene she'd stage to prove it. I couldn't change that, but maybe I could impress her that other people (my father and myself?) might have reasons just as valid as hers for bits of their behavior.

I chose Good Friday evening. Having cleaned, hauled, beaten, swept, visited Father Henry and the Stations both, I felt confident of some credit with her. While my father attended another meeting, I found her alone in the living room. Since she was running her fingers distractedly through her hair, I knew she wasn't concentrating. "Is the puzzle too hard?" I asked.

"Yes. Even Ben couldn't get this one. Tinker, sit down."

I lowered myself onto the rough nylon cover of the armchair opposite her. To ease the conversation, I yearned to pull my chair nearer her around the coffee table. Our bulky chairs, however, did not pull, and edginess stopped me also.

"I'm worried, Tinker. You and I used to be such good friends. What's happened? I hardly know you anymore."

Ordinarily I'd have mumbled, "I'm sorry" or "Well, I'm in seventh grade with Pammy now." That day I felt pleased and flattered by her interest, for I'd determined to try something different. Finally I found my tongue. "Ma, I know you're interested, but it's not easy to talk with *you*. I mean, Nedda always seems to come first. Her problems are the real ones or something."

"What do you mean? She did have a heart attack, and the doctor says—"

"No." *Try again.* "What I mean is, I know she was sick. It's not what you do. It's who you'd rather be with. You don't *enjoy* Daddy or me."

"That's not true, Tinker. In fact, why do you say that? Look how hard I work here. With the baby coming I don't do half so much for Nedda now." Her eyebrows and nose puzzled at me. "I still don't understand what you mean. Of course, I like to do things with you and your father. When he's here," she added. "You know, he and I were good companions, but once you have children—"

Pits, traps, dammit. . . . I changed position over the upholstery trying to devise where to go next. It retaliated by embedding more ridges on my hands and elbows. *Your new dress is so pretty. I like blonde hair.* No. Those were the phony compliments Nedda tried before lowering the boom. "Maybe we could *do* more things together. Like swimming or tennis. Pammy says the new indoor rink is neat and—"

"In April? In my condition?" Sad gaze downward. "Tinker, be reasonable."

"Well, you should get...some exercise," I stammered. *Botched, double botched.* Illness, Nedda, my father, housework: There must be *something* more to talk about. School? Ugh on that, especially arithmetic and civics. A pang of pity for her hit me—never sound, always coping with an absentee husband, an embarrassment of a daughter. Was that truly how she saw me?

"Ma, I have an idea. I was hoping maybe I could explain better to you how I feel about the nursery." She frowned. "Please don't blow up," I begged. "Ma, I didn't know they were...like that when I worked there."

"You *didn't?*" She seemed genuinely surprised, as if lesbians, like lepers, should wear signs warning everybody. Or was it secret disappointment that Eila's and Jody's discretion had permitted not even one orgy or bit of Bill O'Connell molestation involving me? "Well, of course, you didn't, Tinker. Nobody did. But now we know, you should drop them. For your own sake."

"But why? You mean drop somebody just because you find some little thing you don't like? I mean, I could drop this whole town!"

Luckily she ignored my last comment. "What they're doing is not some little thing. It's unnatural and sinful. It's over, Tinker. Forget those women."

"No. Wait a minute. I want to say something."

"Well, say it." *Going wrong.* She checked her watch; I knew she was gauging how much overtime my father would arrive so he could be termed "very" late.

Again I fought the pieces of my idea together, not allowing them to shatter in the face of supposedly worthier topics. "Please listen. Don't get all annoyed."

"I'm not annoyed. Well, I'm nervous. I worry I'm too old for a new baby, it'll be deformed, I can't—" Then without warning she laid her head to the chairback, one hand over her mouth, and dribbled into tears—not dramatic sobs but the steady, hopeless kind as if she'd despaired of solace from anybody.

"Ma, please." Sitting on the arm of her chair, I took her free hand and dredged a kleenex from my pocket. I'd used it to wipe rust off my bicycle seat, but it was the best I could do under the circumstances. I sopped the tears from her cheeks. She seemed too tired to bother.

"Ma, please listen. Try," I begged again—not the way I'd hoped this to go at all. Don't let my father arrive now with the How-dare-you-upset-her-and-risk-a-miscarriage speech I'd got on Monday. Gradually she calmed. However, my neat idea of something I'd wanted her to see was fraying at the edges into its usual clotted mess.

"Ma, I just got two things to say," I announced desperately. "Maybe I started going to the nursery because I didn't have anybody to play with and, well, it was like you weren't here. I mean, when you lie down so much."

"You've got a nerve. I've been right here ever since you were born. Not out working or gallivanting like Pammy's mother." Her reddened eyes glared at me.

But Pammy's mother's happy and you're—hell! What now?...
"Yes, okay, but you're always with Nedda."

"Of course. She's my sister. I can *talk* with her." She blew her nose into my rusty kleenex.

I knew I was giving her a headache, but if I didn't say this then, the next interruption would assure it never got said. I swallowed and plunged on. "Maybe I go see Eila and Jody like you see Nedda. I need somebody, too."

"Why can't you love *me?*" she burst out with alarm. There, she'd hit it. To this I had no answer—except the mystery of human attraction and repulsion. Were she and I fated to remain eternal north poles—those warring animals mounted on silver and red magnets that we sicked on each other in science class? How did people or work so easily leave the realm of loving delight—wildflowers in a summer field—and become a boring chore, like shoveling snow? The process was evil. Inside my head I fought.

"Tinker, I really resent your comparing Nedda and me to those women with their deranged kind of life."

"That isn't what I meant. I meant I *see* them for the same reason. I mean, I like them.... Please don't get so *hurt*. When you're hurt, nobody can talk to you."

"Tinker, I've had enough. You're not to see them again. Father Henry told you that. No more nagging."·

"It's not nagging. I wanted you to see—"

"I do see—more than you at your age."

I gulped two big breaths and sat there, stymied. Defending Jody or Eila would only deepen her anger. Could I be wrong *all* the time about whatever I wanted? Maybe I should locate a different bunch of people who wanted what I wanted. How could I hope to matter in a relationship between Nedda and my mother that had existed years before I was born?

Hands around her stomach, my mother stared at the coffee table that again squatted like a black block between our two chairs. Finally I wiped my palms into the scratchy upholstery and dragged myself upstairs.

To what extent Nedda continued to Help Out, I learned on Easter Sunday. Ten seconds after Nedda's phone call my mother screamed, "Tinker!" from the kitchen. I ran toward her, alarmed at what I'd somehow done wrong, like Friday night's conversation, without even going anywhere. "Why did you lie to me?" Her face was purple. "Nedda says she has a postcard you just wrote to those . . . women. and you signed it Love? How could you *do* such a rotten thing after our talk?"

"Tinker, did you write that card?" My father was onto it now from the other kitchen door. *Why the hell don't they build doors some other direction so I don't keep running into him?*

"No. Yes. Nobody would talk about Sunday. I had to say *something* to them. You wouldn't let me out of here! I wrote it Wed—"

"I told you never to speak to them again. They're filthy."

It was another active rampage of tears, tantrums, cries of "Shame!" and general passion before I got the whole story. Eila must have failed to check her mailbox Wednesday. The postman grabbed the card, assuming it was outgoing. However, after he realized it lacked both stamps and address, he personally delivered it to Nedda two streets onward in his route with, probably, a request that somebody teach Tinker to do a card properly. Nedda waited out the Passion (and our interview with Father Henry) in order to rise on Easter Sunday.

Not only was Nedda clever at heart attacks but she easily qualified as the second biggest gossip in town after, of course, Miss Stanner at the library. Ready, determined, able, at the sacrifice of her own health, to forge family loyalty, forget childhood squabbles and pity her pregnant baby sister in an hour of need, saddled as my mother was for life with that hopeless husband ("although you must admit he's a good provider") and that wicked brat of a daughter. "Of course, if they'd started earlier stepping on that kid for her own good, it wouldn't have come to this pass, let me tell you." . . .

So she told—and wrote—a mouthful of which "spoiling the younger generation now that everything's done differently today" was a mere beginning. The town, including Pammy and two of my teachers, got an earful; I got a bellyful.

The war of whispers against Jody and Eila accelerated.

11

Dear Eila,

I stuck it out through Easter week.

By the time John gets back with the truck and these letters, I'll be in Manhattan for a few days. I know my departure looks cowardly, but so is staying in that miserable town with all those creeps and phonies staring down their noses wondering what you and I do in bed.

"Creeps and phonies" sounds like Tinker, I know, and the other letter is for her. I ask you to get it to her somehow. If I mailed it, Big Momma would burn it. You can read it. I expect the kid is feeling about as great as we are—that is, lousy.

I'm sorry, Eila. I just can't hack playing flower girl anymore to people who sneer behind my back. I know it eats at you in a different way but somehow you take it on the "it'll all blow over someday" theory. I ain't that patient.

You're losing a partner temporarily, but you're gaining a full-time employee. John promised he'll work as much as he can, driving the truck. He says his courses this quarter are a drag, anyway. He bought some nice flowering quince at the show. Hope you like them. I didn't fill him in on why I'm leaving, but guess what his first question was? "Is it something about Tinker? Because she looked real strange at the library last Sunday."

Goddamn that town of yours. You can hardly flush the john without the neighbors speculating on your brand of toilet paper.

Apparently all this hasn't penetrated to the College yet. He says if we want to make an issue about something, he can get *some* brothers (not all) in the Gay Activists' Alliance on campus to march or picket for us, they're always looking for hot issues, and Endfield is such a nothing town that the only real issue in it is that the whole place stinks, etc. He was raised in an even smaller town in New Hampshire.

I told him you're not at all the militant type, that he shouldn't do *anything* without checking with you. I can see you cringe already.

Here I am writing just as if I were speaking to you. I love you, Eila, and hate to think that crappy town is ruining us.

I've mentioned this before and got nowhere, but I try again. Will you consider selling that business and joining me here or in Colorado? Not immediately, of course, though that would be great. Just thought I'd re-mention it in case a filthy capitalist tourist shows up this summer looking for a tax dodge to invest his ill-gotten corporate millions.

I'm staying with Karen and Su on East 69th. The number's in our address book. Guess I'm no better than Tinker at staging an effective getaway. Everybody guesses where I'm going even before I've left. She's right—that town does a job on your mind.

Any chance you'll dump the invoices in the next couple weekends and join me here? You could send a press release to the *Endfield News* that you're visiting a sick sister in the Big A. Wouldn't want the old gossips to lack a bone to gnaw over even for a weekend.

I rattle on like Bob Hope but am kinda sick about all this, Eila. Don't know what to do.

Love you,
Jody

Dear Tinker,

Hey kid. Hope this reaches you. Guess you're being held incommunicado for a while. I am too in a way.

You know, it would have been good that fateful Sunday had you entered the house a wee bit later. I was *trying* to convince your mother of the incredible idea that we never stole you—that you always enjoyed working with us of your own free will and we with you. But I know this philosophy of joy-through-work is tantamount to Communism in them thar woods. (Might as well be hanged for a radical as a liberal.)

Have a good year at school and at the library. Hope it isn't too soul-destroying.

Don't give up on liberating Endfield—Goddess knows the place needs it.

Best wishes,
Jody

12

April 30
5 a.m.

Dear Jody,

I don't know what to say. I never thought you'd do this to me. When we talked years ago about what to do if "it" ever happened, we agreed we'd brazen it down together until they forgot about it. Or we'd go on vacation together. Now you've dumped it all in my lap.

You can guess what's happening. Nobody says anything directly to me—not that I've been out. John is being a godsend buying food and a few things. But orders are vanishing right and left. St. Mary's Church has cancelled their Saturday standing order for three baskets. You know how many thousand $ a year that amounts to. There's a dance coming at Sons of Italy, and I assume their corsages will bloom from the daffodils in Mr. Pelacci's backyard.

John says we should publish an announcement in the *News* that although you've been "called away due to family illness, John Simons has joined the staff as a full-time employee, and Brandi Florist/Nursery welcomes your trade as usual." I think it's too early for that. When are you coming back?

I included your note to Tinker with her last paycheck in a windowed invoice envelope. I'm furious at her for messing up that Sunday. I still don't know what all has happened beyond that.

Jody, if you don't come back, there's no way I can face them down alone. If you do come help me, at least some of them will think it's all just been gossip. *It's no good, Jody, not being able to leave a house I've lived in all my life.* With you here, I feel I could.

I don't want to telephone you. What are you *doing* in New York?

Eila

May 5

Dear Eila,

What am I doing? Well, yesterday I had lunch with a German journalist, friend of Su's. She's here doing "a profile of America" for a German paper, and I'm supposed to tell her about small town life before she sets out for the Midwest. Yecch! They all think I'm on vacation, I guess. Am I?

Love,
Jody

P.S. What about an answer to my questions?

13

Well, on my way home from school, I stopped at the nursery, hoping Eila or Jody would care to talk. When I found the office locked, I walked back to the greenhouse. John was building a couple of baskets of lilies for a funeral and looking equally funereal. He said business was way off, especially with the churches, and that Jody was visiting somebody in New York. He hadn't seen Eila since that morning.

"Is she sick?" I asked.

"You could say that."

"No, I mean really sick. With flu or something."

"I don't know. She's in the house. You know, Tinker, you and your mother really fouled things up here." He turned away and resumed snipping and wiring.

I thought if I depended on John for courage or confidence, I wouldn't get far. I wanted to retort how I had *no* control over my mother or Nedda, finally said nothing. There were already too many not-busy-enough bodies involved in this mess and, besides, I hated posing as last of the bigtime victims—that bitter adult role at which I'd overstudied Ma these long years. I still smarted from that Good Friday conversation and Easter aftermath.

Embarrassed, I walked away. I knocked several times at the back door but Eila didn't respond. I fantasized a note I might leave, but even two sentences at the wrong moment are dangerous in Endfield. *Help. Am held prisoner in a nuclear family. Send an invert.*

That evening the editorial page of the *Endfield News* carried this nuclear blast from our moral guardian Nedda:

VANISHING MINORITY?

To the Editor:

Every community of citizens should have the right to define what kind of behavior should or should not be considered tolerable, especially when such behavior affects young children and other impressionable people within the community. None of us liked, for example, the litter and fire hazard created by summer picnickers, including hippies, on the Ledge so we voted monies for a watchman to supervise the area. And for our children we pay hundreds of thousands a year to obtain good schooling given in a new building by competent teachers.

However, something has gone wrong. It has come to my attention that two people who have made their living in and from our town have not conducted themselves in a ladylike and moral fashion toward each other and toward at least one of the children whom they have hired. I consider that their kind of life, while perhaps tolerated in a big, anonymous city, has no place in an honest community like Endfield, especially when a minor is involved. As the twig is bent, so the tree grows.

Endfield parents still try hard, despite this age of smut, drugs, delinquency, violence, and homosexuality, to raise their children in a Godfearing and moral way. It seems that conscientious parents, raising healthy families, have become a disappearing race and deserve help as "a persecuted minority"—far more so than the outspoken, often vulgar people who presently flaunt their so-called "oppressed minority" lives and illnesses in books, movies, and tv programs.

I ask that at the next Representative Town Meeting, the Board of Selectmen pass a resolution banning the practice of homosexuality and homosexual solicitation from Endfield and recommending religious or psychiatric consultation for any individuals so involved.

Sincerely yours,
(Mrs.) Nedda Howard

Nedda is a widow and can be unbelievable sometimes, nattering on about her son, my oldest cousin Howard A. Howard (that's his name), as if he was God's gift first to Exeter Prep School, then to Yale. A couple years ago he finally married—a Boston University girl his mother considered dull and sloppy. The wedding, which happened under a tree in Vermont, featured a female Unitarian minister instead of a priest. Nedda was "sick about it" for weeks; I thought it served her right.

Nedda's letter to the *Endfield News* seemed particularly vicious because written through hearsay (talking to my mother) instead of questioning anyone directly concerned, such as Eila, Jody, or me. The human thing to do might have been to confront them honestly with something like, "Look, my sister has told me some upsetting stories about you, and she's afraid for Tinker. Are the stories true? How do you explain them?"

That nobody had guts to do this but automatically judged Eila and Jody both "guilty by gossip" and eager to poison my tender twig shows how Old World (Puritan-Jansenist), at least un-American, Endfield truly is. Five minutes after reading Nedda's letter I realized what hypocritical hogwash all that stuff from Mr. Wilson's civics classes was about the glory of America as a land where you're innocent first until (maybe) proven guilty later. Jody and Eila, however, were judged guilty before they ever came to trial.

Later I decided that this innocent-until-guilty bit was another Puritan ideal that got washed out to sea somewhere between Plymouth Rock and Boston. When I reached one semester of college, I read a sociology text with the maplesugar theory that people in small towns are, if anything, schizophrenic—there's a public morality "to which we all adhere" but also a private morality. Supposedly, your private affairs remain your own business so that it's possible now to be a happy vegetarian or skydiver even in an Endfield—so long as you don't injure other people's private property, children included, or force your beliefs on anyone. In this noble view, you can be a happy minority, at worst ignored or scorned, at best catered to by the beaming majority, so secure and tolerant that they let you do your own thing. Sure . . . if you live ten miles outside town, never run a business or talk to twelve-year-old girls—if the town, by tolerating you, has nothing to lose, in other words.

Summer people and Ferncliff students may be "queer" in as many senses as they can achieve because they do spend money in Endfield's restaurants, motels, and gift shops before, blessedly, leaving around June 1 (students) or September 1 (tourists). "Glad to see 'em come, glad to see 'em go." A double or triple standard ever operative about what forms appropriate conduct for "us" and "them."

Part of forgetting that your father or grandfather was a farmer, railway worker, or millrat and your grandmother bore six to twelve children she couldn't prevent is to imagine yourself better than somebody else. Egalitarian radicals, whether Communist, Socialist, or Liberty Union, are wasting their time in Endfield where some men and more women regard their working class origin, with its substandard housing, clothing, and Italian, Polish, or French Canadian dialect of English, as horrors to be escaped, no romantic idyll to be re-embraced. Except for the College, the funeral home, and scattered mansions belonging to the judge, lawyers, and doctors, during the Thirties everybody's house was decked in Early Poverty. Tuna noodle casseroles and homeknit argyles, hooked rugs and wood stoves weren't tourist attractions but stable and staple modes of personal survival for nights and temperatures of twenty below.

Such a hardy, hearty working class community probably did exude ethnic friendliness until Nedda's and my mother's generation. That was the first whose fathers or husbands had accumulated sufficient cash to raise its head or sights into the "lady" category. Ladies, like other *nouveaux riches,* are more apt to prefer hardhearted calculation to hardy friendliness—whatever will do them more good.

Hardheartedness can, of course, coexist with sentimentality in some humans—the sort of emotional bathos that can gyrate into a tizzy over sick kittens, African violets, or the secrets of piecrust while being downright stingy to children, husbands, or large dogs, anything that perpetually gobbles food, dirties clothes, and might not be, well, housebroken. Your soul may be dying but your socks are always clean.

To me, ladyhood with its tenets, clothes, illusions, whether fostered by men or magazines, involves at least one massive contradiction. On one hand, a young lady "who respects herself" is supposed to be worth more on the marriage market. On the other, ladyhood hobbles a woman with an incapacity for life because it assures she has no equipment to deal honestly with the different, the cruddy, the kinky except by cursing or extinguishing them, pretending They Don't Exist. If she can't fight them, maybe she can hide them under the rug, ideally wall to wall.

Right after Nedda's letter hit the fan, my carefree childhood hours at Endfield Regional ("the best days of your life," according to my mother) deteriorated rapidly.

From my arithmetic teacher Mrs. LeBlanc I got pity: "And you worked there four years? What a shame it should end like that. But it's better not to return, dear. Those people, well, they aren't like *us,* you know."

"But Eila was born in this town."

"Oh well, must be she got some bad ideas out in Colorado. Poor girl."

It's all those outside agitators attacking us red, white, trueblue (and lilylivered) hometown folks.

We have met the enemy and they is us....

From Miss Dealey after home ec class, gossip: "Tinker, I heard Jody's gone from Brandi Nursery for good? So it must be true what everybody's saying? Did you...see anything while you were there?"

"My work was writing orders and answering the phone."*Tinker the Grind, just doing her job.*

The worst blow, however, came discourtesy of Pammy. She'd been avoiding me for a couple days after our return from Easter vacation. I caught her at her locker, twiddling the dial.

"My mother doesn't want me to associate with you anymore," Pammy announced. "She asked me all kinds of questions about the nursery and you, and I—I told her what you and I did that night."

My head swirled. Pammy's black hair and white face unfocused. "What?....But that was supposed to be secret. Just the two of us."

"Well, she kept asking. What could I do? She doesn't even want me to talk to you anymore. She thinks if you had more supervision, this wouldn't have happened."

"That's crap, Pammy. This whole town is one supervised eyesore."

"She doesn't like your language either."

"Crap!" *So much for Pammy. Friend of my youth.* Massive blast of self-pity hit me midway between study hall and gym. I could hardly swallow the hot dog and carrot stick lunch that day.

Throughout April-early May I slunk, hating everybody—Pammy, Nedda, my parents, and most of all, Eila and Jody for leaving me to field everybody's nastiness with cheeks stinging, tongue silenced. I envied Jody's adult freedom to cut and run. When one ugly comment about "perverts" popped up, ("Didn't you guess what those women are?"), I got insanely tempted to blab what I'd seen through the window. Luckily for Eila and Jody, the urge passed. It became my test of honor to say less about more.

Gradually I sensed two basic viewpoints among the accusers, present or absent: "Poor little Tinker, what those terrible women did to her. No wonder she's crazy" versus "Well, she's always been a brat. Probably deserves what she gets. There's no telling how children will turn out *these* days." My mother reported regularly on the first variety of Job's comfort while never mentioning the second, probably because it cut too close to the quick of her own feelings about me.

She also landed some sympathy: "That poor woman. What a terrible thing to happen just before her baby comes. Now a thing like that can cause a miscarriage. Let's hope at least the new baby's normal." *Tinker, the Genetic Deviate.*

In late April Nedda came to visit. By sitting on the stair landing I discovered similar two-pronged, run-of-the-mouth viewpoints about Eila as about me.

Nedda: "It's disgusting. Those women living an unnatural life going around hiring youngsters."

Ma: "Eila's lived in this town her whole life except for Colorado. If she never left, I'm sure she would have married the way the rest of us did. I hear Jim Donohugh's coming back to see her. His brother, Roy, is graduating from Ferncliff College in business or something."

Nedda: "Humph. Well, if that's the best the Donohughs could do. (Forgetting my father teaches at Ferncliff.) Howard called last night from Exeter. Got another A on his physics exam, and he's writing for the school magazine. His housemaster raves about him. . . . There are so many opportunities for young people today—*if* they know how to apply themselves."

I stopped listening then. *Tinker, Misapplication Personified.* I wondered what it must be like to have somebody rave good stuff about you. *My Daughter the Genius. Theresa Tharp, well known author and social critic* instead of Tinker, hyperkinetic invert with stringy hair and kinky tendencies.

> *I'm an invert. Who are you?*
> *Are you an invert, too?*

For thirty seconds on those stairs, my defenses crumpled to such a god-awful low I even imagined myself a Good Girl on the way to becoming an Adult Lady. Slinking back to my room, I turned on the news and bit into a used apple.

I plotted how and where to run away, whom I could get to cosign so I could withdraw enough money from my bank account for the bus to Boston. I could live on my last paycheck from Eila until I found a job.

I'd seen the news photo of a twelve-year-old girl in wig, fringy eyelashes, and hotpants who earned a fancy salary as a prostitute. She even had PTA car raffle tickets in her pocket in case the police asked what she was selling on the corner. At the time, it seemed a possible future. Ultra American and female free enterprise was how I imagined it. Maybe if I got a padded bra and a tight dress?

Not the least enticing aspect of this plan was how it enabled a twelve-year-old to earn money for what respectable ladies spent a lifetime supplying free to bored husbands.

Next I scanned the *Endfield News* announcements and ads, trying to discover some activity where I'd feel accepted again.

The Girl Scouts. . . maybe they'd take me back. I saw that Ginny and Sandy had piled up new badges for race relations and camping. Pammy and I had quit Scouts the year before, figuring it was for little kids.

The Gardening Club was sponsoring a bonsai lecture. . . . *Miss Theresa Tharp, noted horticultural dropout.* . . .

Ferncliff College and Endfield Regional were both planning graduations.

The Ferncliff Music Festival was selling tickets. Another ploy to prevent default.

Miss Stanner at the library, of course, had never telephoned me. I read: "Mrs. George Firkle, assistant, helps Head Librarian Una Stanner with book displays and other arrangements for National Library Week. The library's longer hours will be. . . ." Miss Stanner had combed her sausage rolls all to the same side of her head for the festivity. The only positive aspect about my current mess was that I'd escaped working for her. Still, I envied Jane Firkle. What did she have that I hadn't already given away?

In "Around the Village" I read:

Mrs. Mary Garrity believes she has the first Mayflowers to bloom this year. At the edge of her woodlot, sheltered from the cold winds and covered with pine needles, in a sunny spot, she discovered the State Flower, the trailing arbutus, in full bloom.

I'm a gutsy arbutus. How about you?
Are you an arbutus, too?

During that three weeks when we were all coming out together, I saw only one notice for Brandi Nursery/Florist—not the usual spring display ad but a few lines in the closet of the Classifieds:
THE SEASON IS ON
WE HAVE AN UNBEATABLE SALE
Potted Easter Lilies $3.49 while they last; Hardy Primroses 6/$6
Jumbo hybrid Rosebushes reg. $1.69 now 87¢
Delaware Azaleas 18"–24" $7
Pansies $1.19 box; White and yellow onion sets
JUST ARRIVED   JUST ARRIVED
Quince, rhododendron, hydrangea; Hanging gardens $3.98 up
MOTHER'S DAY PLANT—EXOTIC ANGEL
Strikingly beautiful, excellent around the house.
White netted, veiny leaves are attention getters.

Reading all that flora made me nostalgic for my old life. I realized I couldn't begin to feel human or normal again until I managed to talk with Eila and Jody or get them to talk with me about what had engulfed all of us.

After days of planning, counterplanning, and general mooning, I left my room.

14

May 10
Boulder, Col.

Dear Eila,
Did you get my letter? I'm returning on the 28th to march with Dad in the Memorial Day parade. Then there's Roy's graduation and the College music festival. Should I ask him to reserve a seat for you at either? Let me or Mom and Dad know *soon* (before the 15th).

Looking forward to seeing you. Oil and mines are good for a few years, but I think of home sometimes.

Yours,
Jim

15

Early in May I found Eila sunbathing on a quilt behind one of the greenhouses. She looked springy and multicolored in aqua shorts, a green halter wrapped into a sash at her waist, and a straw picture hat. From the tan she'd already acquired in the vernal heatwave (that year's weather went berserk from snowdrifts in early April to 95° afternoons three weeks later), I gathered she wasn't writing many invoices.

She sat up, crossed her legs, and stared at me. Instead of smiling, she frowned. "Tinker, I've wanted to call you. I know you kind of saved our life that day by banging on the window. But I really am furious at everything since then." My heart and stomach sank someplace. "Why couldn't you have handled your mother better? If she hadn't—"

"Where's Jody?" *Why didn't you handle Jody better?*

Eila's mouth flattened to a thin line—the Endfield Special, tough-break-but-solve-it-yourself-don't-bother-me. I expected her to snap, "None of your business!" Instead, her answer came sad. "In New York. She's...visiting some friends."

"But you should go and see her. *Anywhere* is better than here."

"Tinker, if it weren't for you, Jody and I *would* be here, just like any other spring. Weren't you responsible for that letter in the paper? Come on, I want to know what you told them." With one hand she held my chin so I couldn't turn my head.

"When my mother wouldn't let me see you, I tried to send you a postcard. The mailman delivered it to Nedda's house. I know, it was a stupid thing to do. But look, all that crap at school I'm getting. Pammy's dropped me." Eila said nothing so I continued, "My mother and Nedda put together a whole case against you and Jody and me, too." Repressing my confession with Father Henry as another bad memory and the source of Eila's financial ruin, I concluded, "It burns me how they didn't ask any of us honestly what we did. They just assume we're guilty of something or other. It doesn't matter what."

"What did the postcard say?"

"Just apology for talking too much. Oh, I signed it 'love.' That's what blew Nedda's head."

"But I can't go anywhere. I can't leave my own house." Pain crinkled the lines around Eila's mouth and eyes.

Before she dissolved into self-pity, I tried again. "Well, I've made it out to school every day. If you think *that's* fun—listening to all that sneering and hate. You know, you kind of deserted me." There, it was out.

Eila's eyes blinked in surprise. "I deserted *you?* But Jody's deserted me."

"Yuh. Maybe you can go away, too. How about a vacation?" I wanted to beg, take me with you, but guessed that would strike her as the last of the no-good ideas.

"What? With four thousand dollars' worth of new spring stock and and equipment? Tinker, grow up!"

My face blushed at her rebuke. I turned away so she wouldn't notice. "It was just a suggestion," I mumbled.

"Well, keep them to yourself," she snapped. Then she took one of my hands in hers. "I'm sorry. I've hardly slept these last days, wondering what to do."

"You mean whether to go or stay here? Just like me. I've been thinking about running away."

My confession didn't faze her. She answered, "I wish *I* could. I wish it was that simple. Just pack and leave."

"And never have to face crappy comments again."

"It isn't even the comments. It's. . .it's I don't know what to do about Jody." Eila dropped my hand, raised her knees, laid her head on them.

"Well, if she's just visiting, maybe she'll get sick of it and come back. I think you should go and get her."

"I couldn't face it if—what if she won't *come* back with me?"

"But everything blows over in this town. When I got picked up for shoplifting, when I fell out of Whalens' tree. I mean, everybody gabs for a month or so about what a fool you are. Then the summer people arrive who act even stupider, and people forget." I wasn't sure myself I believed all this Pollyanna stuff, but it seemed the kindest thing to say. I felt bad to see Eila drooping there in the sun like a geranium she'd forgot to water.

Her green halter had slipped, and more of her ample breasts were displayed at closer range than even that day at the window. I quelled an urge to run my fingers between them. I didn't do it because she might think I was an invert, and who needed another one? I mean, it wouldn't have done her any good then. *Girls shouldn't make passes at lasses in sashes....* I also felt sharp self-pity at my own cowardice or discretion (I never knew which)—a failure with boys, yet afraid to touch or comfort a woman I'd worked beside for four years. I pictured myself at the only other adult future I could imagine—raising dogs—since I was such a flop at people.

I put my right arm around her bare shoulders. Then I couldn't tell whether she was laughing or crying, but it turned to tears. I found tears in my own eyes. What stopped me from crying was the same realization I always got with my mother: What did it all matter, anyway, because I was only substituting for somebody else she'd rather be consoled by—in this case, Jody?

What if Jody never returned? Maybe Eila and I could live together and continue as before? LOCAL GIRL LOST SIX HOUSES FROM HOME. Imagining her and me in the soft double bed made me overheat from more than the May sun....Big chance, with $4,000 worth of nursery stock pining away for lack of interest by Endfielders who suddenly had more on their minds than rosebushes and Mother's Day bouquets.

With Eila's towel I wiped my face, then passed it to her to hide her crying. Now I sat holding *her* hand, falling more in love with her, second by second. *How do I attract these no-win situations?* No bed with Eila, no Jody to make me laugh, no Pammy to tell it to. John didn't like me, and I couldn't even stroll unnoticed around a town I was born in. The only choice was to straggle back home, the prodigal daughter. I sat motionless.

"Can you and I go to New York and get Jody together?" I asked.

Eila looked up from her towel. "I can't take you anywhere! Your mother—"

"Oh, bleep her!"

Eila laughed. "I think somebody already has, according to you."

"See? I made you laugh." Then I stood behind her shoulders and above her sunhat. She smelled like incense. I leaned over and began to tickle her across the middle. She squirmed deliciously and wound up on her back with me kneeling astride her hips. It was great flirtatious fun, but John was watching us from the greenhouse as I assaulted his one remaining employer.

Suddenly Eila stopped defending herself by tickling and poking me back. Again I supposed my antics either embarrassed or reminded her of Jody. Why couldn't I ever remind anybody of *me?* Reluctantly I climbed off, ending the first fun I'd shared with anybody in a month. The sun shown hot on my face and shoulders. The quilt felt rumpled and soggy under us.

Eila mused. "Speaking of our going somewhere, do you know in the 1920's they had a law called the Mann Act? It prohibited transporting a minor across state lines. It was supposed to prevent kidnappings."

"Hey, I'd enjoy being kidnapped." *If you got the ladder, I got the time. And if nobody claims me in 30 days, I'm yours.* "Did it...prevent anything?"

"I don't know." Eila's weary tone. "Laws for or against something don't work unless the time is right. People are ready to heed them. You have to educate them or make them feel guilty. Otherwise, it's all a failure. Like trying to stop people parking around Park Square. Nobody felt guilty because everybody's left horses or cars there since 1777."

"My mother said overdue parking slips aren't enough. You have to slap on big fines, payable that day at Town Hall, especially for the tourists who park any which way."

"Yes, this town is *so* hospitable."

"What're you gonna do to get Jody back?"

"I don't know."

A brain wave hit me. "The Memorial Day parade's coming. She always got a kick out of flowering up the truck into a float...You know, you looked great as Snow White last year, but *I* had a big problem. If anybody cares."

"I know, I know. You refuse to play dwarf again."

"Yeah. I hereby resign as Chief Dwarf. Pammy, too. Also I threw that pointed green hat away."

"How could you? That was my mother's."

"Tough."

"How *dare* you speak that way about my dead mother?" Mock outrage.

"Well, you bleeped over mine first," I protested.

Eila gazed away to the trees. "I don't know whether they're doing costumed floats this year. Everybody cracks up laughing at all the kids and animals in drag. It isn't very respectful for Memorial Day, considering we all wind up at the cemetery."

"Immediately or inevitably?" I'd heard my father ask that one.

"Both....Tinker, you've really blossomed this year. You used to be so...quiet. What's happened?"

"All the usual stuff. Plus, quiet or noisy, I get into trouble all the time anyway, so I may as well relax and enjoy it."

Eila smiled. "I wish I could."

"Eila, I do have one question. May I ask? It's well, I don't know, how did you and Jody think you could live in Endfield a long time without...people finding out?"

Eila's face went all pained. "But we have until...I guess I thought people knew us so well they wouldn't believe it, it wouldn't matter."

"But you know how scared everybody is of anything different around here. It frightens them all the more because they *do* know you and me."

"Well, they do make us feel about as welcome as cancer or mononucleosis."

"Hey, you can get mono from kissing, too." *As well as an inversion layer.*

"Tinker! How about a bargain? I don't ask you any questions about your private life, and you don't ask me any. And you don't go looking around our windows."

"That's no fair. You know I don't *have* a private life. I'm a sweet little girl innocent as—"

"As twelve going on twenty-five."

"I lost my virginity behind the gloxinia."

"Tinker, shut up. . . . How're we going to get Jody back here?"

"Oh father, dear father, come home with me now.

The clock in Endfield strikes—" (I cribbed that from a tv rerun of Milton Berle.)

And Eila smacked me on the shoulder somewhat like my mother, who also shuddered whenever I entered Overdrive. Suddenly I longed for Jody's sturdier ways. However, I rejoiced that Eila finally understood and forgave my banging on her window as the only way to warn her of my mother's arrival. "Let me write Jody. Or I'll call her," I suggested.

"Would you?"

"Sure."

"I don't know. Let me think some more. Tinker, do you know Jim Donohugh?"

"I know his brother. Roy's graduating. I wish I was graduating. From anything."

"Jim's coming back from Colorado."

"Will he help you get Jody?"

"No. But he might help with a float for the parade."

"Was he your boyfriend?"

"Sort of."

"But Jody told me you were engaged to somebody."

"Well, Jim wanted to marry, and I didn't. So we drifted apart. I had met Jody anyway."

"Did you love him?"

"I don't know." Eila crossed her arms and stared away beyond the trio of greenhouses.

16

"Hello? Jody?....Jody, hi. This is Tinker. How are you? What are you doing there?...Not much. Things are quieter here now. I mean, there was a big stink. I don't have a friend left here but Eila, but it's blown over now. I mean, people are planning for the parade. Will you come back and drive the truck for the parade? Oh, here's Eila. She wants to say hello. I have to leave. Bye for now."

I walked back to the greenhouse so Eila could have the privacy she'd requested. Jody's voice had sounded strained or drained—forced monosyllables—as if we'd interrupted her amid a busy urban evening. I envied her. To stop fidgeting around the greenhouse, I found the glass pitcher and began to water some crates of pink petunias.

When I returned to the kitchen, Eila was slumped there, aligning her address book between the table edge and a few boxes of seedlings. Her eyes stared; she looked stunned.

Since I never learned how to "inquire indirectly" ("A lady always puts others at their ease"), I just blurted out, "Is she coming back?"

"No."

"Are you going to see her?"

"No."

Now my face and spirits fell. I realized how I'd dreamed either that Jody would return or that Eila would take me to New York. I felt exhausted, paralyzed.

On the counter the phone rang. Eila signaled me to pick it up just as if we were working again. Instead of Jody reconsidering, it was a Colorado operator with a person-to-person call from Jim Donohugh. At my repeating his name, Eila's face got alarmed. "Tell him to call back later," she mouthed.

She says she's not here. I could hear Jim crunching around at the other end. It was the first time I'd heard somebody from so far. What did people do there? He didn't talk Western like Jody but Eastern like

Eila and me. *Dumbbell. He was born in Endfield just like you.*

"Yeah, that's right. Please try later. She's out now." Another lie and venial sin on my list that already stretched long enough to wrap around the town. . . . Oh well, what's one more? Just as I was deciding I'd rather be hanged for lying than slander, Eila laid her head on her arms next to the boxes of seedlings.

Poor Jim Donohugh. When he called back, he'd have a floral basket case awaiting him.

When I touched Eila's sweatered shoulders, she shrugged me off. Wondering what to do, forbidden to joke or tease, I sought Endfield's universal solvent. I lit the gas under the red coffeepot. Coffee in Endfield serves the purpose of ordinary water elsewhere. This for Eila, since I've never learned to drink the brown brew, preferring my caffeine as Coca-Cola.

As the coffee heated, I studied the blue gas flames, wondered whether Eila was how people looked and sounded just before they "did away with" themselves, in Nedda's phrase. Imagining life without Eila chilled and panicked me. I cast around for some excuse to stay there until she could perk up and replant herself.

I sugared and creamed the hot coffee and stuck her fingers around the mug. "Tinker, thanks. You're certainly a better friend than anybody else around here."

Flattery will get you everywhere. "Okay. But I want something."

"One thing, Tinker—you're not shy." Eila smirked crosswise at me.

"What I want is maybe sometime when *I* don't feel so good, you'll talk with me."

"You mean about your mother."

I hadn't thought that's what I needed talking about. How did Eila know something I didn't know about me? That must be what acting really grownup involves. . . .

"I'll tell you something. Jody got along tremendously with her mother, but I didn't do so well with mine. I was too much like my Dad. . . . Maybe we can talk about it sometime."

"I'd like that. But I meant something else. I mean I want to talk about you and Jody. I know she meant everything to you. But that's the trouble."

"What are you talking about?"

"I can't say it right, but it's something just like with my parents. When two people mean *so* much to each other—at first it's too much, then it's too little, then it's nothing. I mean there's no room for anybody else."

"Look, you were an employee here, not a relative."

Why does Jody mean so much you wind up beat like my mother?
"No. I mean it's wrong to be so dependent on something or somebody else. It can wreck you."

"All right, Miss Free Spirit, Zen priestess, how do *you* propose I run the business? Not with Jim Donohugh! . . . You mean play silly games to make Jody jealous so she'll come back?"

The thought of that—then the need to reject it—tripped over each other in my head.

"Tinker, you know I can't stand looking weak and whining like that."

"I'm glad. . . . Hey, maybe you can explain it to my mother sometime. About how somebody being full of problems is one way to get what they want, but it makes everybody else feel awful."

"Tinker, my mother always accused me of siding with my father. I never got anywhere with her until I was in my twenties and she was no longer so mad at him. Or I was finally an adult like her then. . . . Actually I miss her now."

"Really?"

"Sure. If you go around hating your mother, it means you hate yourself or one important part of you. Unless you make peace with her, she'll haunt your life."

"And maybe if I was an azalea, you'd be more interested in *me!*"

"Tinker . . ." Eila took my hand. "None of us can solve anybody else's problems for them. Sometimes all we can do is care. I do appreciate all the help you've given me for years. You know I do."

And I let it go for then.

Ever since I'd looked up those terrible definitions in the library (which made me feel like killing somebody because they so falsified the real Jody and Eila I'd known since I was born), I'd tried to find a decent book to sneak looks at. One that wasn't all sneery and pessimistic.

I opened one thing called *The Age of Sensation: A Psychoanalytic Exploration.* The jacket copy almost made me drop it. When one male doctor praises the work of two other male doctors—a neo-Freudian Closed Shop—can you guess their opinion of women?

While the paramount problem of young men is to marshal enough aggression to get by, that of the female is not to get trapped in a disastrous marriage or in the toils of responsibility to the growing child. In either case, you can't win!

So far, so bright.

> Dr. _____ treats in a masterful way the escapes through homosexuality, drugs, and suicide.... He shows how in our confusion we are encouraging the flight into sensation, the numbness, the egocentrism and the experiential acquisitiveness that are driving men and women and family apart. It may not be too late to save the family. It is to be hoped that this study will serve as a challenge to our national conscience.

It probably is too late to save the family, and couples like Eila and Jody who, honestly united for some other reason than babies, may be the wave of our overpopulated future. And doctors like _____ only make people sicker by loading guilt on them. Just like the Church. I say unto you, Repent cringing and we will love you. If you're a wreck, you're never a threat.

I dropped the black-covered *Age of Sensation* back into the New Books section, overcoming the urge to steal it and subtract one volume from the total literature that condemns homosexuals as escapist freaks or suicide-prone addicts.

Where was the sexual revolution that had done so much for (or to) so many? Open marriage, pre-marriage, post-marriage, no marriage. Had it nothing for Eila and Jody or for me who still loved both of them? Was this sexual revolution I'd seen in my mother's *Redbook* just another gimmick to sell jock shorts or birth control pills?

17

FERNCLIFF COLLEGE — EDUCATION FOR THE NEW AGE
May 20

Dear Miss Brandy:

Perhaps you'll remember my sister and me from some time ago. I remember with what care you and Miss Jody arranged the baskets and sprays in the funeral home, at the church and cemetery, and then at our own home after our parents' auto accident. Your real concern and attention to details, especially to the phoning that even the funeral home personnel seemed too rushed to care about, genuinely touched both of us. If it weren't for you, one of our faraway relatives would have missed the Burial Mass entirely.

In two weeks my niece will get married to a young man she met at her school. It's one of the new outdoor weddings that are all the campus rage now. Regardless of how untraditional the ceremony will be, I do want her to have some nice flowers. I want to order two baskets of whatever you recommend, plus a small bridal bouquet. Will you phone me about this?

We know your business has been interrupted due to certain recent circumstances. Whether the topic is fluorine in the water or more parking on Main Street, some people always have too much to say. However, others of us appreciate your work in and for the town.

> Wishing you every success,
> (Miss) Marian K. Dorne

When Eila showed me this letter, she was smiling, her small let's-wait-and-see style. Reading that handwriting under the College letterhead put the queerest lump in my throat. Like my family, Marian

Dorne and her sister were Catholics, but they must have been the agreeably lapsed kind who didn't let a private matter like somebody's sexual orientation forbid some perfectly good flowers to grace an exciting occasion. Though the wording was indirect—and might never have occurred without her niece's wedding—still Marian Dorne had bothered to compose it.

Another bit of unexpected support came from Mr. Ferguson, who runs the Five and Ten on Main Street. In Bill O'Connell's day this store was a tiny, dingy affair full of stale chocolates, dog-eared cards, dusty dolls. Before Mr. Ferguson returned from Viet Nam and bought it, it had always smelled as if recovering from a fire and water sale. Two years before, however, he had plaid-carpeted the bare wood, hung new fluorescent lights from the molded tin ceiling, flattened a wall to expand into the old dry goods store next door, installed a new glass and aluminum front—all part of that New England mirage called "sprucing up Main Street."

However, the old alley behind Main Street, which had lost none of its original smelly charm, remained one of the seedy joys of my childhood. Twelve feet wide from brick buildings to splintered fence, its damp driveway stretched the block from Salvatore's Restaurant to the granite Town Hall. At all seasons it overflowed with excelsior and tissue, rotting fruit and cartons, broken china and toys, the patter of dogs and slither of rats. Truck drivers and garbage men cursed as they unloaded (or reloaded) food and merchandise; townspeople used it as a shortcut.

Since tourists had become Endfield's year-round business, and "up attic" junk, otherwise known as "antiques new and old," had joined babies as a cottage industry, even tourists joined the kids who regularly checked the alley for tag sale-type treasures. And just as regularly, the kids at least were chased away by Pete, Mr. Ferguson's assistant. In fact, the other stores, from the old ladies at the dry goods at one end of the block to the busy Italian cooks at the other, depended on Pete in the middle to Lay-Down-the-Law to us brats and vandals from both ends.

Beginning as a stockboy after the Korean War, Pete had stayed on as a clerk. I still hated buying my mother's sanitary napkins from him because you had to ask for them brown-bagged by name and size from under the counter, like contraceptives or X-rated paperbacks. I rejoiced when the enlarged supermarket began carrying them openly like paper diapers on the new shelves.

So it was Peter, now gray-haired "assistant manager," who stood with Mr. Ferguson in the alley arranging cartons that some "pesty kids," led by Danny Thomas's younger brother, had just knocked over. As I walked along the alley carrying a bag of bread and milk, I saw Danny's brother's tribe in jeans, pastel tee shirts and Indian beaded belts beating it around the fence up the alley.

"Damn kids," Mr. Ferguson muttered as he kicked wads of news-paper and excelsior back into boxes. Although Pete still wore the gray stock coat, Mr. Ferguson was nattier in a yellow golf shirt and green trousers.

"Hi, Tinker," Pete said. Foreheads wrinkled, they both looked frazzled as usual so I was surprised when Mr. Ferguson echoed, "Hi, Tinker. Come here." Since I wasn't doing anything for which he could scold me, I assumed he either wanted me to run an errand or to ask about the boys Pete had just chased. It turned out neither.

"How's your mother doing?"

"Okay."

"You know, she and I went to school together." His eyes twinkled at me. Even Pete smiled. "But she married your father instead," Mr. Ferguson continued.

I never knew Mrs. Ferguson very well. She had beehived blonde hair, came from outside Endfield and, despite her husband's business, didn't mix with us locals beyond saying hello at the market. Did he perhaps regret *not* marrying my mother, who certainly excelled at close, if not always comfortable, relations with half of Endfield?

"Been hearing a lot of talk about Eila and the nursery. I know you worked there a long time." I must have cringed, but he continued his cheerful tone. "I went to school with Eila, too. I was a senior when she was a sophomore. I liked Eila; everybody did. I remember once I drove by a girls' softball game at the athletic field in my new car. Eila was supposed to be catching in the infield. She took her eyes off the batter long enough to wave and yell at me. Well, you know what happened?"

I shook my head no so he would continue the story until I could devise something to say.

"Well, Eila missed a line drive. Whistled right past her ear because she was waving at me. The whole field booed her. I can't remember who won or lost, but she sure was unpopular that day. But she made it up later. She was a good catcher. So thin and quick she could zip anywhere."

I interrupted, "Look, why don't you call her up and say hello? She's feeling kind of low right now."

"I heard. . . . It's sad to destroy a whole business like that just because folks suddenly . . ."

"What?"

"Well, you know. Just tell her this hurts all of us business people. ...Actually we *need* to get these things out in the open and discuss them."

"Okay. I'll tell her. But you call her sometime, too."

Pete and Mr. Ferguson walked inside. I continued up the alley toward Franklin Street. Although I felt frustrated because I hadn't got him to promise anything, still I skipped along happy for the first time in weeks.

So the town had at least two (maybe four, counting Pete and Miss Dorne's sister) people unafraid to deal realistically, if indirectly, with a taboo topic. Like Diogenes, I felt I'd found an honest man—in Endfield of all places.

18

That spring Jody was not the only one who ran away.

Early in May, word rushed along Franklin onto Laurel that Judy James "with those four lovely children" had deserted same plus husband and run off to Texas with Sam the new mechanic at Neilson's garage. I'd been inside Judy's apartment only once to collect for some Girl Scout cookies. Even I could see how a moral, upright life of soggy diapers, jellied furniture, overdrawn check account, and no car could make a ride to Texas look like Paradise.

I imagined Judy fulfilling herself in a neat white tennis dress, instead of bulging maternity smock, lolling in a beach chair with Sam on the Gulf of Something, drinking mint julep instead of lukewarm Coke.

"And I hear he's five years younger than she is. It never works. She'll come back dragging her tail between her legs."

Still intensely curious about what people who "ran away" lived on during and after "it," I wanted to write a letter to tell her how I hoped she and Sam would be happy, no matter how the town cursed them, and how she needn't come back, the kids had probably never appreciated her anyway, did I appreciate my mother, no, of course not, ay-eh, etc., and oh well.

I wrote to Jody instead.

This letter was much harder because I knew Jody wouldn't fall for any platitudes or mush.

Dear Jody,

I guess Tuesday night when Eila called was not such a good time for you. Everything is pretty much the same here. Eila is thinking about decorating the truck for the parade—just the wooden Brandi Nursery sign mounted on top plus some red, white, and blue crepe paper. Nothing fancy this year. Remember how Pammy I were dwarfs and Eila was Snow White last year, and you said you hated chauffeuring all us guys in drag but the show must go on, the DAR needed daisychains or something? Jim Donohugh is supposed to help this year.

Wednesday is the junior high picnic on the Ledge. Judy James ran away to Texas with Sam from the garage. Remember he fixed your truck? Thought you'd like the latest news. I bet she'll have a better time than here. All the news that fits, I print.

Yours,
Tinker

P.S. Somebody you already know will be coming to see you.

19

Okay. I admit I had nothing definite in mind when I wrote that last sentence to Jody. I knew only that my restlessness was fermenting a sort of plan or hope.

So that my parents wouldn't suspect, complaintlessly I washed dishes, picked up my clothes, attended classes, even Mr. Wilson's civics, which so bored me that I retreated to the girls' bathroom at least thrice weekly during it. Mr. Wilson was a high-foreheaded mumbler whose explanations of government process, legislation, and judiciary system pretended, like our textbook, that neither Viet Nam nor Watergate had ever happened. Once when somebody asked about the CIA, he admitted, "It has exceeded its prerogatives." However, that's the most we ever wheedled from him on current events. Like everybody, he feared losing his job, should a student report at home that Mr. Wilson had said anything "radical." Years later when I saw the scribble VOTE COMMUNIST IT'S YOUR PARTY, I remembered Mr. Wilson and how people like him can drive you radical through sheer boredom with small-time alternatives.

His Friday class that mid-May sticks in my mind because after finishing one of his fill-in-the-blank quizzes, I was staring out the window at some newly leaved trees around the Methodist steeple. *Well hell, I'll leave.* Just like that, without considering when, where, or how. A surge of energy buoyed me.

As I gazed at all those thirty students, sighing and rustling in their seats, my brain wheels spun to complete more blanks. Class picnic next Wednesday. Click. Take duffle bag from house with change of clothes. John is driving to Albany to return bushes or stuff Eila can't sell. Click, click.

How many bushes would it take to cover me in the closed back of the van? Hide in a gunny sack. . . . They'll see you. . . . Not if you sneak up from behind the nursery while he and Eila drink coffee in the kitchen.

By the time the bell rang, our tables scraped, Mr. Wilson collected quizzes, I had flash-outlined my plan.

As I hurried from the room, though, I realized I'd forgotten one minor detail: What I wanted to escape was clear, but what was I running toward? What can you reach from Albany on twenty dollars and (I checked my pocket) twenty-two cents? Canada was probably out. I was too young to know draft dodgers remaining there, anyway. Upstate New York, that nest of further small towns, was certainly farther out. That left southward, toward the home of Endfield's tourists if they had such a thing—New York City. Den of Iniquity, i.e., sex and violence such as I'd never seen. I could hardly wait.

During study hall, I found an old cultural tour of Manhattan book in the library and xeroxed its map for a nickel when nobody was looking. The map ended at 57th Street. I wondered whether Manhattan, too, ended there? If so, how could Jody be living on East 69th? Maybe that address was some entirely other part of New York City?

Well, I'd just ask when I got there. The tourists I'd already met at the nursery talked funny, put *r*s at the end of words where none belonged, dropped them elsewhere. But we all spoke English.

Suppose I got lost, Jody was gone or refused to see me? I decided to drop all those Nedda-type wet blanket items. If you imagine failure before it happens, you do a job on your own head.

Then it was Monday. Somehow I walked through those next two days, eating meals, hauling garbage, answering questions, doing homework with the worst divided head ever. I was *in* Endfield—all the familiar houses, people, and problems told me that—but I was no longer *of* Endfield. It was as if parts—my mother's pregnancy backache, my father's complaints about his tiredness and boss—no longer existed. No one asked me about school or my days now. They seemed glad of a respite from all the recent upset I'd caused.

Tuesday night at supper between the peas and porkchops, I began to intuit something new: Maybe the way to get along, if not live, with these people is never again to consider them too seriously, expect much from them. If you don't need them (as they've indicated they rarely need you), then they can't reach you. So you're halfway free. What you've tried to get water from is a stone; that's one reason you needed to drink up Eila and Jody. . . . Or maybe Eila's talk with me about how parents haunt you until you make peace had finally dissolved some submerged part of me.

In short, pieces of Endfield that had nearly drowned me receded like a flood that rushes downmountain, then vanishes, leaving the sun shining.

After supper, I packed my duffle bag with my drip-dry dress and padded bra, a comb and two pearl hairclips, a year-old pair of platform shoes, my wallet and map. In line with my new self: ignore these people, then they can neither make you guilty nor devour you with their problems while ignoring yours, I left the duffle bag openly on the chair instead of camouflaging it under the bed.

I awoke early, thrill and dread mixing through me, focused at my stomach. I washed and dressed. Glancing around my room a last time, I gave the ever-stuck door one joyous last kick (something my mother forbade because it chipped the paint).

As she drank coffee, I kissed her goodbye and said I hoped her backache would end.

"Don't sit on the ground. It's too cold yet," she cautioned as I skipped out the door.

By walking down Laurel, I reached another street that parallels it to a dead end behind the nursery bushes and evergreens. It was 7:45 a.m. I ran now, scared that John would already have left, sentencing me to a day at the school picnic pitching horseshoes and punching boys whenever they flung gloppy lakeweed or tadpoles at us.

Lately the kids had adopted mass giggling fits as the latest spring fever weapon to drive the teachers senile. Although I tried to join, either nothing that spring looked funny or giggling at nothing seemed so childish that I wound up in English class or the cafeteria staring at my hands like some prig. Although Pammy still avoided me, a few of the other kids had begun to notice me again.

"What's the matter?" Sandy and Ginny asked twice.

"I dunno," I mumbled. "Headache, I guess." Already my mother's physical excuse for emotional events. . . .

It was my time to exit Endfield.

In the nursery driveway the blue van still waited, parked back end open and away from the kitchen! Bending over, I scrunched along the path beside the three greenhouses, crossed the driveway, crept onto the metal floor of the truck. On the right, behind the passenger seat, John had piled crates of seedlings and on the left, five green sacks of fertilizer behind the driver's seat.

I folded myself behind the fertilizer and hid my duffle bag behind the boxes. The truck was so empty that I feared John would find me when he loaded more into it.

The kitchen door slammed. I hoped Eila wasn't coming out so I needn't hear her voice and get torn about saying goodbye. Instead, it was John who slammed the back door shut and climbed into the driver's seat.

As we rolled down Laurel toward the Turnpike, I couldn't believe it! Shifting the gears made enough noise so I found I could change position once in a while behind John's back without his hearing. I couldn't see out, except for sky and trees through the back window. So I imagined Endfield flowing by and away. The end of Laurel, onto Franklin, off Franklin onto High in order to bypass Main, then along West (that some DAR wanted renamed Minuteman Parkway to honor Endfield's fallen Revolutionary heroes), through the commercial "changing neighborhood" area to the Turnpike toll booth.

John swerved so fast up the curved entrance ramp that I nearly slid over to join my duffle bag, finally managing to hang on without getting crushed by the fertilizer. Luckily the sacks were plastic and emitted little odor or I'd have got asphyxiated as well as mashed by the wandering cow manure.

I sat up now.

John began to sing a Bob Dylan song about the times changing. I wondered whether he was as excited about escaping Endfield as I. Probably not. For him it was a routine trip to the wholesaler, part of his job, from which he'd return as soon as he finished exchanging and purchasing.

I wondered when we'd get officially "over the mountain" and into New York State. I hadn't traveled this way for a year since my father had come to examine a used car he hadn't bought. I rested my head against John's seat....

When the starts and stops began anew, I guessed we'd reached the Albany outskirts. Suddenly we veered off the road onto a rutty something. I figured we'd arrived.

John turned off the ignition, I scrunched back down until he'd left his seat, then knelt up, and bent my head to the driver's window. When I didn't spot him anywhere around the muddy yard or at the building to the right, I grabbed my duffle bag and eased both it and me out the driver's door. I headed for the red, white, and blue Exxon sign about a quarter mile down the road where I'd find a map, if not a ride.

Luck held; the goddess smiled that day. As I studied the faded map in the office, I asked a mechanic with wild hair and greasy jumpsuit how far the center of Albany was and when a bus came by.

"By here? Nah. For a bus you need the Greyhound station."

"Yes. My father's meeting me there." *If you got it, flaunt it. If you lack it, fake it.*

"Tell you what. Wait fifteen minutes till I finish this radiator job and I'll take you. I have to go by Hamilton."

"Can I use the ladies' room?"

"There's the key." He indicated the grimy white stick with unraveled string attached.

In the ladies' room I exchanged my jeans and shirt for dress and bra, tied on my platform shoes, secured my hair from both sides of my face with my barrettes. Inspecting results in the mirror, I decided I looked around four years older. Sixteen at least and ready for The Big City—if I could remember not to smile and flash my braces. In the 6 × 9 space I practiced different walks, choosing a sort of nonchalant roll over my usual slouch.

Leaving the ladies room, I glanced toward the garden center. The blue truck was still parked there with John if I wanted to change my mind.

"This here lady will take you," the mechanic said when I returned to the office.

And soon I was speeding by the garden center in a bucket seat of my first white Jaguar next to a lady in pink pants who played the radio too loud and chain-smoked. Not having to talk or answer questions relieved me, however.

Ten minutes later I walked into the Albany Greyhound terminal. In ten more I'd bought a one-way ticket and curled myself into a seat on the big bus. . . .

The rhythm and whine must have put me to sleep, for the backfire of a truck woke me just as the half-empty bus stopped to enter a loud tunnel. Next we arrived in a dark platform area. I stumbled down from the bus, annoyed that I'd missed so much of the ride that had eaten half my available money. The other passengers rushed ahead so I joined them down the stairs to the waiting room and lobby. The space and bustle of what looked like acres inside the place stunned me for a few seconds until I picked out familiar needs. Walgreen's lunch counter, a sign to a ladies' room, a bank of telephones.

I'd order a grilled ham and cheese and Coke and call Jody while they fixed it, I decided. Once on my red Walgreen's stool, however, I stayed put and watched a teenager in a granny dress crying to a policeman that her handbag had been stolen. She'd set it down in the ladies' room and when she turned around. . . .

I stuck my left arm through the duffle bag straps and started munching the ham and cheese. It turned out to be wildly salty, as well as costing $1.95 for what I could get for 99¢ in Endfield. The Coke, also strange, appeared in a skimpy little glass.

Beyond my pink waitress, the clock read 12:45 p.m. I paid my illegible check at the cashier and vetoed leaving a tip since I'd sat at the counter and hadn't even got a glass of water to wash down their Salt Flats Special here. *You're always welcome at Walgreen's,* the wall said.

As I made my way to the nearest sit-down phone booth, the loudspeaker voice continued its endless arrivals and departures. However, nobody glanced at me strangely; nobody knew or cared where I hailed from. I decided New York and I were going to like each other very well.

"Hello? Is Jody there, please?.... Well, yes, I want to leave a message. This is, uh, Tinker. Yes, she's...um...expecting me. When she comes, please ask her to wait. I'll be there in—" *My God, where am I?* "Well, I don't know exactly. Say a half hour or maybe an hour. I'm at...Port Authority." *Thank God they print things on walls here.* "And you're on East 69th Street. Okay, I'll be right down...up?"

Su had sounded somewhat confused, like me, but pleasant. I was actually relieved I hadn't spoken to Jody. At least I knew she still lived there. That was enough for now.

Map in one hand and duffle bag in the other, I ventured outside what looked like aluminum front doors. The air rose steamy, much warmer than Endfield or Albany.

When I reached one end of the brick building, the street signs said "8 Av." and "W. 40 St." outside the Rainbow Shop. Next I tried the other end. That side read "8 Av.–W. 41 St." outside one of those phony colonial coffee shops that somebody wanted to build in Endfield.

Aha! If I walked *that* way, I would go toward the top of the map, toward 57th. As I crossed the 41st-marked street, the sun was at my back. I could have told north-south from that.

A shabby man with paperbag, its top twisted about something, lurched out at me. "Hey, girlie, want a good time?"

His face and hands were dirt crusted; I sidestepped him as fast as possible. "No thanks," I answered. "I'm already having a good time." He laughed; I was glad I'd answered. If I hadn't dared, he might have got mad or made me feel I'd lost that round. Suppose he raped me. *Get yourself together, Tinker.* I realized that like O B Joyful, supposed to haunt the Ledge back in Endfield, this one would stumble on his face before he could get it up or together to rape anybody.

Another man in his undershirt wheeled a rack of plastic-wrapped dresses by me on the broken sidewalk. I began to suspect maybe this wasn't such a great neighborhood. By 8 Av. and 42 St., I knew it wasn't.

Unlike the rush of cabs, luggage, and people around Port Authority, here everybody was languid, lolling in doorways, onto the sides of buildings. They reminded me of a stage set. The men were dark, wore platform shoes and tight pants. The women were also dark, wore platform shoes and tight pants. Since they couldn't all be from the same family or shop at the same store, I concluded they must be dressed for somebody and I wasn't it. They all looked through and beyond me.

When a young man in a three-piece suit came toward me, however, two of the women stepped out at him. Underneath all the rouge, scarves, and frizzdos around their heads, I saw they were actually teenagers, three or four years older than myself. When he brushed past them, they slunk back to their doorway.

I felt sorry for them. Were they prostitutes like the one I'd seen in the paper? If so, what a drag to stew every day in the heat on a corner. All that inactivity would drive me crazy. Maybe they work only half shifts on hot days, or maybe this was merely another "changing neighborhood" like the Turnpike end of Endfield.

At 42nd Street I turned right—and discovered people who reminded me of home. Women in rhinestone glasses, nylon dresses, and stockings, on the arms of men in sport shirts and bulging bellies. Everybody stopped to examine movie marquees that were already attracting customers. I could see why. One double bill read *Sex and the Swinging Senator* followed by *Sex and the Whole World*. The most interesting one, where I also stopped, was *Teenage Sex Kitten* and *Teenage Cheerleader*. The leading lady didn't look all that adolescent, however. With her equipment educated and available in the right places, she seemed to know just how to operate with it.

One second story window read:

ENCOUNTER SESSIONS $10
FEMALE CONSULTANTS

I liked that one.

At a corner fire hydrant a lanky black man in candy striped basketball shirt and shorts of satin talked with his white girl friend. He had propped one leg, ending in massive red and white sneaker, up on the yellow hydrant. His dog, corralled by a rope, drank from the oily puddle beneath the hydrant. Farther along I met a fat old man reading the sidewalk while he muttered, "I had no mother. I had no father."

When somebody with a purple turban, followed by two blondhaired blacks dressed in white, flowed by me, I decided I shouldn't take this particular street too seriously. Maybe it was like a parade—you just walk by and that's the end. The people are fascinating but you're not sure you want to know any of them too well. Just like Endfield.

At 42nd St. and the new sign "Ave. of the Americas," I turned left onto it because I like the name. Within one block all the men coming from the glass and steel banks and other buildings now began to resemble my father with suits and pipes and briefcases. And the women began to resemble me in light dresses and platform shoes. I decided New York is incredible—every time you turn the corner, it's another country, even another race, of people.

I continued north, watching the streets flow by on my map, vaguely surprised that numbers from Endfield meant the same as numbers here. I began to hear language snatches that must be Spanish, however, and worried that I was reaching a section where I couldn't understand anything. Now I watched store windows. Next I realized I'd better get on with it; already my watch said 1:20 p.m.

At 57th St. I turned right because this whole area looked so elegant. Here the women especially had changed. They wore flaring skirts, gold jewelry that looked real, high cheek bones under picture hats. They carried crisp shopping bags or grainy handbags that looked alligator.

Suddenly I stopped short, causing a three-woman pileup. After I'd apologized to all of us, I opened my duffle and began to count my remaining bills. I realized I'd neither brought nor bought any present— food or knicknack—for Su and Jody. What would they think? Did everybody, as in Endfield, bring housepresents? I longed to ask one of the blonde, tanned ladies chattering by me but didn't dare....

Actually that was it; only *ladies* fussed over presents and wrappings back in Endfield. Men and ordinary people didn't bother; they just "brought themselves," as we called it. Maybe it was similar here: If only ladies did it, why should I bother? Su and Jody would understand. Still, I continued to stare at the pottery, silver, crystal, and shoes in the summer-decorated windows. When I noticed they lacked prices —always a bad sign—I restarted onward.

The black glass sweep of one facade thrilled me because I recognized it as the bell-bottom building I'd seen in news photos. It looked most grand, poised as if to dance or curtsy. Since the people leaving it didn't look excited or different, however, I concluded it had no particular effect on its inhabitants. What a shame.

Suddenly I found myself walked out far enough to be standing on Fifth Avenue. The first item I witnessed was a near disaster between a cabdriver and a motorcyclist. The driver had turned onto Fifth right across the motorcycle's path. Amid a two-way flood of obscenities the cyclist dismounted, kicked the cab a few times, remounted, checked his cycle, and shot off around the cab while horns flared from four directions.

Further along 57th, before an antique store, a camera crew was shooting a movie. Some of the less fancy chests, chairs, and lamps in the window looked enough like the ones in a few parlors and attics in Endfield and surrounding towns to make me guess their origin. I wondered how the craftsmen who made them a hundred or so years ago considered their work's final destination.

Through a network of greenery I gazed into a building called the Columbian Center, envying what I saw—women in men's straw hats and chunky-beaded necklaces seated at white cafe tables drinking from something that must have been the *demitasses* my French book mentioned. Laughing and smoking, they sat on the chairs and sofas around the deep carpet and drank second cups brought by the maid. I yearned for their leisure and fun.

The long planter box just inside the window, plus the palms beyond in a museum and photo area, turned me sharply homesick for Eila's greenhouses. Surprised, I remembered why I'd come and pulled myself away.

I noticed the 57th St. numbers had grown bigger; it also looked as if there was a 58th St. on my left. Maybe my map was old. I turned left onto a big avenue.

Checking what had become of the steamed over sun, I looked behind me and was restartled at how real and familiar something loomed although I'd never seen it before except on paper. The Pan Am building's glass tower thrust through its hazy hat. *National Geographic* does a pretty authentic job, I decided. One more piece from Endfield meshed into my jigsaw puzzle of Manhattan.

Next I got transfixed by the most fascinating character of my whole trip. Dancerly, she proceeded along the pavement toward me clad in black tee shirt, black anklelength skirt, orange headdress and platform shoes and concluded in bronze tan and swooping black eyebrows. From the front she looked the swinging nun. As she floated past, I caught delicious perfume somewhere between musk and ferns.

When I turned to stare at her back, the shock arrived. She had no back. That is, her clothes had no back. Tee shirt slit from bottom to neckstring as the skirt was slashed from hem to waist. She wore neither panties nor bra. What seat I saw to her skirt was imprinted with a gray mask bearing orange teeth. I concluded that like me, she couldn't decide whether she was a lady from the front or a whore from the back so she'd try half of each in order to please everybody.

I liked her and regretted when she passed out of sight.

Onward. Hot and tired now. I imagined the subway or bus again but feared I wouldn't know where to get off in time.

The best other sight—which I'd tell Jody if she was in a good mood —was the ample lady in magenta slacks and lavender sweatshirt whose front boasted GAY LOVE IS BEST. Lacking even the tentative GAY LOVE IS *BETTER,* this message seemed as bold as the block letters forming it. I wondered where she was meeting whom.

On a corner near some white department stores a boy handed me a card:

MADAM HELGA FOR ESP
TEA LEAF READINGS AND TAROT CARDS

I read and pondered:

> If you are overcome with trouble and conditions that are not natural, I can remove them. Overcome Spells, Bad Luck, and Evil Influences. Remember, I am a true Physic, born with power. Satisfaction in one visit. During many years I have brought together many in marriage and reunited many who were separated. Has the one you love changed? I locate lost and stolen articles.

I wondered how effective she could be if she didn't know the difference between "physic" (the laxative) and "psychic" (of the mind). Oh well, it's probably all one, anyway. I knew the Greeks had devised these words; they must have thought so. Instantly I understood that graffito scrawled on the Union wall back at my father's college: "Reality is the asshole of the Universe."

Onward. An hour had already slithered by.

20

Finally I turned onto the block where, if the even numbers held, Jody must be staying. Now I laughed at myself for imagining this city ended at 57th.

Here was a pleasant street, quieter after the traffic on the big avenues, filled with gold-green leaves on some cemented trees in front of what I supposed were "townhouses." Enameled doors sported brass knockers. Plants and curtains appeared in bay windows. One house even grew a railed front garden. Except for cars parked solid all over and the epidemic of also solid dog droppings, it reminded me of a small town. I wondered whether the people liked or even knew each other. How strange to live on top of so many people and probably not recognize them. Sure reduces the gossip problem.

In the middle of the 200 numbers I pushed a bright red door and found myself in a small fluorescent hallway with checkered floor. When I tried the inner door, it was locked. Stumped momentarily, I noticed an outcropping of black buttons to my left. They must be the buzzer system. I was glad I'd seen so many lousy movies that began or ended in hallways.

I examined all the plates bearing two names and couldn't recognize anything. Finally I saw S. KRANSKY, 5F. That must be Su. Apparently women here didn't advertise first names or even a title to indicate their gender. In Endfield most people were still their husbands' names: Mrs. George Thus-and-So.

I rang the 5F button twice in the stuffy hall. A voice came on and crackled out, "Who is it?"

"It's me . . . Tinker. What do—?" *I do about getting in?* My head was finishing the question when a buzzer sounded behind me. I sprang at the door and opened it just as the buzzer finished.

No elevator. I began the upward trek and arrived panting off the stairs before the door that said 5F. Pressing every button I saw, even the red and yellow one proclaiming *Pray to God and she will provide* under the peephole, I heard the door open.

Su turned out to be a small blonde woman dressed entirely in white from tee shirt and scarf to white circle skirt and straw shoes.

"Is . . . is Jody here?"

"Yes, she's inside. But she's talking to somebody now. Here, wait in the foyer." So that's the entrance hall's name away from Endfield? Su gazed me up and down.

"I like your button outside." When Su looked blank, I continued, "The *Pray to God and she*—"

"Oh yes, that's a joke. Karen got that at some conference. We put it outside thinking somebody would steal it, but so far nobody has."

"Actually I wish it was true—that God is a she and cares about people."

"Oh well." Su ignored this, apparently tired of small talk. "Ah, Tinker, Jody wasn't really expecting you. . . . It's Tinker." Sue raised her voice to some chair noises inside. "Are you coming out here?"

A bunch of blue beads parted; Jody came out at me. I took her hand, and she hugged me quickly.

"Tinker! What can I do with you? How did you get here? I couldn't believe when Su told me."

"You didn't get my letter? I said, 'Somebody you know will be còming to see you.'"

"Yeah, but I thought that was a sneaky way of warning me *Eila* was coming. How did you get here?"

"By bus."

"And do they know you're gone?"

"Jody, you look great. You got a new vest." I fingered her expensive gold and red embroidery against gray suede.

"Su gave me this. One of our friends owns a shop. . . . Look, you came at a difficult moment. I'm in here trying to help somebody with a problem. But come on and sit down."

I entered a brilliantly lit room, intense in tones of white as the hall had been blue-gloomy. Everything shimmered in oyster, pearl, ecru, chalk pieces from yards of snowscape painted on the ceiling, to woolly carpet, to desk and sofa, white-on-white prints reflecting sunlight from windows across the street. The whole effect was creamy as if sea foam or whitewash had just rushed through. I decided Su must be a designer or architect.

Somebody was talking to me. "Hello, Tinker." Dull voice from a large woman in the white beanbag chair. Her face looked streaked, apparently from crying.

"Laura, you don't mind talking in front of Tinker," Jody said. "She's a friend from Eila's town. You can trust her."

I smiled at Laura, but she was fighting her own demons.

"Laura, in my opinion—and you can get mad at me—it's too stingy what you're into. You want to know where she is every night. You want to play Supercouple, and she isn't having—"

"It's not that simple! What d'you care? You don't see. Besides Eila, you've got that German woman keeping you happy. And you haven't lost your job because of it."

I wondered what minutes or hours had preceded this outburst from Laura. Apparently she didn't know about the demise of Jody's and Eila's business.

"Your contract wasn't renewed *six* months after a speech you made, and that still left you six months to teach. That's not exactly being sacked."

"When you're a teacher, everybody thinks you get off your rocks on little girls anyway."

At this exciting new expression, I laughed aloud, then smothered my mouth at Laura's sad, hostile look.

Then Jody laughed, too. "Hey, Tinker. You got any rocks you want off?"

"Plenty!" I sensed, feelings mixed, that I was functioning as comic relief but had no idea what to do about it. Was Laura, like Eila, gearing for The Final Collapse or just blowing some steam about a lousy job situation?

"Laura, why do you want her back if she's not willing? Why not find somebody else only too glad to latch onto a relationship with you where *they* won't have to be jealous?....I mean, if you call her up three times a night checking on her, you can't expect her to feel either good or happy about it."

"But I only did that when she began to avoid me. I still want us to live together. And I do care about her shop. I think she and I would make a great couple to run a business. Like you and Eila."

Jody sighed. I said nothing.

"But, Laura, she's told me she doesn't want that involvement with anybody she works with."

"Then she still hasn't come out far enough. If she's scared her *book-keeper* will find out." Laura spat this out.

"She owns a *women's* dress shop. And most of her customers willing to pay eighty bucks for one of her outfits are straight women. She's scared, that's all.''

"Then how do I unscare her?''

"Well, not by blaming her or staging scenes. Look, if you really care about her shop, offer her something she needs. Ask to buy into it; offer to work there a few days while she's out buying; see if you like it.''

At this point Su reappeared in the beaded doorway. I tiptoed to her and whispered, "May I use your bathroom?''

Truth was Laura and Jody were giving me Endfield-style nuclear family ulcers, and I needed privacy to finish figuring what I'd say to Jody when my time came.

Su's bath hit me like another hunk off the Old Mistress's palette. This room, large as a walk-in closet, exuded shades of blue- and black-grey in carpet, curtains, towels similar to, but darker than, the hall. It wasn't a room that encouraged you to waste time. Maybe that was part of Su's life efficiency program. On the other hand, if you felt like hanging yourself from the shower head, a room like this would just about destroy you.

Suddenly I longed for Endfield's bathrooms of pink and green, overflowing with flowers and frills. Su's soap, however, seemed expensive and perky with a woodland smell. It reminded me of the Ledge in Endfield. Happily I scrubbed my sooty hands and face with it and emerged renewed into the living room.

Laura had left; Su now sat in the beanbag chair.

"Tinker,'' Jody asked, "what do you think? Should people make public revolutionary gestures that get everybody furious, including their friends? Or should they bore silently from within?''

"Well, they sure bore each other.''

Su snickered. Jody slapped her own thigh. "Okay. I shouldn't have asked. . . . Tinker, we have to get around to this: Did Eila send you? Why are you here?''

"No. I came on my own. My own money.''

"And you're not visiting a relative? How long are you staying?''

"I don't know. For a while.''

"Do your parents know you're gone?''

"They think I'm at the class picnic.''

"Which is for today.''

"Yes.''

"Then I think you better go back before they miss you.''

"No. I'm not going back until—'' I stared at her.

"Until what?'' She frowned back at me.

"I have . . . an offer.''

Jody's lips flattened. Her eyes caught Su's.

"I don't understand. You want *me* to make you some offer you can't refuse?"

"No. I have one for you. I'll go home to Endfield today, without even looking any more at New York, on one condition."

"Which is?"

"That you'll come back by Monday for the parade."

"You know I don't plan to come back."

"Then I'll stay. I'll call my parents and tell them you invited me to come."

"Which is a lie."

"They'll believe me because—"

"They think I seduce little girls," Jody concluded.

"That's right. I mean, I didn't mean that like it sounded. Jody, look, *please* come back. Don't let them drive you out. If you come back, it would be like...a statement you're not afraid, you don't care what they think. Eila and you can live again." Then the words, "My dear, all things considered..." from some play tumbled out of me as part of the elegant, witty speach I'd planned back around Albany. I couldn't carry it off, however. My whining little-girlness shamed me.

I finished lamely. "You know, um, at least two people in Endfield have told Eila and me they don't...they think you and Eila should live like you want as long as...you run a good business."

Jody sneered. "New England greed to the rescue. Who are these marvelous types?

"Mr. Ferguson and Marian Dorne."

"Yeah, the golf shirts.... And I remember Marian. Eila and I were just setting up business then, and Eila was watching my every reaction to your one-horse town. So I knocked myself out arranging Dorne sprays all over Endfield." Jody crossed her arms over the embroidered vest and stared at one wall.

"How will you earn a living here, Jody?"

"Well, you got a point there, little girl. They aren't exactly rushing to hire ex-gym teachers these days."

"Not in New York," Su emphasized, "but maybe back in Colorado."

"Actually if you want the truth, I made my own schedule in Endfield. So I enjoyed running that truck around much more than I ever enjoyed running six volleyball classes a day or yoga for overweight Y ladies."

"So why don't you go back?" Now Su asked. "Eila doesn't sound like the type who holds grudges."

"She's not. Eila's the best friend I've ever had. Not to mention lover. Besides a good head on all those tax forms. You know, the IRS has never once investigated us, and we took some rather generous deductions for the new greenhouse and all that equipment. One year we worked our tails off, and still Eila made it so nonprofitable we didn't pay any taxes."

"They only go to blow up people in Africa," I added.

Jody: "I thought it was Southeast Asia."

Su: "That was the last war."

"Jody, people aren't talking about...it anymore. I wrote you how Judy James ran away."

"And now you ran away."

"Well, I mean the tourists are coming. They always entertain everybody. You know, I heard a joke the other day about some traveling salesman" (Jody groaned) "who asked a New Englander, 'Is this a praying community?' You know what he answered?"

"I fear to ask."

"He said, 'Why sure. In winter we pray in the church, and in summer we prey on the tourists.' "

Jody groaned again. Su yelled, "Hire that girl for public relations!"

Silence now. Jody fidgeted. I wanted to ask about Su and Karen but decided that another respite would only divert things further.

Finally Jody proposed, "Tinker, if I get a taxi, will you come with me back to Port Authority?"

"Does that mean you'll come back to Endfield with me?"

"Not this afternoon. I have an appointment."

Was she telling the truth? "Friday night there's a direct bus." Then inspiration struck. "Suppose I work on Eila to stop being all guilty over your lifestyle? I mean, the one you would have if you came back."

"That would help. She's so damn oversensitive to the first bug-eyed look from some old biddy I had to spend half our time placating. After a while it eats you to have the worrying for *two* people." Massaging her neck, Jody worried anew.

"You know, after the parade and cemetery stuff on Monday, I guess there's a women's event at the college. And the Michaelsons' swim party."

Jody's eyes twinkled. "Yeah, their parties are blasts. I had to carry Eila home from last year's."

"Oh, yeah? I heard she carried *you* home?"

"What d'you know, Tinker Toy? You didn't go."

"Sticks and stones will break our bones," I chanted.

"And names will always hurt us," Su finished.

Gloom re-descended.

"All right, Tinker, you win." Jody sighed. "If you go back right now before the Pussy Posse gets you—"

"What's that?" I asked. Su laughed.

"Never mind. If you go back right now, I'll come Friday night. But only for the weekend and parade. Is that clear?"

Was she saying this just to get rid of me? Well, I didn't know how to tell her either that Eila had already asked Jim Donohugh to drive the parade truck so I omitted that.

"How can I believe you? Give me your wallet with all your ID and money in it. I'll meet the Friday—"

"Jesus, you won't even leave me the bloody bus fare? Ever of heard of checking accounts, Tinker?"

"Give her something," Su said.

Jody clicked her tongue. "I don't have anything." However, she rose and strode to another room. I wondered what, if anything, she'd bring me.

When she returned, she had one hand stuck behind her back. "Guess?"

"I don't know. How can I read your mind?"

"All right. My prizest possession. My plastic ski trophy." She produced the shiny black cube mounted with goldish plaque surmounted with chipped skier. It had stood in Eila's living room. About six inches high, it looked worth about $1.99 in one of those souvenir shops I'd passed.

A lady never reveals her true feelings when they discomfit others. "Does this really mean something to you?"

"It's got my name inscribed for downhill slalom. And the shape I'm in, I'm not likely to win another. Tinker, you sure don't take any wooden nickels."

"Or plastic ones either. Okay. I'll meet you at the bus in Endfield Friday night. I'll have the statue in my duffle bag. And I'll work on Eila, tell her you're coming, tell her to be less scared of Endfield."

"Lots of luck. All right. I'll find a taxi and get you over to Port Authority for the next bus."

We all stood up. I shook hands with Su, who remarked, "Endfield sounds like a *great* place. Remind me never to come. Sorry you have to return so soon, Tinker."

"Yuh. So am I. If you ever get to visit us, I'll show you my favorite tombstone in the cemetery. I check it every Memorial Day. Jody and I

102

lay flowers around it. Wanna know what it says?''

Su: "Now *I*'m afraid to ask."

"It says, HERE LIES THE BODY OF SOPHRONIA PROCTOR
WHO HAD A COLD BUT WOULDN'T DOCTOR.
SHE COULDN'T STAY, SHE HAD TO GO.
PRAISE GOD FROM WHOM ALL BLESSINGS FLOW."

Everybody laughed. We went.

I got a semidirect bus, reached the drugstore in Endfield around 7:30 p.m., changed my clothes in Neilson's garage. When my mother asked why I was so late, I said I'd taken a long walk in a different part of the woods. Which wasn't a lie.

However, she remained pleasant about it. Instead of the old, "My God, we were worried sick about you," which had always semicamouflaged "You annoying brat, why do you bother us this way?", she accepted my explanation without comment as if I were grownup.

Then I discovered she'd spent the day busily fixing the room next to mine for the baby and probably had lacked time to brood about me. If the coming baby could continue to divert her like this, however, summer in Endfield might be possible.

My father, as usual, sat in his study behind his citadel of textbooks and term papers.

21

Thursday afternoon after school (I'd told everybody I couldn't make the picnic yesterday because I didn't feel right which, for me in Endfield, was never a lie) I took my duffle bag and stopped to see Eila.

I found her in a sort of maternity smock like my mother's, preparing two large funeral baskets in the greenhouse. I wondered where John was. "So business is blooming?" I asked—a corny joke between us.

"Hardly. The Sullivans just needed two baskets in a hurry for their grandmother, and Mr. Pelacci couldn't supply them. You know what he's done? He's finished his greenhouse in the backyard and set himself up already. He's got corsage orders for all the graduation and country club doings.

"But the worst happened today. Arnold Ferguson called up, which was nice, but he said he met some tourist who'll make an offer of fifty thousand for this business. That's not even *one quarter* what it's worth! The acreage and house alone could bring more than fifty thousand. I suppose Jody would tell me to sell. . . . It makes me sick. I hope those real estate vultures don't get wind of it."

"Mrs. Simpson isn't a vulture. Her office is nice."

"Well, you know what I mean. It's like antiques. They want to grab everything for nothing, then think they're doing you a favor—before they double the price for resale."

"I'm glad I don't own anything."

"Sometimes I wish I didn't." She stabbed vicious snips into the lilies and white satin bows. "Sometimes I want to chuck it all. And live like everybody else."

"You mean sell the nursery?"

"No. I don't know. Live with Jim Donohugh. Marry him or something. He came here yesterday. He says he always knew I was more interested in Jody but now she's gone, he wants to see me. He's quite a man. I mean, not every man would court a . . . bisexual. I guess I intrigue him or challenge him or something. Besides, we're all older now. None of us is going to get our dreams in their, well, virgin form.'' She smiled at me. ''So I agreed to attend Roy's graduation concert with him, but maybe I'll change my mind. I can't face them . . . it yet.''

''Is he driving the truck for the parade?''

''He will if I ask him.''

''I think you're too afraid of people in Endfield. I used to be real afraid of my parents. Now I don't care anymore.''

When Eila didn't respond, I was puzzled but decided she had enough of her own woes.

To shock her into attention, I produced Jody's statue and set it on the worktable. One look made Eila's jaw fall. ''Where did you get that?'' she nearly screamed at me.

''Guess.''

''You found it! Jody threw it away.''

''Uh-uh.''

''Where'd you get it?'' she demanded again.

''Jody gave it to me.''

''Don't lie to me, Tinker. I can't stand it. You're *not* funny today.'' She clumped her hands onto my shoulders.

''I'm not trying to be funny. Jody gave it to me herself. In New York.''

''*You* got to New York?''

''Sure. I can read and count and buy a bus ticket. Endfield Regional isn't that bad.''

''But you've stopped here every day except—''

''Wednesday.'' I nodded. ''It was the class picnic.''

''You mean, you got to New York all by yourself on Wednesday?''

''Sure. Why does everybody always underestimate me? It's horrible.'' For the moment I thought it safer to neglect *how* I got to Albany.

''Why didn't you tell me?''

Now preferring neglect to reproach, I replied, ''Because you would forbid me to go.''

''Well, what did Jody say? How is she? Has she got another job?'' Eila's black eyebrows darted together.

''The hour I saw her she was trying to help somebody named Laura with a big bunch of problems. Looks like people in New York have just as many problems with each other as . . . people around here.'' Eila frowned. ''Okay. I'll tell you. She'll be here tomorrow night on the bus. I'm supposed to meet her at the drugstore.''

Eila sat down and hugged herself. ''I don't believe you.''

''Well, it's only for the weekend. For the parade.''

"How did you do it?"

"Oh, my tremendous personality. I'm just irresistible."

"Or the biggest liar in Endfield." Now she hugged me. I ignored a couple tears in her eyes.

"I don't understand *why* she's coming."

"She says you're the best friend she has. Plus you're a whizz on the tax forms."

Eila smiled. "Boy, how we fought about those. Jody wanted much more amortized and no loans outstanding—oh well, you don't have to know about taxes."

"Why not? I'm already doing a crash course in the other two. Death and childbirth. You wouldn't want me to miss anything, would you?"

"You won't. You're not the type."

"Jody doesn't, well, want anything but, look, why don't you just pretend everything's. . . back to normal? Don't groan about Endfield to her. How about making an ad saying she's returned from a business trip and how the nursery is open as usual?"

"And get it into the paper?"

"No, no. Just show it to her. After you talk with her."

"I'll do something nice. John and I will pick her up in the truck."

"Where is John?"

"Oh, he's at the College studying for finals or something. He's attended a lot of campus meetings because there's so little to do here. A couple hours watering and weeding a day. That's been it."

"Remember. Don't groan about Endfield to her? Agreed?" I felt most grownup, giving Eila directions.

"You know how I *love* the place." She hugged me again.

22

Friday night at seven I just happened to be in Park Square opposite the drugstore and bus stop. I sat on a bench pretending to read one of those monster comix sold at the Five and Ten—the kind that warps your mind before you know you've got one.

Ginny and Sandy strolled by, giggling about something. Because they were a year younger, I hadn't seen much of them now that Pammy and I were at Regional while they remained at Elementary and since Pammy and I had quit Girl Scouts. I'd seen the newspaper, however, and congratulated them on their camping and race relations badges received at the awards ceremony.

I'd quit Scouts because I considered it a sort of volunteer make-work organization that fostered its own dream world. Take race relations, for instance. There's only one race in Endfield—unless you consider tourists a separate subspecies—and even that one race can barely survive each other. If Blacks or native Americans were added to the pot, Endfielders would probably be no happier to melt into bussing or integration than parents around Boston. So a badge for race relations must, of necessity, be awarded for academic or theoretical study rather than practical living.

Ginny and Sandy had both got their braids cut. I noticed Ginny now sported a Janis Joplin mass of curls and looked much older. Sandy wore a sort of shingle style.

"What are you guys doing?" I asked.

"Nothing. What're you doing?" Ginny answered.

"Waiting for the bus."

"Somebody on it?"

I changed the subject. "I hear you're all marching in the parade."

"Yeah. We were practicing with Mrs. Dubois last night. We had band music on the phonograph at the Scout cabin. *I* can march in step but Sandy can't."

Sandy punched her arm. "I can so march in step. You're the one who goofs it up.''

A DayGlo card I'd seen in a New York window flashed into my head:
PLEASE DON'T ASK ME TO KEEP IN STEP
IT'S HARD ENOUGH JUST TO STAY IN LINE
It pictured a parade of three salamanders. I let the topic pass.

"Aren't you sorry you're not a Cadette Scout now? You could march, too,'' Ginny asked.

"Oh, I'll be there, Ginny. I'll see you.''

Two hundred feet away the Greyhound bus pulled in and stopped. The nursery van sat parked to the right in front of the bank. I couldn't see who waited in it. When the bus finally pulled away, it looked as if four people had disembarked. A couple musicians carrying black cases plus a short lady plus—Jody in her new grey vest and (I scrunched up my eyes) a matching grey skirt. Jody rarely appeared skirted; this must truly be an occasion for her.

How to get rid of Ginny and Sandy? "Oh, there's Eila and Jody,'' I said. "I have a package for them. See you guys at the parade.''

"Hey, you wanna hear what my mother says about Eila?'' Ginny called.

"Tell me Monday at the parade. Why don't you believe only half of what you see—and none of what you hear?''

Sandy giggled; Ginny looked cross. Well, I could be nice to her on Monday. In fact, they were both crucial to a certain plan I was already concocting.

By the time I made it across the rest of the park and Main Street, John and Eila had hopped out and both hugged Jody. Then all three of them hopped around entwined. Jody even kissed Eila on the lips. Next they all hugged me; we rehugged one another in varying combinations. Jody whooped. Smiling through tears, Eila blurted, "I thought you'd never come back. But here you are!'' More waist hugs and kisses until I backed off and noticed Eila's face. Beneath the surface excitement, it looked haggard. Jody, however, seemed alert, ready for action. "Hi, Tinker,'' she called.

"Here's your dollar-fifty statue,'' I joked, handing it to her.

"How dare you insult something I just about broke my head over? And you extorted from me in New York?''

"Oh, it's easy when you live here. You learn young.''

Then we all piled into the truck, Eila and Jody in front, John and I sitting on cushions in back on the very spot where I'd hidden two days before. Sometime I should confess to John his own role in kidnapping me.

As elated as I was that Jody had kept her promise, I hoped nobody of the Nathan Hale mindset had seen our dancing reunion to Report All to my mother. Next I decided, that's *her* problem. Nobody could dampen my joy at seeing Jody and Eila reunited.

"I hear Jody's back," my mother said over lunch on Saturday noon. "Mrs. Simpson's mother rode up with her on the bus. Said she'd had her hair cut and looked very nice."

"That's good," I replied, trying to avoid obvious interest.

"Tinker, you've been helpful lately. Very quiet. You don't complain about teachers or homework any more. I think getting away from the nursery work has been good for you. Those women were too old for you, anyway, don't you think?"

Anythingyousayjustleavemealone. "But I enjoyed it there. I miss the excitement."

"I know you do. Look, after the baby is born, your father and I will take you to camp for three weeks."

"A sleepaway camp? Not just the day stuff?"

"Whatever you like. There's one on the mountain and a new one opening this year on Greenwater Pond. My due date is June 23—just about the day you end school. Before the baby comes, we'll visit people at both camps. You can choose the one you like better."

"I want one with archery and water ballet."

"Well, we'll see what they offer. We want one with nice girls, of course."

"How about some New Yorkers? I really like them."

"If they're nice."

Right after that conversation—the decentest I'd had with my mother in months—I walked downstreet and did my special holiday shopping for the plan I'd devised. One box of kleenexes from the supermarket plus some tricolor rosettes and one superjumbo pack of bobbypins from the Five and Ten.

Eila and Jody didn't know it yet, but I'd decided Monday's Memorial parade would be Endfield's most colorful yet. Besides, I'd had it with my career as Endfield's closet brat, known and regretted chiefly by my parents and Nedda.

It was time to go public.

23

Memorial Day Monday I began to tingle with excitement as soon as I awoke. I watched the waving trees do sunlit diamonds on my green wall and remembered Su's white and grey rooms. Since it was a school holiday, I could luxuriate as long as I cared, except that my mother would no doubt require some thrilling chore as soon as I rose. Since the town had recently outlawed outdoor burning of trash or garbage, one of my especially fulfilling tasks had ended. I relinquished it to the new garbageman who sweated and swore from pail to pail on his route to the dump where we all used to go on Saturday mornings.

I speculated on how the Brandi Nursery van would appear for the parade and who (Jody in this corner vs. Jim in that) would drive it. Then I felt sad; it was the first time in five years I would ride neither in nor atop it. I hadn't asked, and nobody had invited me. Too excited to remember, I guess.

Memorial Day (Decoration Day, as a few old folks persist in calling it) retains a special flavor in Endfield. More somber than Fourth of July but more outdoorsy than Armistice Day. For the religious, it's a publicly approved time to commune with the dead—the sister you couldn't stand; that baby who kept everybody awake for six months running until it died ("A real shame, but wasn't it a blessing?"); the parents you liked but, well, you have your own life now. Further festivities featured that parade of merry widows and Gold Star mothers who form the Endfield DAR. Of all days, this is theirs, to don the red-white-blue and socialize.

For the nonreligious, early bird tourists included, Memorial Day combines the excitement of a folkloric spectacle and costume party with a rural picnic and something to keep the kids out of your hair for a few hours. This last item involves a sack race, a tug of war, facepainting at the Athletic Field, and the promise of a swim at the newly re-opened lake beach if sun and temperature cooperate.

That year a pie throwing contest had been rumored. When first the Board of Selectmen, then the Town Clerk, refused to serve as targets, however, the rumor died. Too bad. Now there's an activity with immense community participation potential.

For the patriotic of all ages, Memorial Day in Endfield becomes an orgy of nostalgia for wars I'd barely heard of then. Holiday ritual involves wandering among the granite and marble graves plus laying on of plastic flags, lilacs in crepe papered juice cans, clay potted geraniums. Though a gesture of honor, the flags seemed bizarre to me, as if death notices nationality, or the dead, their struggles over, had begun to sprout stars and stripes.

During the confusion of the Viet Nam period, nobody had much wanted to decorate. Since that "conflict" had ended, however, the florious dead of that war—poor 19-year-olds who never knew what hit them—now ranked equal with all other cemetery military from the Revolution onward. The exact phrase for this, repeated in litany during annual roll call, is that So-and-So is now "accounted for." Which indicates the poor guy is stuck somewhere between the paltry bookkeeping of this world and the real (one presumed) honors accorded in the next.

Endfield's Memorial Parade always ends at the Protestant cemetery because its crypts and stones run older and quainter than the Catholic cemetery that got dug from somebody's back pasture only about 1875.

When the speeches waxed dull (about five minutes' worth) I loved to wander the stones to locate juicy epitaphs. Endfield has a notable collection, favored of grave rubbers. I enjoyed the gallows humor of one located on the far side at the iron railing. Its subject (or "abject"), a sad soul named Molly, who flaked out at 24, always thrilled me as I wondered where I'd be at her age:

MOLLY, THO PLEASANT IN HER DAY,
    WAS SUDDENLY SEIZED AND SWEPT AWAY
HOW SOON SHE'S RIPE, HOW SOON SHE'S ROTTEN
    LAID IN THE GRAVE AND SOON FORGOTTEN.

Another in the center celebrated somebody named Sarah Rivington. Once I actually showed it to my mother:

SHE LIVE WITH
    HER HUSBAND
        FIFTY YEARS
        AND DIED IN THE
    CONFIDENT HOPE
OF A BETTER LIFE.

Having read, my mother termed me "morbid."

I always visited the newest grave. This year it was likely to be Abby Wilkerson. Poor Abby had died, willing all to a niece, her only survivor, while appointing some unrelated body as her executor. Said Niece— part of the angry part—having refused to pay Abby's funeral expenses, left Unrelated Executor—party of the poor part—bereft of cash to cover several hundred dollars of costs attendant upon Abby's demise. The niece's last and oft quoted comment that spring: "Wrap her in a sheet and throw her in the dump."

Such cruelty is not beyond belief. It is merely what happens when an old woman gets ahold of a teenage girl and lavishes compliments, presents, and education upon her, imagining that she is thereby lining up a free geriatric nurse. Ten years later she received instead a scandalous rejection. The unstated, if not unfair, queasiness *(don't you believe young people owe everything to older people?)* of the original bargain creates its own destruction.

Although I felt the girl and her aunt deserved each other, I believed the executor—a simple neighbor woman who never harmed anybody —was the real victim. Nedda, however, declared them *all* foolish. "A pox on all their houses!" Nobody should sign anything, least of all a will, without reading that fine print. Maybe she's right.

As some writer once remarked, "Nothing is unsayable in words, only the living truth." The New England version is, "Short settlements make long friends."

Anyway, while the annual Memorial speeches by the unforensic and untalented living droned on, I communed with the dead—Molly, Sophronia, and Sarah. I dusted their stones, pulled their crab grass, stole nearby glads or flags for all of them so they too could enjoy, although posthumously, holiday treatment. Maybe I'd even rip off something for Abby today.

Once on Halloween Pammy and I dashed to the cemetery to see whether we could induce any of them to rise and appear to us. None ever did. Of course, what was true for the dead applied equally to the living: If you liked them and they liked you, you cared and visited. If you didn't like them, you did them mischief.

Not to be outdone by the town, Ferncliff College was planning its own Memorial festival that year. It was already rumored to combine rites of summer ("I tell you they better watch those girls' dorms") with an unusual cooperative gesture between campus and town women—a crafts festival at the College end of Main Street. Beginning with speeches and arts demonstrations after the parade, it would conclude with a cocktail party honoring some women's movement speakers at a faculty

member's house outside town. When I had asked my father about the
Michaelsons, he said Fred Michaelson had got only a one-year contract,
just expiring, so he hadn't worked too hard to know him. I concluded
my parents would not attend.

I rose, made my bed, and breakfasted quickly. On the pretext of
gathering lily of the valley and lilac from the meadow and woods below
the Ledge to decorate Uncle Matt's grave (Nedda had her gravesite
chosen and financed beside his already), I left the house. On the way
out of my room I filled my duffle bag with what I'd constructed over
the weekend.

As I walked by the nursery, I noticed the Donohughs' brown Pinto
car parked outside the house.

The parade lineup would begin at 9:30 on the College end of Main
Street so I walked along Main. Flag-decked, police barricaded, already
barren of traffic, it reminded me of a war instead of a holiday.

Outside the College Union building I spotted John and about ten
of his friends, mostly men, handling drums and banners. I thought
this uncharacteristically patriotic of them until I realized from reading
their placards that what they were organizing was a (counter) demonstration.

Their signs of white cardboard, lavender felt, and burlap were a
motley lot—everything from NO TUITION INCREASE (left over from
last semester, I guessed) to RIGHTS FOR *ALL* AMERICANS. My
favorite was ENDFIELD—GATEWAY TO YESTERDAY scrawled on
some white wrapping paper which two girls in majorette uniforms were
mounting on sticks.

"Hey, Tinker," John called. "Wanna march with us?"

"I don't know. I'll be either with the Girl Scouts or in Eila's truck."

"She's the only float. 'Way up front near the police and firemen.
They told us we could march 'way at the end if we didn't yell anything."

"The Girl Scouts and kids with bicycles are usually last so I guess I'll
see you. . . . What's Eila putting on the truck?"

"Oh, one of those floral blankets—roses, carnations. No costumes
or decorations this year. Just flowers."

"But floral blankets are for coffin lids."

"Well, you know Jody's sense of humor."

"Yuh," I sighed.

"Hey, Tinker, look at this banner!" yelled a man in leather jacket
next to John. I stared at the ten-foot length of white wrapping paper

on which there was lavender lettering:

SAY IT LOUD

GAY IS PROUD

"What do you think?" Was this a new John, taking me into his confidence? Eila must have told him something good about me.

"Jody'll love it, but Eila'll hate you," I answered.

"I already warned them. Jody's all set."

One of the majorettes called, "Tinker, we'll do you a special banner. How 'bout carrying LESBIANS FOR CHRIST?"

This stumped me as all that noninformation in the books at the library flooded back at me. Was I—or wasn't I? *Aw, it's too early to tell.*

"See you later," I called. Tingling (maybe that medical book was right?), I ran down two blocks to locate the Girl Scouts and get my own plan underway. This was going to be fun!

Along Main Street, early bird crowds equipped with beach chairs, umbrellas, and thermoses had already captured the best curbside positions. Down one sidestreet I saw the high school band and their majorettes practicing.

Farthest away down Main waited what would be the head of the parade—the guys with guns, the police, other uniformed services, fire engines, meter maids, the DAR cars, Rotary and Lions Club and Chamber of Commerce cars, American Legion and VFW people in blue and white.

Marchers now milled everywhere, horsing around, awaiting the signal that never seemed to happen. Then I ran into the Boy Scout and Cub Scout sidestreet with one pregnant den mother and perspiring den master trying to line them up.

Crossing between members of the Ferncliff College band already out on Main exercising their tricolor-decorated bulldog, I reached the Brownies' and Girl Scouts' sidestreet opposite the Boy Scouts. Ginny and Sandy stood joking in the Scout bunch, a bedlam of everybody making faces, shouting hopscotch riddles, doing jumping games.

In the year since my resignation from the Scouts, dress codes had definitely relaxed. Only a far-out minority now wore the traditional green beret and uniform, red neckerchief, oxford shoes, or white gloves. Senior Scouts now wore mint green dresses or miniskirts, long pants, no pants, orange kneesocks, blue sneakers or earth shoes, green gardening gloves.

Excellent for my purpose.

I sought Mrs. Simpson, the only troop leader I could spot, as she bent over tying a Brownie's shoes, then a succession of pony tails.

In my jeans I stood beside her until she noticed. "Where's your unif—?" she started to ask. "Oh, hi, Tinker."

My stomach did one nervous leap, but I had my speech all prepared. "Mrs. Simpson, I know I'm not marching this year, but I want to do something. So I made these holiday flowers for everybody." I opened my duffle bag.

"What have you got there?" she asked. Now Ginny and Sandy and a bored half dozen others crowded around. I brought out a handful. "You wear them in your hair," I explained, holding up a sample. Each bobby pin held half a lavender tissue in wing formation, surmounted by a glued on red-white-blue lapel rosette.

"I don't know, Tinker. They don't match our green uniforms. So few girls wear a whole uniform now I don't want to make it any worse. It was thoughtful of you, though."

I had my answer ready. "That's all right. They're . . . like one of the badges on your sash. Lilac's for spring plus red, white, and blue to honor the holiday."

"They're fun. Let's wear them!" Ginny yelled and grabbed at them. In five minutes fifty were distributed and mounted on Junior, Cadette, and Senior Scouts. "You wear them over your left ear," I instructed. In another five minutes the Brownies, dressed in orange and chocolate, were clamoring for their supply of forty more, which didn't match their uniforms either, but their leader, a Mrs. O'Hare, also accepted my explanation.

Wherever I looked now, lavender bits flowed from sashes, bobbed on heads, dropped over ears. Some girls got triple rosetted in all three places. Surveying my work (which had killed the flashlight batteries in Saturday night hours of rosetting my bed), I beamed everybody a big smile and walked back to check on John's adult version of my groups.

Next the Grand Marshall in red, white, and black with gold braid sounded his bugle. Everybody bounced into place. In a few seconds I distributed more protest rosettes to John and his group, who stared at me, then at my bedecked Brownies and Scouts, howled and hugged me.

All in all, I decided that Jody and Eila driving the head of the parade plus the Girl Scouts, John's College group, and me bringing up the tail would make one neat lavender encirclement of Endfield's holiday celebration. My time to get even with everybody for painting all of us—Eila, Jody, and me—evil that spring. If I had to live condemned to my mother's bleep pool for the rest of my years, I at least wanted to go with a public splash. What heroic dreams I'd invested in bits of kleenex and ribbon!

I distributed my last batch to Sonny Thomas's tribe of skateboarders and bicyclists, whose wheels held crepe streamers and playing cards mounted to make noise in the spokes. By now the sun had vanished behind clouds of mist, making everybody perspire dark lines under uniform arms and helmet visors.

The College band started along Main playing *Yankee Doodle* and *Battle Hymn of the Republic* followed by *Bells of St. Mary's*. Boy Scouts and Cub Scouts swung out from their sidestreet, trailed by Brownies and Girl Scouts, all green, brown, and lavender, followed by John and me leading his group.

The banner between the two of us was my favorite: ENDFIELD—GATEWAY TO YESTERDAY. Behind us, every two people held other banners: NO TUITION INCREASE, then 3-5-7-9 LESBIANS ARE MIGHTY FINE and LESBIANS IGNITE, ending with WE ARE THE PEOPLE OUR PARENTS WARNED US AGAINST. One bass drum, played by a tiny woman I'd never seen before, concluded our College contingent. Must be an "outside agitator."

"Atten-tion!" We stopped marching, then stepped off again.

We got exactly one block down Main to the library before violence broke out. Two guys in jeans, built somewhere between apes and tanks, rammed their way off the sidewalk and into our group where they grabbed one GAY IS PROUD and began ripping it. Since all the police were rounding the park at the head of the parade three blocks on, we had to handle it ourselves.

Somebody who knew judo surprised one of the guys but not before John and I, protecting our YESTERDAY banner, found ourselves pinned under the other guy, who seemed to weigh two hundred pounds of sweating tee shirt and muscle. He smelled like an auto mechanic. My cheek and arm scraped and burned against the hot asphalt.

Next Danny Thomas and his bunch of high school thugs, plus assorted skateboarders eager for action, took them on, freeing John and me to wrap GATEWAY TO YESTERDAY back around its sticks and continue. By now, somebody had rammed one of the guys in the gut with an enraged brass eagle atop one of the nine-foot flagpoles grabbed off the curb.

Although a few old ladies screamed, most people seemed to consider the quick scramble akin to Halloween fun—a free-for-all joke. Somehow we regrouped and marched on, trying to catch the Girl Scouts who bobbed lavender and green a full block away now.

So the spectators spectated. I was too dizzy from being dumped upside down to distinguish particular watchers except Mr. and Mrs. Ferguson chewing gum on one curb. Beside them, Pete waved a KEEP THE SPIRIT ALIVE flag.

Suddenly I realized the fate for myself and John's group: We formed entertainment, the parade's ragtag "dessert" end, at which spectators felt free to laugh, having endured the meat and vegetables of the solemn ranks of former WACs, velveted colonial dames, weekend warriors, and other arrayed marchers with pointed scotty hats and bulging uniforms. We followed like street clowns or court jesters, although lacking even their caps and uniforms.

Rage tore through me. Lacking time to think, I still realized I'd counted on my lavender flower gesture to catch Eila's and Jody's notice (at this rate, would they even see it?) and also to scandalize the town, twit them into dealing with a reality they preferred shoved under the collective rug. Ungarbled, my gesture could have said, raise children decently with love to spare. Otherwise, you'll end by banning the Girl Scouts as a subversive organization . . . . More rage.

Four Air Force Guard planes swept over Main Street, the perspiring crowd, the overdressed ranks of marchers. Everybody's neck tilted backward.

"John, what can we do? They're not paying attention." My arm ached; my mouth tasted grit. I began to cry and immediately bit my lip.

"I know. What the hell's the matter with them? We get our skulls cracked back there, and they laugh. . . . Hey, don't cry." Above the banner John reached a hand toward me. I grasped it in mine.

I wiped my nose across my left sleeve. "Maybe it's because they don't know any of us—except me. I mean, the College students don't live here." Although I tried to sound grown-up, I felt like screaming and running. Did adults really have to be people who never dealt with anything sensibly on time? If John were some big sports or rock star who also happened to be gay, our reception would have been different. He'd get respected like some tv celebrity whistle-stopping in Endfield on his way to a new season.

Finally I ached myself into deciding that Endfield's laughter was preferable to the agonized shame of "How could you do this to us who tried so hard?" that I usually received. If harsher, it was cleaner, anyway.

Now the band beyond all the Scouts launched into *Way Down South in Dixie* followed by *Yellow Rose of Texas*. Having just studied the Civil War, I resented this historical mishmash that Yankee playing of Southern Rebel songs represented. Was it for *this* that Confederates died and Lincoln got shot? (I'm glad I'm neither historian nor politician; the responsibility would paralyze me.)

At the end of Main Street we rounded the Park, waited at the KEEP RIGHT sign, then continued up West Street toward Burying Hill Road with its DEAD END sign. Today somebody had stuck one of my lavenderized rosettes to it. Which made me laugh enough to walk farther. although my right arm and cheek still stung from the asphalt bruising.

As John and I carried GATEWAY TO YESTERDAY past Sophronia's and Molly's graves, the sun came out, further steaming up the morning. When we neared the podium under the central Liberty Oak, I helped John roll our banner. Then I grabbed the last chair between two blacksashed DAR ladies wearing heavy perfume and Chinese red patent leather shoes. I tried to relax and enjoy the clash of scents somewhere between Lily of the Valley and a newer chemical aura.

Behind the podium the lavendered Girl Scouts were gathering between the Boy Scouts and the group of worthy politicians, priest, and minister assembled to speak.

To my left somebody unhooked and rolled up a tricolor Rotary banner with its Four Way Test:

(1) Is it the TRUTH?
(2) Is it FAIR to all concerned?
(3) Will it build GOODWILL AND BETTER FRIENDSHIPS?
(4) Will it be BENEFICIAL to all concerned?

Such noble ideas made me think of Nedda, then of burning it on her front lawn. I grew hotter and sadder.

After the honor guard of colors from the four uniformed services had presented, the speeches featured the usual assortment of "that this may never happen again," "our struggles are meager compared to theirs," and how "those who served the nation in war were then called to eternal peace."

Throughout it all, the Boy Scouts goofed off, twisting neckerchiefs around forefingers, passing a dirty picture card from hand to hand. I squirmed and pained: Please, God, destroy these ceremonies or make people speak or sing well enough to hold a crowd's attention. In a small town, neither ever seems to happen.

Then the local DAR's Child of the American Revolution—Heidi Spencer's four-year-old swathed in pink gingham and pigtails—tottered forward with a potted geranium for one of Endfield's decomposed Revolutionary heroes. As several of the audience murmured, How-cute-isn't-she-sweet?, I rose and strolled over the graves. The Spencers lived down Laurel from us; remembering all those maternal hours spent screaming at Heidi to get out of the road and back onto the porch overwhelmed me. Well, why begrudge the kid the one moment of glory she'd likely ever get?

The Michaelsons lived further out West Street. So after the new Liberty Tree and time capsule paintings and before the color guard's gunshot and taps finale, I had to leave. The two volleys of shot always gave me a headache. The second was all right, but even staring at the guns never readied my ears for that first one. I wondered how soldiers stand it.

The fighter planes reappeared, roaring above all of us.

As I left, Minister Walker from the Congregational Church was asking, "You may wonder why all this is necessary, since everything we say was said better a century ago by Lincoln at Gettysburg." Then he surprised me by making the only good point I'd heard all day: "The dead died defending something, and it is right that we honor them today. However, we cannot let their struggles, illnesses, or deaths blind us to this simple truth—life is for the living."

Hurrah for Mr. Walker! I didn't know much about his family but supposed that one too many ailing relatives or parishioners had landed on him lately with their quota of headaches and backaches trumped up to resemble Calvary. The cemetery at least was honest, holding the results of real Calvaries from war and other diseases. Maybe I'd sneak into his Protestant church some Sunday morning after Mass and hear more of him. He seemed sensible.

24

My next surprise, beyond ache at how my parade gesture had fizzled, occurred in the Michaelsons' backyard. I must have expected a semiboring, semiadult party of drinking men flirting with under- or overdressed women. I came because I knew Eila and Jody would arrive so we could celebrate Jody's homecoming and Eila's outcoming more properly than at the bus stop.

Instead of a private party, however, a massive public-political rally had started with chairs and microphone along one side of the aqua pool, drink and food tables on the other. Benches of craft items stood against a row of evergreens.

"Hi, Tinker. You're Bennett's daughter? Fred Michaelson. Political science." A thin man shook my hand.

"Yes. I'm Tinker." I had to clear my throat twice before I could talk.

"Glad to see you. Is the parade over? What'll you have?" Fred Michaelson was doing his bartender thing. He had sandy hair and a worried face but seemed friendly, even without my parents' presence. I liked how he had shaken my hand.

"Well, people are still at the cemetery. It was pretty dull." *Tell him how awful it was?* "Um, I'll have a triple martini with a beer chaser."

"One Coke coming up!" He clunked ice into a glass. We both laughed.

"What's doing here today?" I asked.

"Marge's group and the women's union decided to hold their rally and talks here instead of on campus. Although..." (he looked upward) "if we get a thunderstorm everybody'll wish they were back in the auditorium. You never know what'll happen with a crowd these days."

I know just what you mean. "Well, guess I'll move around a bit. Thanks for the drink." I thought that exit line sounded like the polished person I aimed to be. Luckily he hadn't noticed my scraped cheek, torn sleeve, or teary eyes—what freedom to deal with somebody used to

Early Poverty-looking students.

I gathered that of the fifty people, mostly women, standing hip deep in conversation, nobody but me had attended the parade or knew the scuffle John and I had endured. In fact, those few minutes before Eila and Jody jounced into the driveway with the decorated truck passed dreamlike as if Endfield had cracked in half and the two hunks would never meet. Wiping my cold, runny glass onto my jeans, I devoured stuffed celery and cheese cubes and stared around. Nobody was using the microphone yet. They must be awaiting arrival of the parade contingent. Nightmare-like, my personal parade was receding.

Among the ladies, including the college students, grasslength cotton gowns or handwoven tops and sashes from Africa or some other exotic wear had replaced jeans and work outfits. Marge Michaelson was engulfed by a beige tent dress. A chocolate kerchief confined her blonde hair. I wondered why such a trim woman would hide under such a garment. My wrinkled jeans and rose tee shirt embarrassed me over to a convenient evergreen.

I thrilled when the blue nursery truck, dripping red and white carnations over its windshield, sped in, followed by a good hundred people—John and his group, more faculty with attached families, a few townspeople with low-level College jobs, several women with flash cameras and notebooks, a few scruffy town kids (hanger-on types whose presence reassured me), plus the usual canine assortment, poodle, setter, shepherd, dashing and barking at every new car. No Girl Scouts —and none of my relatives; so far, so good.

I pushed to Eila and Jody outside the truck. Surrounded by John's group, they were backslapping and laughing. Jody hugged me. "Hey, Tinker. You were great! Where'd you get the idea to beflower the Girl Scouts? When we saw you all at the cemetery, we rolled around in our carnations laughing. It was perfect."

I basked in her praise, trying to hide my injuries.

Then Eila added, frowning, "John told me how you got attacked. Of course, if you parade with signs like that, you can expect attacks."

This floored me. "What d'you mean?" I blew up. "You were *leading* the whole thing! I did it for you . . . and Jody."

"And not for yourself?"

"I don't know. I get so fed up. Everybody thinks I'm a brat. So I did something *really* bratty. Ah-h, I'll talk to you later."

Eila seemed stuck in one helluva self-protective, self-pitying mood. For the first time in our whole life together, I hated her momentarily. My face flushed enraged purple; what could I say before all these milling people? *Aw, she's nervous as a bat outa the zoo, worried what Jody will do.* But she misunderstood my whole effort!

Jody continued joking. "Well, kid, you succeeded. Do you know how many mothers'll hit the Girl Scout ceiling when they figure out what lavender means and who it came from?"

Everybody laughed. "Never tell Mother more than she can bear at one time," John yelled.

As we shoved along toward the food and liquor, I said to Jody's shoulder, "Make Eila understand." Then I asked, "Are you glad you came back?"

"Don't know. Can't get through to her yet. Jim Donohugh's there. That always—"

I missed the rest of it. By this time Jody was whooping and hopping somewhere between tense and hilarious, talking too loud, overreacting continually. If meant to reach Eila, it was wrong plus embarrassing. Well, who was I to warn either of them? Beside the pool I savored further brief acclaim and applause for decorating the Girl Scouts as John's news spread. Even if the rest of the day continued disastrous, at least I had some joy to recall.

By early afternoon the speeches droned. The first few I had liked— handsome women in print robes telling jokes, then tackling the business of advocating legal and campus medical reforms, lowcost abortion, the ERA amendment, rights for homosexuals, even birth control devices for men which I'd never heard of. (Bill O'Connell of the old Five and Ten could have used his consciousness raised, I decided.) Although the ideas and speakers were limited to ten minutes apiece, they did begin to repeat themselves. A cut above the parade, but with hard chairs and sticky temperature, a less than fascinating way to pass an early summer day.

I hoped either Jody or Eila would speak. When Jody did rise, however, it was to beeline for the liquor table where she hovered and joked and clowned some more. I could see that plans for liberating women from housework, small children, and overbearing husbands failed to touch her problems or Eila's either. I debated urging her to line up for the microphone and speak her viewpoint. I'd developed a tense need to get one or both of them to go public so I'd feel less lonely, less foolish over my part in the parade.

A florid lady topped by a green straw hat stepped from the front row and began. First she thanked the Michaelsons for their yard and "facilities." (Whenever I heard this word later, I imagined people dancing naked in the bathrooms.) Next she noted the presence of so many invited guests "plus you news reporters." Thirdly, she declared it "time to finish the unfinished revolution of American women." This intrigued me; I listened on only to discover she'd sneaked back to the standard, martyrized topics of "menial housework and the young mother's average work week of 108 hours. This has been documented. . ."

I wanted to interrupt: Suppose a woman isn't yet, or any longer, your ideal (pathetic) young mother? How to identify with it? I couldn't, and I noticed some College girls staring off, too. Would the Man of *their* dreams sentence them to 108-hour weeks chasing soggy diapers? Of course not, they'd find one who didn't; according to my mother, young girls never listen to mothers until it's too late, etc. I watched Eila in the fourth row ahead of me, our backs to the pool, stare away from the speaker toward the flowers and trees.

Where was Jody?

Before I learned the answer to this, I heard—with all the back row of us drenched by—a whopping splash. Somebody had dived in, was thrashing across in a combined butterfly-crawl. First I saw a dark blue shirt like John's. At the center of the pool the figure righted, treading water, caught its breath, and flung its hair back. It was Jody!

Unbuttoning the workshirt away from her ample front, she dragged it off and flung it onto the feet of Fred Michaelson as he cowered at the liquor table.

Barebreasted, Jody finished her fifty-foot lap across the pool in a crawl, flopped over, and retraced her swim, this time in enthusiastic backstroke, arms flung wide, breasts bobbing, mermaid-like, for all to see.

My first reaction was shock. Then I began to giggle, wondering crazily when and whether my pancake breasts would approach Jody's in grandeur.

The speaker in hunter green hat had frozen. Giving us a crooked smile, she continued, "As I was saying—" Next Marge Michaelson leapt up, grabbed a towel from behind an evergreen, flung it to her husband, who had sprinted to Jody's shallow end of the pool.

"It's a great pool!" Jody yelled as she grabbed a surfboard and straddled it. Around the edge Fred chased her until he caught the gold surfboard and forced it back to the shallow end. Jody splashed his leisure suit into dark patches. I was hoping she'd pull him in, but after a couple bobs up and down, she exited with jeans slung at low mast around her bottom half, her upper half dripping. The weight of water in fabric would have exposed a thinner woman, baring pelvis, legs, and a few other items. Somehow Fred muffled her body into the flowered towel and led her through a petunia bed toward the house.

At first everybody played it cool, turning briefly, pretending not to stare, pretending to return attention to the outraged speaker. "Right on!" yelled one man. John seconded it. "Liberation now!" called somebody else. "Right on!" Everybody began rotating glances from the speaker, to Jody, Fred, Marge, and back again. The Michaelsons did resemble two wretched parents stuck with a hopelessly unsocialized brat. A confusion of triumph and chagrin, I squirmed on my chair.

"And now, how about a song?" the interrupted speaker finished lamely. "Now we have a song for you. The guitar, where's the guitar?" Frantic motions to the first row.

And soon we were singing, "We shall overcome...." as if all were united with the speaker or one another, as if Jody's plunge had never occurred. Again I watched Eila stare, face white, jaw fixed, unsinging. She dropped her face into her open palms. Finally she rose and followed Jody's drying trail into the house while everybody crooned, "We shall live in peace..."

I wanted to rush after her but couldn't imagine the least thing to say that could ameliorate—except how gorgeous Jody's homecoming Baptism had looked. Instead I, too, sang how "We are not afraid. ...We'll walk hand in hand...someday."

Some day. Yes, ma'am.

25

Well, between my purple parade finally (rightly or wrongly) under-stood and Jody's semi-skinnydip, the bleep hit the *Endfield News* fan for several weeks. I pasted a few letters into my scrapbook; they proved so horrifyingly perfect of their kind. They also illustrate what happens when well-meaning people try to help and worsen things by widening or confusing issues.

My first clipping is the *Endfield News* editorial on

MEMORIAL PARADE UPROAR

We find it sad that Main Street on Memorial Day resembled more a free-for-all battlefield than a public event honoring the dead and dignifying the living. On a day when all Americans should unite to praise and remember their country's heroes and history, such a scene of disorderly dishonor is both painful and dismaying.

We try not to blame the organizers of the College contingent of demonstrators, Mr. John Simons and Miss Katrina Williams. As a minority, though an exceedingly vocal one, they have a right to state their beliefs and preferences publicly. However, they must then also accept responsibility for the fact that many will disagree with them, some to the point of violence. . . .

How sneaky-slimy! This view so easily becomes: If you hate me, it's somehow my fault—never that perhaps your hatred is unjust in the first place and produces what it can then justify hating.

The next one really blew my mind. It was from somebody in End-field who hadn't even attended the parade.

DON'T FRIGHTEN THE HORSES!

To the Editor:

My wife and I heard with distress how Endfield's Memorial Day parade degenerated into a brawl with a group of homosexual marchers attacking their college, Endfield, and our whole American way of family life plus insinuating themselves through decorations into the Girl Scout and Brownie marchers. If they received violence for their efforts, probably this is not be be regretted. It will teach them not to try such tactics a second time.

The family remains the bedrock of all society. Yet in America's popular culture and media, marriage and the family are incessantly ridiculed by the proponents of the Playboy philosophy, homosexuality, the commune, and the Cosmopolitan Girl.

Many artists, writers, soldiers, scientists, scholars, and statesmen have been homosexual. However, I believe they achieved their praiseworthy work despite—not because of—their affliction. To allow homosexuals into a public parade dedicated to other ends means that we condone such an affliction, and only a sick society would render tribute to a sickness.

Such people ought not to be harassed or blackmailed in private. I believe the State or the police should not involve themselves in the private affairs of consenting adults as long as they do not do it in the streets or frighten the horses. But it is another thing altogether to elevate homosexualism—often the consequence of a damaged home environment—publicly to the level of a praiseworthy lifestyle for all, especially the young, to view.

Has America passed beyond maturity into decadence?

Sincerely,
Albert J. McElwain

The final letter I saved is curious because it was written by a tourist/outsider whom you wouldn't expect to care:

TOUCHING

To the Editor:

As a physical education and yoga instructor, for years I've deplored our near-touchless environment where physical expressions of affection and comfort are reserved for lovers, small children, and relatives. It is as if the fear we initially have for our own bodies leads us automatically to fear others.

I happened to see the homosexual and students' rights demonstration that formed part of Endfield's Memorial celebration.

The violent response to it saddened me because I fear such reaction will unleash a whole new wave of antihuman and antibody sentiment.

When people now in their 50's or 60's grew up, homosexuality or lesbianism weren't words ever to be uttered and, paradoxically, women related to women, and men to men, *more* freely because the fear of homosexuality did not exist. Homophobia increases as the openness, if not the incidence, of gayness increases. Today two women holding hands, even living together, are immediately suspect. Yesterday this was not the case.

Just because a woman, for instance, enjoys touching another woman need not and does not mean she is a lesbian. Liking to touch other human beings is a beautiful and natural thing, given the fact that we all both body and soul.

Fleeing from homosexuality or going overboard about it are both bad because they render us excessive and uptight in situations where we might achieve other, more liberating reactions based on accepting our own bodies and other people's.

In hope,
Jane S. Fremont
Port Washington, N.Y.

I realize now with something like terror that *any* incident can be endlessly embroidered from as many viewpoints as there are viewers. Sometimes this is exhilarating, but mostly it's confusing. So I'll return to the facts as I lived them.

Luckily my parents, womb-deep in coming birth details, baby's room, baptismal party announcements, etc., remained immune to this newspaper storm, since my name never appeared in print. Either the editors and spectators assumed John had flowered up the Girl Scouts, or they dismissed the event as a juvenile joke. Relief—and disappointment.

My parents had already chosen the baby's name. Daily it alternated between Ian Alexander Tharp and Alexander Ian Tharp. When they asked which I preferred, I almost questioned, "But what if it's a girl?", then decided not to be so mean. Obviously they'd failed with me and could use the consolation of a boy this second time around.

Anyway, when my mother discovered from Nedda my role in beautifying Endfield's young women and marching with John, it did not create its usual volcanic effect. After all, I hadn't consorted with Eila and Jody, had I? The fact that she was daily swelling with my father's yearned-for heir (to what? I wondered) had upped her self-image. She no longer let Nedda's gossip ruin her day. Even the fact of

Jody's swim at the party was ascribed to heat and drunkenness. Not that my mother liked either of these; rather, for the moment, she grew immersed in her own world of body waiting.

One night after dinner my father did comment, "Fred Michaelson says your friend Jody took a pretty spectacular dip at his party. Guess she couldn't stand the speeches either, huh? I avoid these events. Still, it would have been fun to see."

"Dad, Jody was drunk but she's not . . . sick."

"I dunno. She and Eila have kind of messed it up around here this spring."

A straight account of Fred and Marge's party did appear in the *Endfield News,* done by an intern society reporter who, after summarizing several speeches, naming guests and describing their clothing, merely remarked that "one of the female attendees decided to take a brief but splashy dip in the Michaelsons' pool—apparently a humorous, summertide protest against a speech given by one of the visiting celebrities. Music began. Then Ms. _____ continued her speech in favor of wages for housework and childcare, plus other means to elevate the status of America's housewives. . . ."

As I read, I speculated whether Eila's post party fury would again drive Jody from Endfield. Eila could turn cold and sullen when she chose. I kept thinking all these adults should know how to handle such events better, then realized I had no solution either for how to salvage a ten-year relationship that had exploded into dismay and disgrace. I felt horrible that all my retrieving Jody from Manhattan had achieved was to re-enable her to blow up and leave like before.

But what could I do about it?

26

Events rushed along. Next thing I noticed was the campus covered with flyers about a TEACH-IN ON HOMOSEXUALITY AND RELATED OPPRESSIONS. A three-line announcement even appeared in the *News* "Public Notice" section, disguised as:

DISSATISFIED WITH YOUR LIFESTYLE?

Learn about others. Teach-In, College auditorium.

Thurs., June 12, 8 p.m. REFRESHMENTS SERVED.

Assembling extra shreds of courage, I dropped a flyer on my father's desk. I fidgeted through a magazine until he noticed the pink paper. "Daddy? Oh by the way, are you going?"

"They already asked me, Tinker. They wanted somebody from the history department to say something."

"Will you? But why history?"

"To lend respectability, I guess. No, I don't participate in these political frays."

"Well, if you're not speaking, are you going?"

"No. A classroom's one thing. A mob is something else."

"But they're not—"

"Tinker, I'm staying home with your mother while we wait for that trip to the hospital. But I know *you* want to hear Eila and Jody or John speak."

I granted my father the point. I realized that my attempt at nonchalance had failed to hide my hunger to learn who would speak, what they'd say, and the net effect on Endfield. Or perhaps I'd dissembled well enough, but my father wasn't as oblivious as he usually endeavored to appear. Maybe a son's birth would reinterest him in our family life, at least for a month or so, until it cried too much at night and my mother complained again. Or maybe it would prove the dream baby I hadn't been—no allergies, diaper rash, nightmares, or teething problems. Just smiles, coos, and wiggles. Secretly, however, I pictured

128

it growing into another red-haired brat like me; then I'd not feel so alone. At least there'd be *two* brats for Nedda and my mother to despair over. When I caught myself daydreaming a string of such fantasies, I understood why my mother walked around fixated elsewhere that June.

In her ninth month, she lived as two people, neither fully there yet. I wondered whether they'd let me into the hospital to see anything happen. From a conversation I overheard, I gathered my father could go if he'd attend special classes; he hadn't wanted to. This made me vicariously sad for my mother. If *I* gained thirty pounds producing somebody's kid, I'd sure as hell want that somebody there while I unloaded his thirty pounds. But my mother, still into feminine modesty and other crippling notions, didn't agree or agitate, I guess. My mother's "talks" with me about sex had been pathetic, unrealistic affairs so I didn't want to embarrass either of us or spoil her joy by pressing new questions. I could have asked my father, but what did he know about it? All he had was the other set of equipment—whose job was over—not the female set around which all that future action would transpire.

On June 12 I stopped by the nursery right after school to ask John whom he had scheduled to speak and his defense plans against the thugs. The campus police would have to handle it. Endfield had refused any police protection, which pleased him. He always believed uniforms provoke violence. After the parade, however, I decided lack of uniforms also provokes violence. Not daring to inquire about Jody, fearing he'd say she'd run away again, I loitered inside the greenhouse piling boxes and sweeping the floor until I roused enough nerve to enter the kitchen.

I found Eila and—surprise—Jody seated at the table, both looking hung over. When they said together, "Hi, Tinker," I appropriated this as sufficient welcome to sit down. Although I remained angry with Eila for ignoring me and my parade gesture, I hadn't devised any way to broach the subject. I worried I was becoming one of those refined cowards afraid to mention something unless somebody else is "in a good mood." That is, probably never, so that I then congratulate myself on "not fighting" with people. The whole cycle repeats, not to mention self-destructs.

"How's Little Miss Fix-it?" Jody asked. "Lavender Menace of the Girl Scouts?"

"That's *not* funny," I objected. "Nobody got the point anyway except one guy in the newspaper.''

''Well, we got the point. What you did made me feel good—a really funny welcome-back present. Plus John's group. That's a dozen more people. Tinker,'' she continued, ''I'm afraid you've interrupted a big event here. I'm trying to rig a bargain with Eila. I'll stay a few more days—if she'll speak tonight at the teach-in. But right now, she doesn't even want *me* to speak.''

''Why?''

'' 'Why not?' is the question. Afraid I'll make another ass of myself, she thinks.''

Eila stared fiercely into the table. ''I don't think. I *know*.''

''In ten years here did I ever insult a customer, did I ever seduce a child, did I ever lie or cheat you? Well?''

''If either of us speaks tonight, it'll totally kill my business.''

''Well, the damn thing's suffocating now. What've we got to lose?''

I rejoiced when nobody asked me what I thought about this one. I found myself divided enough to squirm, startled to discover their tension afflicted me like my parents' similar bouts—with depression, knotted stomach, surprise that nobody had solved it (whatever) yet, determination never to trap myself in such a relationship.

''Eila, we *have* to do it, and we have to do it here in Endfield. No place else matters. I mean, what courage does it take to stand up in Manhattan and yell you're gay if nobody knows you, nobody could care less?''

''I don't want to stand up anywhere. You stand up in Manhattan.''

''Oh, you know what I mean. Don't go catatonic on me.''

''Why do you of all people suddenly think Endfield matters?'' Eila persisted. ''Yuh, I know. It's a great place to visit, but you wouldn't want to live here.''

I laughed; nobody else did.

''Eila, will you at least come tonight? Even if you hide in the curtains, that would be something. Look, I'll try my speech out on you before time so you can censor it. Will you come?''

''Why do you want me there?''

''Ah-hh!'' In one exasperated collapse Jody dropped her head onto the palm of her right hand, then the whole arm onto the table.

Silence.

I longed to suggest how maybe John could say something for each of them. Finally I decided they needed to settle it themselves. Tinker the Coward. Then I asked, ''What about Jim Donohugh?''

''What about him?'' Jody repeated.

"Maybe Eila won't speak because she wants him."

"Oh Christ! Do I hate these gay relationships that become parodies of the nuclear family. Complete with adultery. If she wants him, she can have him. I certainly don't want him."

"What *does* she want?" I asked.

"Okay, Eila, what do...what does Woman want?" Jody mocked.

"I don't know. I need more time.... Do you want to sell the business for fifty thousand? That's the only offer I've had."

"No. I agree it's worth four times that. But we've been *through* all this."

"Give me till six o'clock."

"Eila, the thing begins at seven. John needs—"

"Give me till six."

Suddenly I longed to stand between them, take one each of their hands, and rejoin them again—a triple linked human chain against Endfield. Dismissing that as over-mushy, I swallowed my confusion, fumbled my arms around both their shoulders, and left.

27

"Hi, Tinker. How are you?"

Later that afternoon I was standing in the First National debating between the last leaky half gallon of milk (my mother's order) and some uncrushed gallons when Jim Donohugh strolled behind me. I turned around. "Hi. I'm doing okay. I'm getting bread and milk for my mother." Should I mention the imminent baby? Aw, skip it.

"Want a lift home? Or I have a better idea. May I buy you a milk-shake? 'Frost'—I guess you still call them here?"

I hardly knew Jim or his brother Roy, but I was sunk so low any pickup looked welcome. Since the drugstore next door had just raised its frost price from fifty to sixty-five cents, I was torn between fighting inflation and having a fun time. "Okay. Let me go through the check-out line." I paid the cashier's total and met Jim outside the glass front door.

Jim is a short man with dark eyes behind tortoise shell glasses. That day he wore a khaki leisure suit that made him resemble a vacationing safari hunter. It reminded me of Fred Michaelson's—minus Jody's wet spots.

"Eila has mentioned you. I wanted to get to know you....Well, you're all grown up compared to the little girl I remember," he re-marked. The first part I liked; the last part struck me like Klass K Korn, but I couldn't figure out how to counter it. We settled into a scarred back booth and ordered maple and strawberry frosts from Estelle, our white-ruffled waitress.

"What's new?" My all-purpose, verbal hide-and-seek question.

He laughed. "Can you keep a secret?"

"Sometimes....I saw Eila just now. She asked for time until six o'clock. Do you want to buy her business?" I blurted this out, shock-ing myself because gossipers ranked lower than snakes on my list of worthy beings. In fact, I hoped a special wing of Hell would be devoted to them.

"Tinker, I'm no florist. I'm an engineer."

Try again. Playing games. I felt challenged. "Okay. Then you want to marry her."

"Tinker, you are full of. . .extreme solutions. I had no idea you're so outspoken or such an activist. By the way, I saw the parade."

I slumped farther into my booth. "I didn't like the parade. The speeches were dull."

"Among other problems." Jim winked at me. "Look, I hope you'll help me with something."

"I'm really busy. I'm going to a teach-in tonight; my mother's having a baby; and school isn't out yet."

Jim smiled. Our frosts arrived, foaming at their walnuty and pink mouths.

I couldn't stand it anymore. "Well, please, what's your secret?"

"Will you deliver something for me?"

"You mean something of Roy's? Roy was in my father's class this spring."

"Yes, I know that, but there you go—jumping again where angels fear to tread." Another Mona Lisa face. Maddening man. *And the angels are all in heaven and the fools are all dead.*

"Well, what *is* it?"

"Will you deliver a letter to the nursery for me?"

"No. No more letters. I'm sorry, but I got trapped in a big mess this spring over a postcard. You don't know my aunt Nedda."

"Of course I do."

Dammit! No rest for the wicked in Endfield. "Well, once warned is twice warned or something like that. With her."

"Tinker, someday you'll make a good lawyer. Or something like that." Another wink; he was the winkiest damn man I ever met, including Bill O'Connell.

"Will you stop making fun of me? I can't stand it."

"I'm sorry, Tinker. I apologize." Now he sounded genuine. I could relax a bit into my maple frost with my mother's milk souring next to my feet on the floor. As I stared at Jim, I realized he probably wasn't used to picking up twelve-year-olds in markets; maybe what he'd tried on me was his social-ha-ha mask, which I should ignore. Then I realized he seemed genial, handsome, young, together compared with Bill O'Connell. And somewhere in my midsection began to speculate how it would feel to have a man like him really interested in you for a long time, instead of diddling you a bit for Sunday recreation or a woods weekend. I saw now why Eila walked around confused.

"Well, if you won't deliver my letter, I'll just have to deliver it my-self, won't I?"

"I guess so. I don't recommend the mailman. He's kind of nosey, too, and drops things in the wrong places. That's what happened to me."

"Tinker, don't you wonder what's in the envelope?"

"You mean you want me to *read* it?"

"No. What I had in mind was that you'd keep it a few days."

"Until you're out of town?"

"You could say that. Well, at least until the seventeenth. That's a couple days after Roy's concert and all his finals are over."

"I don't understand why you can't just mail it. From wherever you are."

"I'd prefer it hand delivered. You emphasized yourself how that avoids...accidents?"

Oh hell! Trapped.

From the flap pocket of his jacket he produced a manila vellum envelope, deckle edged, altogether an expensive, toney job as large as Ferncliff diplomas. It resembled a wedding or reception invitation.

Why do people stick me with stuff they can't manage themselves? "All right. I'll keep it safe at home. Then I'll give it to John for Eila next week. How's that?"

"I guess it'll have to do," Jim answered.

Then he paid the check for our frosts and drove me up Laurel Street. I asked, "What's being an engineer like?"

"Well, it's like everything else. Fine for a few years. First I worked for the U.S. Geological Survey, then for an oil company. I've been consulting on other people's projects, but this fall I want to get my own business going."

"Running your own business must be exciting. Do you have a lot of money?"

Jim laughed. "That's precisely what I'm trying to figure out."

"Well, good luck," I said as I hopped from the Pinto, carrying the envelope inside my shirt away from my mother's leaky milk. I won-dered how much Eila's six o'clock deadline involved Jim. So nobody would conclude I snooped like Nedda, however, I hid Jim's fancy letter, still sealed, under a shoebox in a recently cleaned section of my closet. I could deliver it next week.

28

For the next hour until supper I stared out my bedroom window. At first I watched roving kids and dogs gang up on Heidi Spencer's little Heidi. Within ten minutes they dispatched her home screaming, knee scraped, to validate her mother's fear that the kid's future lay in victimhood. Big Heidi had already complained to my mother about "neighborhood bullies."

Somehow I'd escaped that problem. When I was Heidi's age, I'd dared to kick the shins of a girl and boy team about twice my age, causing an irate call from their mother. When I refused to apologize to their mother or mine (who didn't want "any trouble"), I noticed they stayed clear of me, having been warned by their mother that I was a brazen tomboy unfit for association . . . .

That afternoon before the teach-in, I must have sunk into one massive gloom. Whatever had buoyed me from the parade on through the meetings with Jim, Eila, and Jody had drained, like a rain barrel that finally bursts. Worst of all, I had nobody to commune with. I saw Pammy once a week at lunch—if I was lucky. She ate with a girl from South Endfield named Marcella. My parents remained transfixed in excited waiting, Eila and Jody in gloom and nagging.

Not since early spring, when I'd sat disgraced in my room, had I dared face how I felt, about Eila and Jody especially. I began to realize how I'd been bleeding in opposite directions—half trying to disengage myself from the women now that they and their nursery had become forbidden pleasures, like sneaking chocolates despite your acne or cavities. For the other half, I yearned horribly to love and be loved and noticed by each of them, depending on which I'd seen last or—these days—successfully. At any rate, the fear that I'd soon, again, permanently lose one, maybe both, of them to depression, business failure, or New York sickened and chilled me.

I tried to recall Heidi-like pain and discovered it had been physical

—stubbed toes, broken arm, hunger, wailing during a spanking. My new pain that spring, however, was mental, lonely—and unchanged by crying. Was such agony what growing up meant? Should I accept my mother's and Nedda's suspicions about me? How can you be a lesbian if you lack the essential—a willing somebody to do it with? Should I like boys although I lacked one of those, too?

At six p.m., Eila's deadline hour, while my mother fried porkchops and potatoes, I imagined tiptoeing to the phone extension in my father's study. To say what? Bite my lips, twist my hair, I couldn't devise anything whole. If I reached Jody, it would be how I hoped Eila would get the guts to speak this evening or at least let Jody speak. On the other hand, if Eila answered, I'd have to sympathize with her desperate hopes that the evening would go as she wanted—no speeches, fuss or muss.

What crushed me as I contemplated on the bed, arms propped under chin, was that I couldn't see how either solution—Jody or Eila speaking tonight or not—would fix anything. Jody was correct on that point: Everybody in Endfield Already Knew so what did it matter, the next move would be Endfield's, anyway. Whether Jody, for instance, spoke or not would wind up interpreted against her. "You know how it is with women like that. Always mannish and outspoken, like somebody's persecuting them." Or maybe: "I heard Eila and Jody were supposed to speak. Just as well they didn't. People like that shouldn't expose themselves so much. Enough of it around New York."

To dam up my mind, I rippled through summer camp booklets. My father had scheduled one camp interview for the next afternoon. At the moment, though, I just couldn't get it together for the "mature, experienced staff" I was supposed to meet or even for "fine arts, drama, and overnight sleep-outs." One camp's location "on the *backside* of Queechy Ridge near friendly, historic Endfield" did strike me as appropriate, however. Repeatedly I failed to concentrate on stuff like "skill centered," "individual growth through group living," and "furthering your daughter's sense of social responsibility through realistic and meaningful involvement." . . . Maybe I could run their snack bar and embezzle enough money to escape Endfield entirely. I could join that Labor Day group of knapsacks and guitars that stared left from the overhanging porch of the drugstore awaiting the Boston-and New York-bound busses. I could—

"Tinker-r. Where are you? Will you get the plates for me?" My mother's voice from the kitchen above the pork chops, ball bouncing, and radio sounds. My mother's front had enlarged until she no longer carried stacks or sacks of anything—newspapers, plates, groceries—for fear she'd tip over. Yet my father and I both helped her easily now because she seemed so *cheerful,* compared to that other woman of brooding, illness, and gossip, who had needed help but rejected helpers as awkward stupids. Nedda must have hinted or even told her what she thought of a woman over thirty producing a new baby. Why, only dirty old ladies do that, and what about the danger of mongolism?

Anyway, one healthy result of these months seemed to be that she'd weaned herself from Nedda's helpfully destructive influence. No more ambivalence about Nedda that swung from "She's so good to me" one day to "She'd talk the tin ear off a mule" the next. Maybe my mother would acquire a life of her own that could benefit all of us. I hoped so. In fact, that spring began my unexpected process of *respecting* my mother, for I saw her, despite discomforts of pregnancy, refusing to degenerate into the baleful nuisance my grandmother had become. Turned "difficult" and "peculiar," Grandma had died following a series of strokes—plus two years of being waited on and whispered about by her daughters. That period of living from one collapse/medical bulletin to the next explained when and how my mother and Nedda had got extra intimate.

My uncle, Forrest, who owned a business in Canada, avoided it all except for ritual Christmas visits and the funeral in March of the previous year. I thought him a genius to have moved so far away. Was it because he's male—or merely gifted at prospering on his own? I never talked much with him. He stayed with one of his high school buddies, spent more time socializing than grieving. Yet nobody criticized him. Finally I guessed why: Nobody in Endfield really cares how you feel so long as you *appear* tragic or joyful at appropriate funerals or holidays. Appearance is 90%, and hypocrisy maintains the rest of the social order.

At the other end of life's spectrum, my mother's current optimism was de-emphasizing all the childbirth fears I knew formed a part of her. For this I was most grateful and—

"Tinker!" Now two frantic voices.

Suspending myself between the upper bannisters and opposite railing, I jumped myself down the stairs a few at a time, a game I hadn't played in two years. That way took longer to arrive but provided more satisfaction in case a grilling awaited me about attending the teach-in. I never should have mentioned it to my father.

29

As it turned out, my father questioned me more about the teach-in than my mother. However, at 7:15 I escaped the house having promised to come home early, do my homework, and not "sit with" Eila, Jody, or John. Although sitting was forbidden, nobody had mentioned *standing*. Maybe I could do that, especially if one of them spoke. I could cheer them on from backstage or something.

In the entry hall to the auditorium I dipped up a paper cup of tea punch from a bowl, took three vanilla cookies, and walked the center aisle toward the stage. John and his group were unfolding metal and wooden chairs onto the basketball floor. At that time Ferncliff lacked money for a new sports building; the gym still served as auditorium/prom hall despite complaints that street shoes ruined every fresh coat of shellac the janitors applied.

"Hey, Tinker," John said, "I'm surprised to see you. I thought you were grounded for the next year."

"Well, they didn't want to let me out, but here I am."

"Wow, that's a good idea for tonight. Maybe: 'Out of the Closet, into the Crowd'?" Katrina spoke up. She had traded her majorette uniform for plaid minidress and scarf.

"Knock it off," John warned. "It sounds too near 'Out of the Frying Pan, into the Fire'."

"We-el?" Katrina questioned.

I saw her point, for it was exactly Eila and Jody's present impasse. Again I caught myself viewing events through their eyes, rather than my own. How was I learning, though painfully, to be *me* in all this, and who would that turn out to be?

"Remember, the point of this evening is making *us* feel good—and making the audience feel good about us feeling good. If they decide to feel rotten, that's their—"

I interrupted, "What if you don't know *how* you feel? I mean, you're mixed up? You're not sure who you want to be?''

"Tinker, would you like to speak for a couple minutes? You're the 'impressionable child' everybody accuses us of seducing.'' Katrina was staring at me.

That's really crappy, calling me a child. Then I began to panic. "I don't know. What would I say? I don't want to be seduced by anybody. I mean, I was already, and it's fun for them, I guess. Anyway, I just want to live somewhere with no hassles from my parents. I don't know yet whether I like men or women. Maybe I like both. It's just I don't wanna be *nagged* about it.''

"Great! Will you say that? How you want freedom to choose your own lifestyle?'' John insisted.

Again I'd trapped myself with Eila's and Jody's problem—how to summon the maximum+ courage it takes to act outrageous in your native town, compared to some anonymous city. Did this mean I must resemble them more than my parents—if I kept suffering their dilemmas?

To divert John, I finally promised. "I'll try to write a couple sentences. Maybe I can read them.''

Accepting his pencil, I positioned myself on a stool behind one side curtain of the stage to observe who was arriving. If it proved mostly students, I'd try to speak. If it wasn't—

By 7:45, however, I'd done only doodles on Katrina's notebook page, no words at all. My stomach was also fluttering to and fro in tango duet with my heart. Is this what politicians and priests go through? Well, they know what they're talking about—or they're supposed to. My mind drew a blank except for set of proverbs I'd gathered as a reading project the year before—some from *Farmer's Almanac,* from Nedda, an old calendar, and, of course, the newspaper.

NEVER TELL PEOPLE GOOD NEWS— IT ISN'T WHAT THEY WANT TO HEAR.

VOLUNTEER—IT'LL MAKE YOU A BETTER HUMAN BEING.

IF YOU FEEL LIFE IS ALWAYS SNIPING AT YOU, AT LEAST GIVE IT A MOVING TARGET.

BE PRO-LIFE! BABIES ARE GOD'S OPINION THAT THE WORLD SHOULD GO ON.

IF I WASN'T MARRIED, I'D HAVE TO ARGUE WITH TOTAL STRANGERS.

This last one stumped me: I couldn't see how Eila's and Jody's personal relationship differed at all from my parents' except that my parents produced babies while Eila and Jody produced a nursery. If anythings, over the years Eila and Jody liked each other better than my parents. As long as everybody does something useful that they enjoy, what difference does it make who they do it with? Happy adults are so scarce, anyway.

At five to eight I wrote these last sentences on my paper between the doodles.

By now the auditorium held about 75 people, milling and sipping under the basketball hoops and vaulted ceiling. John had pulled yards of navy blue shades, preventing kids from peeking in the windows. *This performance is rated UFO: Unidentifiable Freaky Object.*

Where were Jody and Eila? John's group remained the only people I recognized. Perspiring, I wished I'd worn my new skirt or a wig/purple nailpolish/platform shoe disguise like Ginny. What if, when I stand up, my jeans fall down? I drew my alligator plastic belt tighter, ripping another notch.

When the square clock at the back read two minutes to eight, John called, "We're beginning now" to all quarters plus outside. People began to stroll in and settle. Who were the other speakers? I noticed Katrina fingering a paper in the front row.

John doused the houselights, illuminating the brown podium with microphone poised above it. He climbed the steps to the stage and began to welcome people like a minister or principal starting a new year. Instead of fatigues, he wore a tweedy suitcoat, which impressed me. I imagined Nedda remarking, "What a waste. Man like that would make some girl a good husband if only he'd put his mind to it."

"Well, ladies and gentlemen, I'm your master of ceremonies tonight through default, mostly because nobody else wanted to do it" (guilty giggles from John's group) "but I'll keep my remarks short so we can end the formal part about nine and have time for discussion and questions.

"As you leave tonight, you'll receive a list of changes we hope to see both in the College rules and in the town laws. It's the pink sheets that'll be handed out. Take them home, think about them. My address is there, plus Katrina's address and phone in South Endfield. Let us know what you think. Help us make this society, Ferncliff College, and the town of Endfield something *all* people can live in—not just those who happen to be white, straight, and Republican.

"At this point in U.S. history, a few advances have occurred. In more than twenty states, nearly 50 city and town governments have now passed gay civil rights bills. These bills prohibit discrimination in some combination of things like public employment, accommodations, real estate and credit practices. Some also include education in this package, and some cities—like Boston—not only ban discrimination but even have an affirmative action program for gay rights.

"Yes, Boston. Shock, huh? Because most of the others are in California—" Hoots and hollers sounded. John raised his hand to quiet the crowd. "And we hope that Endfield through this meeting here tonight will be one of the next to do this.

"However, only *five* states have enacted such laws statewide," he continued, staring at outspread fingers on his right hand.

Only five states of the whole U.S.? I found John's figure both sad and fascinating. I hoped his talk would make at least the College paper, maybe the *Endfield News*.

"But an additional 23 states at least do not consider adult consensual sex acts against the law. And that includes heterosexual acts. Sodomy laws should affect heterosexuals as well when they engage in anything defined as 'unnatural practice.' In reality, however, the law persecutes or prosecutes heterosexuals only for rape and prostitution."

Was this true? What about Bill O'Connell? Was Jody right that he lost his job for entertaining little girls?

"In Western Europe ancient laws governing sexual conduct in private between consenting adults have ended. We hope the U.S. will follow suit.

"Regarding employment, I have here a packet of letters from personnel managers of corporations that do not discriminate on the basis of sexual orientation and have even publicized their stand in company publications. More than 200 companies have now responded in some affirmative way about gay and lesbian rights in their organizations. We hope that Endfield College will be one of the next businesses to pass such a rule for both faculty and students.

"There are many myths about lesbians and homosexuals that we must combat. At the most we're now tolerated. That hardly means acceptance. When you and I hear anti-gay jokes just the way we used to hear anti-Black jokes, I have to think, well, that's how they'd feel about me—if they knew. Well, now they do know.

"The media picture us as sick, demented, or dead. Other myths are that we hate the opposite sex, are promiscuous or mentally ill. This despite the fact that even so conservative a group as the American Psychiatric Association has removed homosexuality from its list of mental disorders.

"We believe fear campaigns can be countered with honest and factual education. Civil rights for all should not be a debatable issue.

"Okay, our next speaker will be Katrina Williams of the lesbian group on campus."

While Katrina found her way through the dark, John sat down on the bench beside my stool.

"John, that was good. I mean, people are really listening," I whispered. "Better than the parade."

"Yuh, they're listening," he agreed. "But I wish more of the town was here."

However, to get *anybody* out on a minority topic like this in Endfield during mid-June just before exams and vacations amazed me.

When I tuned in on Katrina, I heard her statistics. "Did you know that in 1969 a CBS television poll revealed that two out of three Americans regard homosexuals with disgust, discomfort, or fear? And one out of ten regarded them with outright hatred? A later Harris poll concluded that 63% of Americans consider homosexuals 'harmful to American society.'

"So my first question is what do we as students, Americans, human beings who happen to be homosexual *do* about such statistics? If we demonstrate like on Memorial Day, we're accused of being militant crazies. If we keep quiet in the closet where some of us have lived for years, we're accused of passivity or sissiness.

"I won't describe the particular events of my life that made a lesbian relationship as natural to me as getting married and raising kids is to other women. I do want to give other people a chance to tell their stories tonight.

"Among the demands on the sheet John mentioned, I'd like to see a gay group have the right to meet *regularly on campus*. So we have some legal place to be ourselves away from constraints to act somewhere between Miss America and Miss Ferncliff Coed.

"At Ferncliff I major in sociology. Someday I hope to be a teacher. I do well enough in my courses. I don't see why I should transfer to another school merely because the relationship I have with my roommate got revealed during the Memorial Day parade. Yeah, like *True Romances* or some soap opera. Yet I expect after tonight, both of us will be asked to leave the College by the dean of women.

"Is this what should happen in America where everybody came three hundred years ago to build a free life? We need your help. Thank you."

Moderate applause as if the audience sat either groggy or unbelieving. Did the clapping hands belong only to Katrina's supporters? Or were people present that night who hadn't known about her but believed she voiced the desperation of all minority groups in a majority culture?

A young man spoke next, describing a march for homosexual rights he'd organized in San Francisco. I relaxed when he had no horror stories or beatings to report. It had gone well; he planned to transfer to a California college that fall because he found the whole environment "freer and friendlier than around here." I seized his point that the rigors of New England winter epitomize the people's souls—hardy humans used to all weathers and fighting so hard for their livelihood that they have little to spare for others, especially if those others look strange or, in the case of homosexuals, act strange in private. "In New England the quality of mercy is never strained because it exists only for a few family members, and even those mustn't act shiftless or their payments get cut.

"Somebody encourages us to hush up. Even Presidential candidates claim they have 'other priorities' than enfranchising ten percent of the population. If our 'problem' or 'sickness' does get known, then we're treated like unwed mothers forty years ago—with scorn, scandal or forced marches to religion or psychiatry."

Although I liked his spirit (espcially his recalling my forced march to Father Henry), he got less applause than Katrina. The audience evidently didn't know either of them well.

A woman student came now and read a poem about someone's love for her friend or mother, how the bad moments of nursing her during some illness recalled the better times they'd been close, especially during a spring walk in the fields. Somehow the nursing alleviated both their fears of death. The poem ended sadly.

After that meditative note, John's roommate, Phil, walked up. His talk flashed by deft and witty—impossible to remember—as he mocked standard jokes about homosexuals, hippies, women drivers, and the priest who swung a lighted censer until somebody told him his handbag was on fire. I could remember only bits of ideas: How enduring such a barrage of gossip, insults, and reverses makes strong people of homosexuals. Also that preferring members of your own sex should not be considered proof of general incompetence—any more than race or religion automatically disqualify people any longer.

When he hit a dull historical stretch about male homosexuality in Greece and Rome, however, I tuned him out for the same reason my father's classes bored me: Whatever men achieved in history seemed to aid women but little. There my mother was right. It was only because women remained willing to stay home, cook, and babysit that men got out at all, but nobody wrote history about *that* as if domestic life didn't matter. All Phil's wittiness couldn't conceal the fact that, to me, he was expounding a bisected view of human civilization.

Now I slumped, thoroughly confused. Who was right? If not Phil, then Jody and Eila? Or my parents and Nedda? How could I decide with nothing but hungers eating me? John must have noticed me wiggling on my stool. "You're on next," he whispered.

"But where's Eila and Jody?" I felt trapped.

"Jody was supposed to come, but they're not gonna show, I guess."

I gazed toward the section of audience I could see. I noticed Mr. Ferguson and—surprise—Mrs. Ferguson wearing her teased hair. Now nobody could dismiss solid business people like them as hippy-dippy radicals who needed either a good licking or a tar and feathering. At first I imagined I saw Eila in the audience. Then I recognized the dark-haired woman as Miss Sanderson who had just bought a Cape Cod house on that new street with the funny name—Tanglewylde Drive.

Just as my hope for Eila and Jody died, one of the auditorium back doors yanked open. Jody strode in. From the angle of her body and the length of her paces, she appeared miserable but determined. Someone propped a chair into the door. By straining, I distinguished Eila leaning at it.

By this time Phil had finished, the audience was murmuring, and John rushed to recapture attention. "Ladies and gentlemen, we have a special guest tonight, who is willing to appear here despite considerable. . .opposition after events in the town this spring. Here comes Jody Foxx who, as you probably know, runs Brandi Nursery with" (John paused longer, bit his lips) "Eila Brandi." A few claps, a lot of head turning and whispers. Eila continued the door ajar although I expected her to slam it any second.

Wearing her ceremonial outfit—the grey suede skirt suit and flowered blouse—Jody climbed to the podium, adjusted the microphone, and began. "Well, folks, I've had a sort of rugged day like some of you, I expect. I won't keep you long. When John asked me to speak, I answered I don't give political speeches about the need for revolution. I always figure revolution, like charity, should begin at home. Revolution isn't a matter of what you say or how much violence you promise. It's rather what you are or what you can become in your daily life. Because that's the only life given to most of us. In a way, nothing else matters."

Jody regripped the podium and continued. "I'm a lesbian, yes, I'm a lesbian to those of you who've known me ten years but never known me, so to speak. I didn't have a mixed up childhood. I loved both my parents, especially my mother. I don't hate men. I have always and simply preferred women, especially one woman. Love and need are the essence of lesbianism, just as they are of heterosexual marriage.

"However, don't you dream that acknowledging this privately or publicly has simplified my life. I've never been, well, politically correct anywhere. I've never been anticapital enough for the Marxists nor Marxist enough for certain feminists, and I wound up being too lesbian for the lot of them. Either they run you out of town or you leave before they get around to it." I laughed to John at this idea. Jody's courage thrilled me.

"Even the present women's movement is buying its own ticket into mainstream America at the price of disowning us, making us look like freaks. Whoever claims that being a lesbian is a cop-out because it doesn't change or risk any institution has never tried to live—and earn a living—as a homosexual human being in this country.

"Maybe someday we will live in a loving, or at least just, society. I assume that's why we're here—to continue the effort.

"Some of you have known me for years. I recognize your faces because I've fixed your flowers, delivered your bouquets, helped you grieve or celebrate depending on the passing seasons and changes in your own families. Now I'm asking you for something. Not acceptance or tolerance, although I've offered you these qualities in the past. Nor do I ask forgiveness like some kind of sinner.

"What I do request is neither complicated nor revolutionary. I ask that you help Eila and me continue our life and work at the nursery as you have in the past before you knew or guessed...about us....

"You've heard and will hear, I'm sure, slanders against homosexuals. Some of them are true for individuals, others just prejudice. When you hear them, I ask you to discern carefully which is which....Eila and I have been happy in this town. We don't dislike anybody for the shape of their head or the cut of their clothes. We hope to remain in Endfield. But we *need your help* and the help of your families and friends. Thank you all."

Then Jody didn't walk so much as wander toward John and me. I gave her my high stool; John sat her down. She dropped there, arms between her knees, exhausted and perspiring.

Applause rose and ebbed in waves. Fighting tears in my eyes, I couldn't speak. I took her hand and held it while John leapt forward to regain control.

"Our next and last speaker will be Tinker Tharp. Tinker?"

Who, me? My God, I'd misplaced my paper. Jody must be sitting on it! Suddenly I felt fresh evening air. Behind me in the wings the stage door had opened. There stood Eila. Clutching the iron railing, she made her way up the steps, head lowered.

"Well, while Tinker gets herself together..." John was battering and bantering his way onward. "I'd like to read the list of requests we're making of the College and the town..." I lost the rest because when Eila got near Jody, suddenly three of us formed one solid, speechless hug, erasing some of my bad hours. Next Eila was standing between Jody's feet and legs.

John finished the last of his list about further use of campus facilities, a course on homosexuality in the curriculum, a new town law prohibiting discrimination. Then he was dragging me out into the spotlight and podium light. At first I panicked. All those people! How had Jody spoken for so long?

To forestall collapse, I shoved my knees into the furniture, cleared my throat, and tried to begin. I discovered if I stared sort of cross-eyed at the microphone before my nose, I needn't see the audience at all. This steadied me.

"Well, uh, I'm not used to speaking in public. And I got extra problems today, because, well, Jody just sat down on my speech notes I was gonna read—" Bursts of laughter interrupted. "But I'll do the best I can. Mostly I want to say I've worked at Brandi Nursery four years until this spring and...haven't been seduced yet. At least not there," I added quickly. More laughter. My face blotched hot and purple. I was botching it up!

I stopped, then continued bug-eyed at the microphone. "Well, that's what everybody worries about, isn't it? Anyway, what people my age would like is some *freedom* about who?...whom? they'll associate with, whom they want to marry, and generally just not be forced in any direction before they're ready. Thank you, everybody."

The last part came out whispered stupidly, but I couldn't manage any other ending. Uncrossing my eyes and leaning into a khaki curtain, I stumbled backstage. And then it was over. John replaced me at the microphone to begin questions. Eila, Jody, and I made another triple hug, all our faces red and white and running. Still nobody spoke.

Next Jody and Eila half carried me down the stairs behind the curtains. "Tinker, c'mon with us." Jody wiped her face and neck, dragged her sweated blouse from her skirt, and waved the tails. "Wooh! We're going to a real party. To make up for Memorial Day," she whispered.

We got ourselves to the truck outside the stage door. At that point I didn't even care how or what I'd ever explain to my parents.

30

"We're going to a fraw-lic at Bridgwah-tuh's," announced Jody in mock Boston-ese.

"Where's Bridgewater's?"

"You'll see."

The three of us climbed up into the van front seat. Jody lit a cigarette and we veered out the driveway.

After all that effort of nerving myself to speak, my insides were a rage of emotions—exhaustion, relief, curiosity about our evening plus the familiar excitement at sitting again between Eila and Jody.

Eila wore something I'd never seen before—a three-piece velvet pants suit of a russet color whose folds luminesced brown, wine, grey like the sheen on a plum or stained glass against angles of evening sun. She also wore potent but delicate perfume somewhere between wisteria and lavender that recalled springs and falls of nursery smells.

"Jody, I liked your speech." I didn't know what else to venture for fear of angering Eila. If I expected one of Jody's zanier replies like "Pretty good for the town pervert, huh?", I didn't get it. Silently we drove through the twilit gold-green streets.

"Tinker, what time do you have to be home?" Eila inquired. Another bunch of conflict filled me—her care at inquiring, followed by anger at my parents' rules that, as usual, subverted an evening before it even began. Or was she concentrating on me to avoid dealing with Jody?

"Oh, I'm supposed to be home early," I mumbled.

"It was brave of you to get out there and talk." Now she took my right hand.

"Well, uh, John *dragged* me out. I mean, I didn't offer to speak."

"You're not the only one!" agreed Jody.

Then Eila blew up. "What d'you mean? That's ridiculous! Jody, Im still furious. You ran out of the house."

"How else could I get away?"

"Don't play smart-ass!"

"Well, I'm glad it's over, anyway," Jody tried to conclude.

"It's not over." Eila released my hand from her knee.

"All right. It's not over. But let's have a good time tonight, huh?"

Eila's answer came as a trickle of tears, which Jody ignored. Finally, however, she reached a comforting hand around the back of Eila's bent head. I sat and sweated, unsure what to do. What good were tears? I suspected this particular argument with its impasse had been dress rehearsed frequently, explaining its sudden dropping by both of them.

Avoiding the main road to South Endfield, we had cut through back lanes bordered by maples, stone walls, and meadows to King's Land Road. "Do you know how King's Land got its name?" Jody asked. "I actually read it once." She was attempting to sneak a change in topics. When neither Ella nor I answered, she continued, "Well, for those of us who care about history. Before the Revolution the deacon of First Con Church in Endfield lived along here. During the War he about bankrupted himself supporting the rebels against the King. Afterward the new government's taxes hit him as bad as the King's. Owning the strip here meant he had to pay upkeep on the public road, too. When they came to collect, he yelled, 'I'll not pay a shilling. Give it back to the King.' And he drew up a quit claim deeding it back to England."

"What happened then?"

"When he still refused to pay, these three acres sat as common land a couple centuries until the state claimed them last year for the new highway."

Eila burst forth. "Oh fine, Jody. Any more great ideas? And when we go broke, we'll mail the nursery back to Queen Elizabeth?"

"Why not?...Oh, Eila, it's just a story."

Cool, mossy twilight had settled over King's Land. "There's the third picket fence. Turn!" Eila ordered. I admired her efficient recovery. Could I ever do as well? I saw now why Jody had ignored the tears.

Jody screeched brakes, swerving us onto a dirt road at the right. "Why the hell did John give picket fence directions? There's one on every rock around here."

"There's the Chinese money tree. Left, on the lawn. Remember the day Bridgewater bought it?"

Squinting across Jody's front, I studied a handsomely shaped bush in blue-violet flowering under the sun's final rays. It reminded me of winter nights in the greenhouse when I hated to extinguish the light on such a palette of tropical colors. We negotiated the winding driveway. At the hilltop, bits of radiance showed a cupola atop a square-rigged white monstrosity of a house—full of porches, pendant eaves, skinny windows.

"It's also called Honesty."

"What?" Jody asked.

"The Chinese money tree. You don't remember?"

"Was I here then?. . .But I like that. Prob'ly on Halloween End-field'll drape it with toilet paper and burn it down for being Communist."

I giggled.

"More likely capitalist," Eila commented.

"Sweetie, I'm glad you're doing better." Jody had stopped the truck and reached behind me to touch Eila's shoulder. "Hey, kids, do you know there's a parasitic British plant called Lesser Broomrape?"

"I thought it was Greater Broomrape."

"Yuh, Eila. It feeds on broom and gorse." No reaction. "Well, one rape's as good as another." I giggled. "Maybe it's related to that plant you read to me about? Creeping Lady's Tresses? You know, all those veins with scented flowers in a spike on one side of the stem."

"Very funny." Eila was continuing her sardonic mood.

I stared back over Jody's shoulder to what I could see of the Honesty tree. "Is this place haunted?"

"You could say that. Okay, kids, out," Jody ordered. How could I end her insistence on "kid" this evening? We ran up two levels of concrete steps and jangled some brass bells at the door. No one came. To the right on greyish clapboards hung four wicker bicycle baskets—maiboxes, I guessed. Whoever our hosts were, they must be multiple.

The black door swung open. At first, however, no one seemed to stand there. Then I sensed something lightish in the murk a couple feet from me. I picked out a hand, then a face on about my level.

Next we crowded inside, greeted by a whispery woman so hooded and draped in dark satin that she seemed to emanate from the varnish-work. If she's not a ghost, she must be an artist, I decided. From a room on the left I heard muffled bumpings as if somebody was being beaten.

Eila faced left and reached out. The woman pulled her arm back. "No. They're rehearsing. Come on into the bar." Somehow we stumbled our way around a staircase, through a swinging door, into a tiny candlelit room. From the long steel counter with sliding panels atop it, I guessed this must be some variant of dining room off a kitchen farther back.

Eila and Jody knelt on plump cushions around napkin size tables. Each table sported a fat jade god with green candle sprouting from his dome. I plunked down on a beanbag hassock that squeaked and felt like corduroy.

"How did it go?" the woman asked.

"I don't know," Eila answered. "We left before the questions."

"What d'you mean, you don't know? Tinker and I were marvelous." Jody blustered. "Actually, Ardath, we don't know. The audience clapped a lot but, as Eila said, we cut out early. I hope it has *some* effect. It cost a helluva lotta effort."

"You are a bit early. I can't show you the stage until Myron finishes rehearsing everybody. He gets paranoid if you interrupt him."

"What does he want? I mean, the stage flowers," Judy asked.

"You better talk directly with him. In the meantime how about a drink? We have scotch, gin, juices, Coke." After Eila and Jody had ordered Scotch on the rocks, I said, "I'll have a Tom Collins, please." When everybody stared at me, I amended it to, "Well, never mind Tom. Just the Collins part." I'd got that at my father's departmental party.

"Uh, Ardath, this is Tinker. Our right-hand lady until this spring. Tinker, on that hassock you look like Little Miss Muffet."

"Don't call me Little Miss Muffet. Or kid," I protested.

"Why, you're taller than I am," Ardath noted.

"Ardath, everybody's taller than you are." That remark from Jody must have finished Ardath off, for when I looked up, she'd disappeared, apparently into the wall.

"What is this place?" I asked.

"One of the lit professors, Bridgewater, went on sabbatical last fall. He rented to some people from dance and drama who wanted more practice and rehearsal space. They're doing a play next month for the Endfield Arts Festival. They live here."

"Oh, c'mon, Jody. Tell her the truth."

"Okay. Gay people meet here on weekends. For parties," Jody added. My eyes widened. "Does Endfield *know?*"

"Well, according to Ardath, the neighbors suspect . . . . Ah, what the hell, what's life if you spend it crouching in the closet—"

"Don't, Jody!" Eila begged. "She—"

"I won't tell anybody. I promise."

"It's not that, Tinker. I mean, that's happened already. It's just we don't want you hurt by mixing into—"

"I won't get hurt. . . . Well, I do get hurt when you get all gloomy like my mother. I do things for you, and neither of you even notices me." There it was out. I should have shut up, but I continued, "I don't understand. If you *like* your life, why're you so scared?"

"For the same reason you're scared," Eila answered. "Only you got a place here no matter what you do. We haven't. Any longer."

I bit my fist. Jody sighed. We all crunched around our cushions. I took possession of another angle on the beanbag tuffet. How had my desire to help both of them got twisted into a three-way barrage of criticism?

"Of course, we need you, Tinker, and appreciate you but—"

Eila ended when Ardath reglided from the wall bearing a silver tray of glasses. "I think Myron and the crew are finishing. There's a real quiet part just before the end. That's why they aren't knocking anymore."

"I'll come with you," Jody announced. Grabbing a hunk of Ardath's robe, she followed her through a drapery of the same rosy leaf pattern as the wallpaper.

I munched some odd-tasting nuts and brooded into the limey depths of my Collins glass. "Cheers," I said, tilting it crookedly. Eila offered me a sad smile, then tested her drink. Candlelight had softened the white tenseness of her face, playing the melody of warm browns that formed her suit, hairband, beige scarf at her throat. I gave up—and lay down on the cushions beside her. She surprised me by reaching out and gathering my head into her lap.

Behind my eyes ruby and brown lights blinked. I relaxed in this embrace of velvet and scent. As I stretched my arms around her middle, I knew this night was melting away every rotten event from all that spring—frustration at my parents, fury at the town, ostracism, shame, confusion, even my hurt rage at Eila from the Michaelsons' party. As I rooted around wordlessly, trying to prolong the peaceful moment, my nose hit a sharp object—the zipper head on the front of her pants.

"Dear? Tinker?"

"What?"

"When you get away from Endfield, I hope you meet—"

Figuring what the hell, I raised myself on one arm and kissed her on the cheek and lips. *Please don't let her go dead like Pammy.* At first she moved backward startled; then I felt her kiss me back. I touched her throat.

I'd just settled down past her breasts to her lap again when Jody and Ardath returned. If Eila wanted to pretend I'd fallen asleep, she didn't get a chance. "What's doing here? Jesus, Eila, how can we return Tinker to paths of righteousness if you seduce the kid?"

At first I jumped. How real was Jody's anger? Then I began to smile. Regardless of subsequent penalty, I'd *finally* achieved something personal in both words and touch from Eila to mull over in sadder moments.

Eila surprised me by saying nothing.

In a flash I concluded it often doesn't matter what you do; it's what other people make of it that plagues you. I rolled upright onto the soggy hassock. "Jody, I'm not a kid. Remember?"

"That makes it worse. Okay...Miss Muffet. Ardath, she needs a rhyme." Jody began reciting,

"Little Miss Muffet

Sat on her tuffet—"

Ardath continued, "Eating her sesame seeds and whey." (So that's those nuts?) "Along came a spider

And sat down beside her—"

"And turned Miss Muffet astray?" Eila finished with a question.

"I'm not Miss Muffet! Knock it off." By now my whole body blazed back at them. "Like I tried to say to John—I want to experience everything. Then I make up my mind."

"Ah so. Chinese menu theory of experience—choose one from column A and one from column B."

"And wind up with nobody," Ardath concluded, blasting what had seemed to me an ingeniously good idea—to like *both* men and women so nobody gets jealous.

"Jody, don't," Eila asked, shaking her head.

"Tinker, all right, I'm sorry. Are you okay?" Jody seemed truly contrite as if my feelings mattered as much as Eila's.

"Uh, you can come in now," Ardath announced. "Myron wants to know what you have that's cheap and orange? Tiger lilies or maybe geraniums?"

"Tiger lilies grow wild. We don't deal in them. Does he know they die right after cutting? And geraniums aren't orange, but we have red and pink ones." Eila returned to business.

"Oh, shine an orange light on the pink ones, Ardath. Or how about white mums? They'd take any color light."

"Come look at the stage," Ardath suggested.

"All right, but only for a minute," Eila said. "We should get Tinker home."

While they negotiated and inspected with Myron, I knelt in the candlelight, finished Eila's and Jody's Scotch, which tasted dreadful, and mooned over my Collins minus the Tom....

"Who *is* Ardath?" I asked as we stumbled through the night down the front lawn levels.

"Katrina Williams' roommate," Jody answered.

"Why wasn't she at the teach-in?"

"She's Myron's stage manager for this play. He's a perfectionist."

"Jody?"

"Yes?"

"Don't ever call me Miss Muffet or kid again in front of people. Promise?"

"I do promise. From what I saw, you're all grown up."

"You're not mad at me?"

"For seducing Eila? Yuh, I'll sue you tomorrow. Replaced by a twelve-year-old. How'll I ever live it down?"

"I'm thirteen in two weeks," I announced.

"Really? Eila, if she's like this at puberty, what can we expect at twenty-one?"

"I'm afraid to guess and, besides, it's all your fault. Let's go home. I'm exhausted."

As we piled cozily into the front seat, I reminded Eila of her deadline that afternoon. "What were you waiting for?" I asked.

"I found another offer to sell the business."

"Who to? You mean, you may leave here?"

"We have to decide. Soon. Jody! You almost hit the Honesty tree. Why don't you let me drive at night?"

"Sorry... Well, why not bash it? We could sell them another one."

"Not if we kill the one they do have. What kind of business ethics is that?"

On the road back, we honked at Katrina's station wagon just coming out.

"Hey," Jody said. "We missed the party."

"No, we didn't," I concluded.

31

That night I slept no more than two hours, at first from sheer excitement, then helplessly—unexpectedly—from rage. I'd never felt more alive, every sense and nerve vibrating at how, having dared to seize some small initiative, I'd won some loving attention from Eila, despite her problems. It flooded me as the very item I couldn't remember achieving in years from my mother because there seemed no way in that situation for my emotional needs to matter. I thrilled to imagine more such scenes for the future of what I'd do if Eila did...

'Long about three a.m. when dawn's first birds were beginning to vie with First Con bell tower in noting the hours of this nearly longest day of the year, I suddenly went cold under my thermal blanket. A couple other facts hit squarely in that limbo between hopes and dreams.

The first fact was Jody. How I *hated* myself now for going to New York and fetching her back to make Eila human and happy again. If she weren't living with Eila, I might move in and refuse to leave, I might— On the other hand, if Jody left again or permanently how could or would Eila remain in Endfield at all? I tore my bed sheets trying to solve that dilemma. Suppose the nursery went bankrupt and Endfield won, forcing them both out? I'd shatter trying to stay alive with nobody left to care about.

Maybe I could get trained or educated enough to replace Jody to Eila? *Who the hell wants you around? If they had, you wouldn't be in this fix now, trying to matter with two women, neither needing you because they have each other.*

Where could I go? Whom could I tell? Who would believe it—all my desires to help run amok and awry? Already through watching my mother, I'd discovered that precisely the moment when you most need consolation, a healing hand or word, is when people withdraw fastest: You've verged into becoming A Problem—their problem. Even my mother liked me better in the last months of that spring since I stopped being a pest (that is, a needful human being) and settled into some subnormal region where she could ignore me in honor of the coming baby.

Eila's caressing hands, however, had recreated every hunger for further human parts, savored at peace, that I must have yearned for since I was born.

Nedda's voice drilled through me: *There's no pity like self-pity. You know, Jane, only children are a bit odd. Howie had problems, too. It's just a stage. Don't pay any attention to her.* Goddamn that woman, always better-guessing everybody, and goddamn this family that screwed me before I could walk or see straight. All my attempted nonchalance, nurtured so carefully that spring as a way to ignore my family situation, dropped away with each toss and twist among my bedding.

While the birds chirruped in another summer day, I fell asleep uncovered at the foot of my bed, my head on the windowsill. I'd not been asleep two minutes when I met a witch of the grey green variety who was attempting to stuff me down a dismal cavern, a manhole in the woods, while she shrieked, *There's no pity like self-pity* at me.

At 7:30 a.m. I awoke, sweaty, exhausted, my neck and spine cricked. Yearning for a day home from school with no one to face or answer stupid review questions about Civil War highlights or African capitals. However, if I stayed home, what to tell my mother and father?

"Well, I had this marvelous evening with Eila." "You're not supposed to see Eila!"

"I've fallen in love with Eila again." "You're not supposed to do that either."

"I've got a stomach ache." "It's just nervousness about exams. Now go to school."

"I don't have any friends." "Why don't you call Pammy anymore? Oh well, you'll soon be at camp anyway." *Camp Anyway.*

Somehow I threw some clothes on, washed a few areas, stumbled downstairs to breakfast. Maybe if I snap a leg crashing down the last landing?

At the table my father noticed. "Tinker, are you all right? Your face looks blotchy." My mother got a hand onto my forehead. Although I appreciated her attention to the juvenile physical, it had become the adult emotional that tortured me.

"No. I don't feel good. I didn't sleep right. Can I stay home today?"

My father interrupted, "But we'll have to reschedule the camp interview."

"Huh? Is it today?"

"Supposed to be. Anyway, I'm glad you didn't like that camp last week. I thought that guy was just making money off a bunch of run-down shacks. Even the float in the water looked—"

"Oh, I don't care!" I burst out at them.

"What d'you mean you don't care? Seven hundred dollars for the summer and you don't care? What the hell's got into you?"

"Lemme go to school." Then I raged out the door, having chosen the lesser of two miseries, torn between wanting to tell them the tangle of emotions regarding Eila/Jody/Nedda clawing me vs. hating myself for having gone downstairs at all that morning before I'd got my face structured. I shouldn't have rubbed it so hard with the towel. Pimples had just begun to sprout around my mouth. I imagined them swelling until they burst into my plastic teeth braces—an orgy of adolescent leprosy.

The idea of my face as leprosy plant was so grotesque it verged me away from self-pity into black humor. Such humor was a mental weapon I often used against Nedda's engraved phrases. Whenever she ordered, for example, "Sit up straight," I'd add internally, "And die right." Never solved anything but made me feel better.

By the time I'd climbed the last street to the former horse pasture from which Endfield Regional thrusts itself, I could focus on the outside world again.

32

I passed that school day in further frazzled fantasy of what would happen if— If Jody left, if Eila and Jody both left, if my parents died, if I never had to see nor live in Endfield again. Mr. Wilson had to call my name twice during his review about Congress and the President before I even focused on what he was saying.

When I finally dragged myself home, ready to sleep about twenty years, I found my mother lying down—not unusual—except that she reported having cramps since noon and maybe she should get to the hospital?

"Ma, uh, I want. . . . Well, maybe we could talk sometime?" I'd nearly decided to tell her about last night.

"Yes, Tinker, what is it? How're you feeling? . . . Oh look, will you call your father? Ask him to come home? I asked him not to leave this morning but he went anyway. And while you're downstairs, will you peel the onions and potatoes I put on the sink? I'll come if I can. We're having liver tonight. Take off your school clothes first. That's a good girl."

"Ma, I—okay." *Never mind,* I mumbled at her doorjamb. In my room I flung open my closet, dumped my dress over a chair, and found my old bandana skirt. When I phoned my father's department, the secretary said he was out. I left a message that probably sounded frantic about how somebody should find him soonest because my mother was getting ready.

At the kitchen sink I peeled the potatoes, chopped the onions onto a board, nicking only one finger in the process. The routine work soothed me. In my long skirt, now that I no longer needed any stool to reach cupboards or counter, I imagined I was already adult, peeling my own potatoes in my own—

At 4:30, just as I finished setting the table and dumping the peelings mess, my father arrived through the front door. I heard him upstairs phone first the doctor, then the hospital. Next he organized my mother plus her green plastic suitcase and handbags into the car. I saw them all to the outside, receiving some rushed hugs and my father's promise to get back "soon." My mother's forehead wrinkled and un-wrinkled in fits of concentration upon her contraction cramps.

As they drove away, I began to cry into the formica dish cabinet this time—for nothing in particular or for everything dissolved or ruined that spring. I felt desolate as one of Lonetown Road's abandoned houses. *There's no pity like self.* To quench it, I wadded a kleenex first into one eye, then the other, and set about frying the onions and pota-toes, imagining I'd eat them. I tried to kid myself that too many onions had provoked my crying fit. I failed, realizing I'd never been the eye-delicate type whom onions affect.

Since I'd set the electric stove dial on High, forgetting to lower it in time, the margarine scorched, followed by the whole steel pan of vege-tables. By this time the smell had sickened me. I turned off the stove, dropped the whole charcoaled confusion into the sink, and fled upstairs...

"Jody? Hi. Can I come over? Uh, I have an envelope for Eila."

"We're having a big talk here. How 'bout leaving it in the mailbox? We'll get it."

"Jody!"

"Oh, yuh, last spring....It's Tinker," Jody announced away from the mouthpiece. "Eila thought your call was somebody else."

"Jody, my mother just left for the hospital."

"You're not scared, are you? Is she doing okay?"

I bit my forefinger at this maddening conversation. "Jody, can I come over? Maybe watch television or something?"

"All right. But Eila's still not doing well. I warn you."

At the last minute I replaced Jim's envelope under my shoebox. I'd promised him to wait at least a week before delivery. If Eila was upset, no sense flustering her further with news from somebody who'd skipped town.

I washed my face, slobbered some cream across it, combed my hair, and walked to the nursery where I turned up a tv jungle program in the living room to drown out Jody and Eila in the kitchen. They haggled over figures on a six-column sheet. I hadn't believed they'd sell the nursery but Eila seemed red-eyed and determined.

Around seven p.m. when I couldn't stand the suspense any longer, I poured milk from the refrigerator and heated cocoa for the three of us, tending it carefully in Eila's battered aluminum pot to redeem my-self from the onion and potato disaster. When they continued talking, ignoring me, I finally blurted, "Are you really leaving?"

Eila erupted into tears and fled to the living room. Jody yelled. "Tinker!" And of all my interminable days in Endfield, I judged that evening the living worst—no good to myself or anybody, it seemed.

Jody and I sat, brooding into the cocoa.

33

My brother, Ian, did not get officially born until the far hours of the next night, Saturday. My mother did not return from the hospital for ten days. The problem, according to Nedda, who moved in with us to seize control during the week before Howie arrived home, was that our family physician, Dr. Bellfield, "acts like a small town quack. He ought to be delivering kittens, not babies. How could he let Jane suffer all those hours without doing a Caesarean?"

When my father mumbled through a mouthful of toast that no one expected a second birth to be a complicated breech event, Nedda merely harrumphed and stared out the window. Once beyond Easter's miserable postcard crisis, she and I had existed on good terms mostly through my mother's reports of my improved behavior. I intended to keep it that way, neither confiding in her nor allowing her to pry tidbits from me about the nursery, my teachers, or my father's flaws.

Because my mother slept most days following the ordeal, I did not actually see her until the following Wednesday evening visiting hours. The receptionist nurse emphasized she'd except me from the "No-children-under-14-admitted-to-maternity-ward-and-only-to-maternity-lounge-on-Sunday" policy if we promised to stay just ten minutes. We promised and received two pink adult passes. It seemed futile to protest my thirteenth birthday soon approaching. To such bureaucrats you remain too young, old, _____x_____ to meet any requirement they have already devised for the purpose of discriminating. If you protest, it merely confirms their view of _____x_____ as both disturbed and disturbing. As part of a group nobody wants, do you have to prove supercompetent to get anywhere at all—as Jody claims?

From Nedda's descriptions, I'd feared what my mother would resemble. When I reached room 217, however, I found her propped in bed, quite the same person, although with black-circled eyes and droopy strands of hair about her neck where her bouffant had collapsed. I kissed her. She smiled and asked a couple questions.

Then my father and I walked to the nursery where an attendant lifted some bunched bedding that contained my brother. With a shock of black hair, yellowish skin, eyes scrunched against the light, Ian wasn't much to glow over. When my father's eyes lit and his fingers tapped the zoo glass, I put in a few seconds' enraged jealousy, wondering whether he'd been that thrilled over me. He answered, "Your birth was different. Your mother was in better shape. You don't understand —your brother almost didn't live."

"What about Ma? Is that doctor as bad as Nedda says?"

"Well, he let nature take its course for too long. That's for sure."

Knowing nearly nothing of the mechanics of birth in people, as distinct from Pammy's kittens, I tried only one more question before dropping the subject. "But why doesn't nature fix it easier?"

"I don't know, Tinker. I guess Dr. Bellfield thought your mother should do it by herself since this was her second time around."

"Oh." The whole topic of Natural-Unnatural had been a mental morass to me since my Easter campus library trip. I couldn't assemble it even for a further question.

As I followed my father from the hospital, I decided since any version of sex seemed such a pain in the neck, besides other places, I'd do well not to marry anybody of any gender at all. Then remembering Eila's hands on me, I got sweaty and newly reconfused.

34

On Friday, June 20th, school ended at noon. Although my home-room teacher had capped her remarks in True-blue Pill style with a peptalk selling us on being "big eighth graders in September"—as if the summer was over five minutes before it ever began—I dropped her from my mind like wrinkled lunch bags and saran wraps from my locker. I told Pammy of my summer plans for Camp Wohe-lo, said goodbye to Ginny and Sandy on my way home. As usual to reach them, I had to sneak through their entourage of older boys at the bus stop.

Although I was relieved, as usual, with another year of makework school assignments ended, I found myself depressed, worrying how I'd do in a camp full of strangers. My trip to New York seemed the escapade of some other personality—the one who'd been sure she disliked her mother while she loved both Eila and Jody and ran driven with the absolute goal of reuniting them. I'd succeeded but now realized I'd failed at the larger job—restoring the happy four years when they lived hidden and I lived loving each differently, wanting both as delightful friends, exciting older sisters, mainsprings of my life who always rendered me welcome and valuable.

Now I hated retreating to camp with pieces of my puzzle spread across Endfield—Eila and Jody at odds, the town gossiping anew after the teach-in, my mother fretting already at coping with baby duties once she got home.

Although I liked Ian and enjoyed wiggling and rocking him for the few minutes the nurse allowed me, I couldn't imagine spending whole days doing nothing but cajoling him out of crying and choking fits. While I sympathized with my mother, I resisted her insistence that I stay the minimum camp session, save that money, and come take over Ian. Despite honest attempts at patience I found myself re-mired in exactly the problem that had opened that spring—my interests and hers always competed, never matched. Well, I'd "see when the time comes,'' as Endfielders put it. Maybe a miracle would render Ian a placid baby, my father an attentive husband, my mother a contented woman, newly independent of Nedda.

That noon of school dismissal my mother remained at the hospital. I'd brought Jim's envelope in my duffle bag between a used notebook and the comments half of my report card. My father had already signed the marks half. The verdict read:

Tinker is unusually bright for her age and shows progress in several subjects, especially geography and English. However, daydreaming prevents her from doing better work. Her attention is definitely elsewhere than in the classroom.

I recommend a talk with the guidance counselor in September.

So much for Mrs. LeBlanc, my math and homeroom teacher! If they expect people to pay attention, why can't they make classrooms more like life, with true problems and challenges, not toy tasks printed in a workbook? . . .

I found Jody, high-spirited, in the greenhouse watering carnations. ''Did you hear the good news?''

''You mean, my brother got born? Nedda just left? Oh, I don't know. I just got a lousy report card.''

To all this, Jody registered a quartet of emotions that delighted me. ''No-o. No. Or, yes! Congratulations, Tinker, on your brother. We need a toast to you. . . . Now what's that about the report card?'' She dropped the hose nozzle and put an arm around my shoulders. When I didn't answer, she continued, ''No. *Our* good news. It's coming up tonight.''

''What?''

''What d'you mean, what? The Board of Selectmen vote. Arnold Ferguson got an antidiscrimination amendment onto the agenda. Just like we hoped. John and I are attending to make sure they vote it tonight before everybody gabs so much they won't dare pass it.''

''What happens if they don't pass it?''

''Tinker! Whose side are you on?''

''I don't know. Everything's so messed up.''

''You sound really far down. Here, help me roll up the hose. I've been on the phone with a lawyer. What the town has done these three months amounts to a killing boycott of our business. Whether the town passes or doesn't pass the amendment tonight, we can sue the whole place for restraint of trade if we want.''

''Will you?''

''I don't know. The teach-in was my zenith, I guess. I get more tempted all the time to listen to Eila, cut our losses, and get out. I just work Eila around to selling; she changes her mind and stages another fit.''

''Take me with you?'' I asked this desperately—and blushed at how silly-hopeless it sounded.

''Tinker, I'd like to. You know that, but you don't want kidnapping added to my sins, do you?''

''Who is it?'' Eila called from the kitchen.

''I've got an envelope for you,'' I yelled back.

''Hi. How's the new baby? I heard your mother had a rough time.''

I didn't answer but held out Jim's large envelope toward Eila. I found my throat choking because that moment overwhelmed me: how much Eila resembled my mother—eyes dark-circled, coping with monsters beyond her control. She was wearing her spring halter outfit, the one from our day on the quilt when I'd imagined bliss if I just got Eila and Jody reunited.

As Eila slit the envelope, I tried a sally nobody found funny. ''Bet it's an offer to buy the nursery for a million dollars.''

Then Eila exploded, scaring me. ''Look at this! He runs out of here. Me in a mess, and he imagines I'm going all the way to Colorado. Goddamn him! Read it,'' she ordered Jody and me. When she flung a letter and engraved card onto the counter, the envelope fluttered to the soily floor.

For a moment the italic script defeated me, but I deciphered:

**YOU ARE CORDIALLY INVITED TO A RECEPTION AND
PARTY INAUGURATING THE OPENING OF
DONOHUGH CONSULTANTS, INC.**
**AT OUR NEW OFFICES, 115 ALTAMIRA ST., DENVER, COLORADO,
6 TO 10 P.M., THURSDAY, SEPTEMBER 22, 1976.**
R.S.V.P.   **JAMES A. DONOHUGH**
                                                ROY P. DONOHUGH

Dear Eila,

Here's a sample of our official invitation for when Roy and I really get started. Snazzy, huh? Will you come? It's *before* Christmas or whatever other rush you decide to have.

It's your choice.

Jim

By this time Eila had fled to the front of the house.

''I guess he still likes her,'' I said to Jody and a tray of planter pots.

"Jesus, Tinker, I was on such a high before you brought this."

"I'm sorry." My voice whined. "I mean, I promised him I'd deliver it this week. What could I do?"

"It's not your fault. In a way, it's good. Takes him out of the picture. Maybe I can even convince her it was Roy he came home for, not her."

"Why would that help anything?"

"Tinker, you do have a knack for hitting our worst moments around here. I think you're bad luck."

"Don't say that," I begged, stung and miserable.

"Okay. I apologize. Whatever happens, before we go bankrupt or hang ourselves, I reckon you have done one big thing. To or for us—I don't know. You made us stand up to this town and declare we exist. We never would have done it."

"Will you take me to the Selectmen meeting tonight?"

"Uh. . . . I think it's better you don't go. According to John, there's a reporter with a camera at the ready when everybody starts screaming in the Town Hall. Look, I'll call you tomorrow and tell you what happens. How's that?"

"All right." I sounded unhappy but realized immediately it would perk up a dull morning spent alone at home while my father collected Ian and my mother from the hospital. "You promise."

"I promise," Jody answered.

35

"We won, Tinker. We won!" At 10:05 the next morning just as my parents were due home, Jody's excitement crackled over the phone. "I had to drag Eila with me again. The meeting took an extra hour and messed up their agenda. John came armed wtih some wording they could use, and Arnold Ferguson spoke about how it's bad for Endfield to allow a 35-year-old business like our nursery to be boycotted out of existence.

"John was gorgeous. He even had copies of letters from the Minneapolis City Council and the mayor of Alfred, New York. Both those places did it and survived."

"Did what?"

"Tinker, aren't you listening?"

"Of course, I'm listening. But my parents are arriving with Ian in a couple minutes. And I'm worried about this summer camp I'm supposed to go to."

"Oh. . . . Well, we have a new clause in the town bylaws. An amendment really. Endfield's wording is so outdated they hadn't even prohibited racial discrimination in the Sixties. They hadn't discovered the Civil Rights Act yet except for a fight about whether the 1972 Equal Opportunity Act should apply to women town employees. They haggled the whole thing around for an hour."

"But you said they passed something."

"You bet. After everybody spoke, they wound up with two clauses somewhere between equal rights under the law and no discrimination in housing, employment, or education on the basis of race, religion, or sexual preference. John was real strong on the education part. Eila and I said some stuff on how our business has got strangled. Two Selectmen claimed they hadn't heard, so we refreshed their memory."

"How many people came?"

"About a hundred. Mostly because some hunk of the school budget still needed voting, and a lot came to oppose additional expenditure.''

"Well, they could begin by dumping some of those lousy teachers like Mr. Wilson.''

"Tinker, you want poor Mr. Wilson to starve? Anyway, after Arnold Ferguson proposed the amendment as part of the Civil Rights Act, people haggled some more. Eila and I repeated that without the security those few clauses would give us, we couldn't see going on in this town at all. Eila hates me to look pained or persecuted in public but I did—to make it sink in.

"Finally the three Selectmen voted the amendment, and about fifty people ratified it. Not a landslide but, anyway, it's done.''

"But people will find out.''

"Of course. But they're gonna look silly unvoting an amendment to a piece of national legislation they tried to ignore years ago. It'd make them look like the asses they are.''

I laughed. My morning began to shine a bit. Just as I was going to ask, "How's Eila?'', I heard my parents' station wagon crunch along our driveway. I'd failed to straighten the living room, wash the dishes, make my bed—all tasks to be accomplished before the double home coming. I began to squirm.

". . . .So we'll send you an invitation. Now that the thing's official, Eila's looking forward to it.''

"What?''

"I knew you weren't listening.''

"My parents just drove in, and I haven't done a bunch of stuff.''

"To our summer open house and sale. We're reopening publicly.''

"That's exciting. . . .Jody? If I can get out tomorrow night, can I come talk to you? Maybe after supper?''

"Sure. You don't have to make an appointment with *me*. Is something wrong? The baby or Nedda?''

"No. Yes. Well, the other night I got real mad at you because everything went so screwed up after you came back. I really hated you. But you know what I found out?'' *Say it. Before anything else happens.* I felt myself blushing and stammering. "Jody, I love you.'' Out rushed the words.

Silence. More silence. "Tinker, that's beautiful, considering we haven't treated you all the best. Look, come tomorrow night. We'll do a little party.''

My heart happily thrummed around my insides.

Then: "Tin-ker! Where are you? Come on out.'' Next I heard the baby squealing. Nedda was right; Ian certainly lacked an adaptable or chuckly sort of personality.

"Jody, I'll come at seven. It'll be fun. I have to go now. Bye." I hung up abruptly, eager for the party, angry that I felt so guilty at needing to talk with somebody. When I tried to rise off the kitchen phone bench, I nearly ripped the bottom cord from the wall. Without knowing, I'd wound it all around my sneaker and ankle. Like white plastic ivy, it clung, wearing floral balls of dust.

I blew them at the wall and ran outside.

36

To the Editor:

We don't understand how it happened. The Board of Select-men's ruling that favored those far out people at a Town Meeting called about the school budget is the last straw.

Why are those people making Endfield the homosexual capital of New England—and hiding it under the school budget? What has become of democracy when these things happen because some weird minority passes something without the other 99% of us present?

Wait until election day in November when we all get to say yea or nay to it.

The ERA is already controversial enough, provokes arguments between people who used to live and let live. Why do we need more? Especially if nobody gets consulted about what we do need like lower taxes, better schools, return to moral codes.

Sincerely,
Emmett T. Hollander

Ferncliff College
Department of Government
June 28, 1976

To the Editor:

We, the undersigned faculty in the Departments of Govern-ment, Philosophy and Religion, Theater Arts, Literature, and Psychology, protest the letter by Mr. Emmett Hollander published recently in the *Endfield News*. We do not agree with his position, the repressive ideology behind it, nor with his melodramatic sus-picion that Endfield after this amendment will function as gay dating center of the Northeast.

We believe such claims can be based only on fear, and we ap-plaud First Selectman Cuttner and the Board of Selectmen, aided by John Simons and Jody Foxx, for taking this dramatic extension in human rights at this time.

The first Friday evening of the coming summer session at 8 p.m. in the Union Building the faculty council of Ferncliff College will hold an open meeting. Members and audience will discuss how to insure that full civil rights for homosexuals becomes an official part of College policies for hiring, promotion, and job classification. We invite all interested persons to attend.

The rights of one group, no matter what its number, affect the rights of all.

Best wishes,

This letter was followed by ten signatures, which seemed to me a remarkable number. My father's, or anybody's from the history department, did not appear.

Around July 1 Nedda brought a petition to our house. While she and my mother commiserated upstairs over Ian's already irregular and sloppy habits (he ate when he should sleep and vice versa, I gathered), I sneaked a look at the petition. The wording was modest, un-Nedda-like: "We, the undersigned, disagree with the amendment to the Town Bylaws passed at the Board of Selectmen's June meeting. We request a future general Town Meeting to consider its speedy repeal."

When my mother arrived in the kitchen alone and began to read the paper, I decided to attack. "Ma, it's mean to sign that. Are you going to?"

"Well, Nedda's all purple and green about it. I guess I better. Actually she thinks they should have published the amendment in the paper first. Then people wouldn't feel it was sneaked by them."

"Why don't you do what *you* want? You still listen to her too much."

"Tinker, don't be fresh. You and I talked about that already. Nedda's been a big help to me." She must be referring to our spring conversation where I tried to make her see how similar my interest in Jody and Eila was to hers in Nedda. Did I even believe that anymore?

I was lousing it up. "Look, Ma, if you don't sign it, I promise I'll babysit for you every afternoon till camp begins." This was dumb of me—trying to barter what I was supposed to do anyway. But I was desperate. Actually it took less courage than demanding $1.00 per hour for looking after Ian, which they'd reject on the theory that I must love my brother so much I'd be happy to do it for nothing—exactly what I was getting. She'd forgotten her promise to increase my pocket money if I quit the nursery.

How could I get both my parents to stare Nedda in the eye and refuse to sign her irate petition?

Unfortunately Nedda entered the kitchen, ending negotiation between my mother and me.

"Jane, I think Ian looks fine considering what a time you and he had. His skin color is improving, though if he doesn't schedule himself better after a few days, you're in for a year of it." Nedda, my dear aunt, the optimist's optimist. "Ah, look what time it is. I have to drive Howie to the shopping center. I swear his feet will never stop growing. . . . Oh, did you sign this?"

"Let me think about it, Nedda. I want to discuss it with Ben. He knows more about it than I do." Was she lying? Or truly doing something because I'd dared to ask?

"Well, pass it on to Heidi Spencer after you and Ben sign. All right?" I almost expected her to add, There's a good girl, as if my mother were still the child. And what nerve—automatically assuming my parents would sign. Nedda tidied her bangs over her forehead and left. Lately she'd adopted a Miss Stanner sausage curl style. *It must be spreading.* I felt depressed.

"Ma, why does she wear her hair that funny way? And then she complains about *my* hair."

"What funny way? Oh, she's letting her perm grow out for the summer, I guess. She doesn't complain about your hair. She just wants you to brush it."

"You won't sign her petition, will you?"

"Tinker, why're you still so interested in this? You know those women were always too old for you. They have. . .different ideas."

Internally I muttered away. That morning I realized something else had changed about me—if growing up meant perpetually calculating, never antagonizing people because you might need them later, you could say I'd begun to mature. Hating myself for it, I desired the time just three? six? months before when I yelled or thought, "Oh crap!" to whatever she or anybody said that I didn't like. Then I'd sulked until my father arrived to apply another installment of Don't-hurt-your-mother. So problems festered unsolved, and I wound up the town brat to Nedda. Now I found myself re-reduced to rage at how little I said, could apparently say, that wouldn't shock or horrify her.

"Oh, crap!"

"Tinker! C'mon outside and help me fold the laundry."

37

HOLIDAY OPEN HOUSE
BRANDI FLORIST / NURSERY, LAUREL ST.
JULY 5, NOON–7 P.M.
END OF SPRING SALE. NEW SHIPMENT
ORNAMENTAL SHRUBS AND TREES. BRING A
PICNIC LUNCH. ENJOY OUR MOUNTAIN VIEWS.
+   +   +

ENDFIELD BOMBING

July 3—Police Chief Steven Munce admitted today he has "no leads" in the bombing that took place yesterday at Brandi Florist/Nursery on Laurel St. The mailbox and tree limbs overhanging it were destroyed when a bomb of "the Molotov cocktail type," according to Chief Munce, exploded shortly after dawn, alarming the whole street.

Despite a police cordon and questioning of neighbors, no one has been apprehended. The *Endfield News* was unable to reach Miss Brandi for comment, except that plans for the Brandi Nursery open house on July 5 will continue as scheduled.

"It's vandalism, criminal mischief. There's no conspiracy involved here," Chief Munce assured this reporter. "But we are continuing investigation."

Parts of the aluminum mailbox, covered with sunflower decals, and the white post on which it was mounted were thrown as far as 50 feet by the blast. Anyone with information is asked to contact Chief Munce at Town Hall.

38

Despite my immediately renewed intentions not to anger my mother, by 10 a.m. of a baking July 5th with steam trim, she and I had already fought about my attending the nursery open house.

She'd half planned what she called "a real family outing" to Greenwater Pond although for some reason she'd neglected to secure my father's agreement first. He disliked holiday driving. Maybe she considered me easier to convince, since I generally enjoyed escapes in any form. However, as soon as I realized a couple basics—first, it was too late to invite Pammy, who'd developed an uppity way of refusing, on principle, any short notice invitations, and two, my mother planned only cold drinks and tuna sandwiches, nothing grilled—I lost interest. "But I'd like to do something else with all of us," I sympathized.

Whereupon she blew first up and then down, sobbing nobody ever did what *she* wanted.

Guilty sorrow trickled through me. If only I'd flooded away with it. . . . "Nobody ever does what I want either. I hate you. I hate this whole house!" I found myself screaming back as much at my own glut of rage as at her. When I could see again, I realized I'd just nullified weeks of good behavior and days of Ian sitting. I slumped onto a kitchen chair next to her, confused and pitying both of us.

My father rushed in yelling, "Tinker! You stop that." Just as my mother ran sobbing upstairs toward Ian, the phone rang. Torn between ignoring and hoping it could solve this miserable day, I lifted it on a thumb and finger. An especially cheery form of Nedda's voice asked to speak with my mother—if she wasn't busy.

"Uh, they're upstairs. Taking care of Ian." I stumbled through an answer.

"Tinker, is everything all right?"

"Oh yeah, sure," I lied.

"You sound strange." *Try strangled.* "But you're going to the lake, how nice," she burbled.

"Oh yes, well, thank you for calling. Goodbye." I hung up, knowing I'd hear about "such rudeness" later. At the moment, however, turning somebody off—if only electronically—lifted me a couple inches off the gully bottom the whole day had become.

I checked the kitchen back window. Already the insurance company's thermometer ("You're *safe* with Allstate") read 93 °. I longed for Eila's air-conditioned office.

Again the phone insisted. Again I forced myself to grasp it, begging some miracle to erase the whole day.

"Tinker, I'll forgive you for hanging up so fast. I know everything's upset there. Poor Jane, she tries so hard to cope. . . . Actually I had an idea I expect you'll like." Me like one of Nedda's ideas? "I'm stopping by the nursery to look over their flowering shrubs. Would you like to come?"

Split three ways into rivulets of fear, suspicion, and curiosity, I panicked. "I don't know. I mean, my mother says I can't go there anymore." I bit my lower lip. My free hand twisted a knob of hair behind an ear.

"But you have been going there, haven't you? Several times, in fact." *You witch, you bitch, frustrated old cow.* My mind threw insults while my throat choked. "Never mind," she cajoled suddenly. "Let it be our little secret, shall we? If you come with me, I'll take you out for a snack. A milkshake or something."

Did she know of my meeting with Jim Donohugh, too? Was there anything she missed?

"I do want to have a friendly chat with you. Those five days at your house we never got around to it. Did we, dear?"

"No. Uh, I'm very busy today. Helping my mother." Again I lied, hating her for forcing me into it.

"Well, *all* right," she grumped at me, having guessed I was lying. "Have your mother call me." She finished gruffly and hung up.

Crap. Double and triple crap. A subterranean day now plummeted to absolute depths of summer hell by threat of Nedda's company. How could I escape? Hide at the nursery? Run to the woods? Act a case of scarlet fever?

I poured a glass of grape juice and stared out the window. The hydrangeas between my parents' property and Mrs. Curtis's drooped already. I know just how they felt. Now my mother's voice drilled my imagination: *Go with her. She's so good to you. Being a parent isn't easy today. . . .*

"Ma, I'm sorry I blew up. I'm sorry you got all upset." I remained mad at her but couldn't figure out how to avoid a day of Nedda without enlisting her aid. *Tinker the Selfish Brat.*

"Well, Tinker, you have got all moody again. Just like last winter. But Ian's upset everybody, I guess. I'm trying to breast-feed, but I'm so exhausted."

Relieved at this honest statement, I answered pleasantly, "Nedda wants you to call her."

"Okay. What was the second call?"

Ugh. I had no explanation ready. "Oh, she called twice. She wants to know if I can visit the nursery with her this afternoon." I said this brightly, assuming my mother would not only veto it but fume at Nedda for suggesting a visit to that "den of sin."

"Why, that's a fine idea—going with Nedda." *What?!* "Your father has agreed to take Ian and me for a drive, which I know doesn't interest you. So it's nice for you and her to visit. I mean, she was so good while I was at the hospital—all those salads she made. You hardly ever talk to her. You could see your cousin, Howie, too. Wouldn't that be nice?"

"What'll I talk about?" I bit hard on my grape juice glass until I could taste the decals. "You know how she pries stuff out of me about you and Daddy."

"Oh, you're exaggerating. Nedda means well. I'll tell her you'll be ready after lunch. We'll eat early."

I drummed my forehead. To my room I slunk. Why did my mother approve this meeting? Did she imagine my nursery appearance with Nedda would warn "hands off" to Eila and Jody? That Proper Moral Surveillance had finally entered my life? Maybe I could collapse with some handy disease like bubonic plague or smallpox between 10 and 1. Maybe I could tumble out the window and fly to the moon. Maybe . . . .

Down the hall Ian cried again. I knew what he was suffering—the Fifth of July heat rash blues.

At 12:55 p.m. Nedda appeared, straw hatted, orange sashed, minidressed, with an extra layer of apricot makeup and lipstick against the temperature. I dreaded an outing with her, not to mention introducing her to Eila and Jody after she'd sneered and contrived against them. Determined to look cheerful to avoid questions, however, I even managed a compliment. "I like your hat."

My mother arrived downstairs into the front hall. "Well, don't you look nice and summery! Tinker's all ready. Here she is."

I trudged from behind the hall coat rack. Minus coats for the summer, it was useless as a hiding place, anyway.

Nedda had parked a couple wheels on our lawn, which wasn't going to thrill my father. It's *her* fault for making me go. If I get him tonight, maybe I can mangle her character and the lawn simultaneously. *Tinker the Stool Pigeon.* This town really does a job on your head. . . . "Where's Howie today?" I asked as we walked ourselves through the heat waves into her front seat. Shock of roasting red vinyl hit my haltered bare back. *Must be what hell's like.*

"Oh, Howie's visiting a school friend of his. The boy's parents have a club membership. They invited Howie for swimming. *Very* nice people."

I said nothing, brooding on why Nedda wanted this trip. Since our dislike must be mutual (right? why *should* she like me?), she must have. . . . A welcome, then eerie, chilled prickling ran along my spine. She must be. . . planning something. What? How could I stop her?

As we entered the nursery driveway, I noticed somebody had piled mailbox and limb shatters around the jagged white pole, then topped the rubble with potted geraniums. The whole looked most brave. While the neighbors on Laurel feared the bombing because it might spread to them, the clandestine viciousness of it had earned Eila and Jody sympathy points among a few people like Mrs. Curtis and Heidi Spencer.

"How long are we staying?" I asked Nedda.

"Why, just a little while. Tinker, before we get out and meet people, I want to have a little talk with you." Right I'd been—dammit! What could I do now? Her agenda careened onward. "Your poor mother isn't up to it. I realize, Tinker, you've tried hard this spring, but there's a couple points you're missing. It concerns Eila and Jody. I know you're continuing to see them regularly."

"Well, what about them?" My attempted nonchalance just sounded edgy.

"Don't be fresh. I have your best interests at heart. It isn't easy being a parent today. You wouldn't want your father finding out you're still seeing them, would you?"

"I don't know," I muttered, miserable. How had I already lost the chance to shut her off? What was wrong with me that I constantly attracted people like her to run my life? "My father knows. I told him, and he said I could go to the teach-in."

Somehow this failed to deflate her. "And to South Endfield afterward?'' she asked, cocking an eyebrow at me.

"How'd you find out about that? You bitch! You witch!'' Screaming my favorite fantasy words straight at her, I lost control for the second time that day. Helplessly I jerked the door handle. I'd snapped down the lock button myself; Nedda always insisted on locked buttons.

I slumped back, scalding my neck on the seat.

"Tinker, for a girl your age, your language is atrocious. I'll answer your question, but it's more than you deserve.'' Instead of relieving me, her patience merely increased my guilt and nausea. "Mr. and Mrs. Evering—they live across from the Bridgewaters—have been...unhappy for some time with the quality of people who visit there.'' I imagined old lady Evering, binoculars trained round the clock on Bridgewater's front door, with infrared lenses for twilight.

"Tinker, I want you to tell Eila or Jody or both of them *today* you won't stop here anymore or go anywhere with them. Nor will you phone them. Will you do that? Tinker, your whole future is involved. You don't realize that. You've preferred these women with their outrageous life to any friends your own age. Naturally you're lonely. You ignore your mother. You won't babysit for Ian unless somebody forces you.

"I don't know what's to become of you, Tinker. Unless you change some high-handed ways. Now, will you tell them you're not coming here anymore?...I'll take you out for dinner afterward. Would you like that?'' She put her forearm on my bare left shoulder. "Such a pretty halter you've got on. I wish *I* was young enough to wear all the new styles.''

Then I did something I hadn't done publicly in years: I began to cry, unable to bite my lip to shut it off. Rather than risk her comforting me, however, I found the car button. I yanked it upward and flung open the door. Past the office and round the first greenhouse I sprinted, hoping to fling myself into the waves of side meadow grass until she'd driven away.

Had my parents left yet for their outing? Maybe she'd be too scared to report at all if I never returned. Knowing Nedda, however, I realized she'd make it all my fault: "Tinker and I were having the nicest, friendliest talk when all of a sudden she said the nastiest things and jumped right out the door. Jane, a disturbed girl like that should see a psychiatrist as soon as possible. In your condition, don't try to handle it any—''

Rounding one glass-framed corner, I smacked into John and sent his stack of boxes flying. "What the hell—Tinker!...What's the matter? You're crying.''

"Oh, it's Nedda." Gulping back sobs, I picked myself up. My left knee, however, had contacted shards of green glass and clay pot along the path. Blood coursed along the new hairs down my leg, sluiced itself round my ankle, and finished in my leather sandal.

"You better come inside. Eila and Jody are busy getting ready, but I'll find something to put on it."

Whatever mess this spring had wrought, at least John no longer ignored me. "Do we have to go on the driveway? She's there."

"Who?"

"Nedda."

"We'll go through the greenhouse into the kitchen. Can you walk?"

"No. Lemme just sit here. I can't move my knee." Incessant stinging had replaced the shock of fall.

"But you can't let the blood run like that. I'll help you." One arm round my middle, John dragged me along the path, into the greenhouse, through the office and kitchen. At the office window I glimpsed cars besides Nedda's now. I couldn't believe we'd met nobody. They must be picnicking under the apple trees or hiding behind the evergreen rows.

As we passed the sink, I grabbed a paper towel and wadded it into my sandal to absorb the trail of blood before it reached Eila's parlor carpet. My knee was already swelling and stiffening.

Then John carried me to the second floor that I'd seen only once— when I accompanied Eila for Christmas decorations. The landing window still showed its magic glass that turned the landscape blue, rose, or yellow depending on which pane you stared through. In the bathroom John sat me on the toilet, removed my sandal, and stuck my left leg into the tub. The whole thing was a mess of red, black, dirt, and sand. Examining it flipped my stomach.

"You got enough stuff in this to start a garden," he joked. "We're not supposed to be up here. It worries Eila."

"I know," I answered. That seemed to be my July 5th purpose— upsetting people. Recalling Nedda, I shuddered. Cars and voices sounded from the driveway side of the house.

Rifling through the medicine cabinet, John arrived at Band-Aids and bandages but no iodine or mercurochrome. He sighed. "Let's wash it off first." He ran hot water onto a clean cloth and swabbed my leg until only the three-inch gash area remained to treat. "I don't know how to get the dirt out of this. Maybe Eila should look at it. She fixed an infected finger I had once."

"No, no," I wailed. "I'll do it. Don't bother her." I feared rousing

Nedda in addition to Eila. More voices entered the open grillwork of
the heat register on the bathroom floor. Choosing between kinds of
fear, I took the washcloth and stuck it directly into the cut. (A doctor
should have eased out the dirt with cotton swabs. To this day I own a
grit-speckled left kneecap where scar tissue has formed over those bits
of Eila's nursery.)

When I yowled despite attempted bravery, John yanked the cloth
from my hand. "You've started the bleeding again. What're we gonna
do? Here, lie down on the floor, No, don't get up. I'll get a pillow or
something." When he returned with plaid blanket, embroidered
cushion, and *Home and Garden* magazine, I felt already in the doctor's
office. "C'mon, lie down. Now just *stay* here. Wait'll the bleeding
stops. I'll come back and help you."

"You won't tell Eila or Nedda. Promise?"

"Okay, kid." I was so eager to believe him I didn't even mind the
"kid" part. I lay back, stared at cracks on the white ceiling, remembered
Su's apartment, smelled my hard pillow. When I tried to angle it
better under my ear, it lumped on the floor. John had grabbed one of
those New England jobs full of pine quills that crunch instead of
feathers that plump. I examined tiny cross-stitched lettering on the
satin case, green on white:

While I slept, life was beauty.
When I awoke, life was duty.

Reading it, I grew desperate in addition to pained. Cheery bunch,
Eila's mother and ancestors. How did she turn out so friendly and normal, fun to eat and work with? Not the Eila of these last gruesome
weeks but before...when I was eight or eleven. Not normal, Nedda
says. Ah, fuck Nedda. I laughed at the thought.

I rolled an ear near the floor register to glean what was happening
now. Although inner and outer iron gratings restricted my view to a
three-inch peephole, I could hear enough. Nedda was there! In the
kitchen with Jody.

"Why no, Mrs. Howard....haven't seen her. You know she doesn't
work here now? Though if you brought her, I'm sure she'll turn up
when it's time to eat. Jody laughed. "We told everybody to bring
lunch. Eila, have you seen Tinker?"

Muffled answer.

Then Nedda's voice again: "Miss Foxx, I've never approved my
niece working here. I told her mother that years ago. She's a most difficult child, really too much for my sister....But I can see from people
already here today and from your floral displays, you know your

business. I mean, the town would be poorer without your business. So I'll bargain with you. I didn't want this, but I have no choice. If you promise to send Tinker home when she shows up here or calls for any reason, I'll ask Father Henry to begin ordering from you again." Nedda stopped. She must have planned this speech carefully, "Well, do I have your word? I'm sure if Father Henry with the largest congregation begins to order, other churches will follow. Well?"

Jody, no, Jody, don't do it. No, please! Silent screams into the expanse of white enameled bathroom and black dusty grate. How clever of Nedda. No mention of morality, homosexuality—just business on this holiday weekend dedicated to reintroducing the nursery to Endfield citizens as a viable establishment. And what business needs embarrassing scenes staged in its kitchen?

"Mrs. Howard, I assure you we haven't invited Tinker *here* for anything since her mother visited last spring. The one exception was a half-hour the other night when she sounded low because everybody was busy at the hospital. I had some cake and Coke with her. Since we don't entertain much, we don't intend to invite her."

This hurt. I felt both dumped and foolish over my love speech to Jody that Saturday morning.

". . .though if she stops here, say on her way home from school, how can we prevent it? You know, Tinker has a fine interest and knack for business. She was a real help to Eila with the accounts and me delivering orders. I hope her talents do get appreciated whatever she decides on."

"But—" interrupted Nedda.

"Please let me finish. Now about Father Henry and the church orders. Eila and I both spoke with him Friday morning. He's discussing with the pastor, but he expects they'll order if we give him a better price than in the past. Sunday collections always drop off in early summer or something. So we agreed. The first orders would start with the Feast of the Assumption, middle of August."

"You've thought of everything, I see."

"Except one thing. Or one person, I should say."

"What's that?"

"I hear Tinker's going away to summer camp?"

"Yes. And Bennett's negotiating with some excellent private school people to get her into an eighth grade class near my son. She'll have to pass the test, of course."

"Then may I ask something of you?"

No response.

"See the school has some good teachers—women, men, any kind you want. But make sure *she* likes them, not just you and Bennett. See they have something to teach her. Her feelings matter, Mrs.—Nedda? I'll call you Nedda. If you ignore her feelings, naturally she thinks you don't like her and she responds in kind—"

"But she's only a child."

"*Is* she?" This sounded like Eila's, remembering our evening at Bridgewater's.

"But I like the child," Nedda continued. "Jane and I have got much closer since Tinker was born....Actually I believe children shouldn't be sent off to school so soon. Ninth or tenth grade is early enough."

At this news, I began to choke and cough. My knee, however, had stopped oozing. Maybe the old what-you-don't-notice-goes-away proved true, at least for knees.

John returned, washed his hands under the tub faucets, cleaned more grit from my leg, and began to paint it fluorescent red. When it didn't burn, I relaxed. With gauze and tape he bandaged it gently—a total operation crisscrossed around the whole knee and lower thigh. "If I do just the knee, it'll pull off when you walk."

"Where'd you learn that?"

"First aid course. Phil and I took it last year at Town Hall. Comes in handy during demonstrations. If anybody's hurt."

"You mean, like the parade."

"Yuh."

"Nedda's down there. I heard her. They're making peace by deciding not to invite me anywhere. Do you think Nedda's really making peace?" I confessed one part of my dilemma.

"Why should she? If she didn't have you to save, she wouldn't have anything to worry about. Don't fight—it'll only strengthen her."

"Well, *you* don't care. You're not related to her."

"I do care. Remember I got my own Disneyworld of a family back in New Hampshire."

"John, why don't they wanna see me anymore?"

"They do. We do, Tinker. The thing, though, is try later. When you're grown up. Then it's your own choice what you do and who you see. And Nedda's off your back."

As I stood up and tested my knee, I remained desolate. I found a country Western song tripping through my head—the tearjerker with that mournful chorus, "Will you miss me, miss me, miss me? WILL you miss me when I'm gone?"

Seems I'd have to go to find out.

OUTLAND
The Present

39

Well, that spring proved my last in Endfield—through little fault of my own, with all names changed to protect the guilty, etc.

When I performed adequately making friends and "entering the program" (lingo of Camp Wohe-lo), my father proposed a definite re-routing of my future, despite my mother's protesting my "critical age" ("Jane, all the more reason to get her away!") and my value as baby-sitter.

Camp Wohe-lo (acronym for Work-Love-Health) wasn't an unqualified success. My swimming couldn't meet the precision requirements for water ballet routines, but I did well enough at archery, leading the team in number and accuracy of bull's eyes. I decided it must result from four years of shooting tulip, hyacinth, and onion bulbs into Jody's prepared holes—whenever Eila didn't notice enough to yell about kneeling down and doing it right. I remembered Jody's tales about bulbs named Sam and Erna (sometimes Mimi and Jacqueline) that used radar to figure out which direction to grow. I believed them until I was eleven and studied enough about radar in science class to debunk this myth.

I'd assumed my father hadn't noted the different Eila and Jody functions I attended. However, he had merely bided his time and now used my "mixed" report card as battering ram. "Jane, we've got to act. If she's bored and daydreamy now, she'll continue with a bad crowd. Then we'll have twice the problems."

"Well, wait a year on private school till she starts ninth grade. She's so young to be away so long." My mother's defense of me genuinely touched me as I listened from the dark stairs. I fantasized myself pining at school for her and Endfield, homesickly losing weight, teams of attractive female teachers and students gathered at my bedside. The total image made me giggle.

"What's that noise?" my mother asked in the living room. "I better check on Ian.''

"Wait a minute. . . . So I'll get an interview for her with Frank at Briarwood. See if they have a September opening. If they don't, I'll try that Catholic school.''

He did; Frank did; I went. On August 30 I began my Five-Year Plan at Briarwood, nicknamed "Firewood" by generations of us alumnae who slept in the row of clapboard dormitories. One December night the inevitable occurred. Somebody knocked over a Christmas candle in her room, igniting the curtains, not to mention the whole end building. After we evacuated, the fire department unfortunately saved it. After that, cigarettes, matches, and candles were forbidden in all dorms.

Frank, known to us as Mr. Saybrook, the headmaster, is an amiable man able to run the place without losing his temper at students, staff, or secretaries. After our initial interview I liked the little I saw of him— assembly presiding or bicycling among buildings.

My favorite teacher was Mrs. Leahy, who lent three of us her private stock of novels and plays, inviting us to her apartment for weekly readings and literature discussions. However, she never played favorites. I was rarely alone with her as I'd been with Eila. Much as we speculated on what tragic fate had befallen Mr. Leahy to produce his perpetual absence, Mrs. Leahy avoided personal questions by diverting them to plot discussions of the classics. As the first in the class to finish *Moby Dick,* I concluded to my roommate, Linda, one night that Mr. Leahy had got rammed in a sailing accident. Linda settled on divorce as more realistic.

During my second year at Briarwood in this ecumenical age, the school admitted its first boy students, as my father had calculated. I suspect that as the reason, besides the tuition reduction teachers give each other, that I attended Briarwood rather than Thomas Aquinas, which remains an all-female academy to this day. Certainly uniforms of any kind would not have suited me. Although Linda got a boyfriend whom she lent me on nonstrategic occasions, I preferred swimming, skating, and archery to hanging out in the snack shop snaring boys. Sports, with their structured rules, performance, and prize system, always seemed a more tangible accomplishment than the hours of gossip that a captive community like Briarwood (or Endfield) can generate.

However, in my senior year I met Russ, bound for Yale, who became my companion for ranging walks across the hills. We still write and meet whenever he comes to Boston. After Bill O'Connell's introduction to these matters, Russ turns me on physically despite some shyness, born of Briarwood's restrictions, that haunts both of us. When I'm with him, I'm half in love with him. But when he leaves, I don't know what I feel about him. . . .

When the school rented itself out for summer conferences, I began vacation buswork in the cafeteria, Swain Hall—Swine Hall to the initiated. In my graduating class of fifty a couple years ago, I was one of two rebels who did not continue immediately to college, secretarial school, or art study in Europe. The other, Rosemary, had already begun her notable career as unwed mother, the valiant kind who keeps the child rather than aborting it or plastic wrapping it under her dorm bed. I just got a letter from her. She lives on welfare and some surreptitious waitress work in Manhattan rather than accept money and comments from her parents. She claims she still waits for Ted to finish some Army course and marry her. Maybe they'll visit me here in Boston and see my new life.

My brother, Ian, who never did learn to schedule himself to either Nedda's or my mother's liking, is nearly eight years old, a devotee of fiberglass guns and tv monster movies. His favorite food is pickles. Without being critical, I doubt he fulfills my father's dream for an intellectual genius who will discourse on philosophy and history in a few years. A couple months ago, he nearly flunked arithmetic and spelling. With Cs in math and behavior, he seems to follow my pattern although he manages to avoid the scandalous messes I attracted. That is, he's never swallowed buttons, shoplifted, broken an arm, or hired himself out to work.

Since he's a boy, he easily loses himself in airplane or naval model-building, thus avoiding my mother's complaints and illnesses that have returned with the full force I knew. Often when I glue some tricky balsa or plastic piece for him, I envy his self-absorption. I know he fares better in that house than I did, for he already imitates my father's pose of obliviousness. Nor does my mother expect Ian as her confidant, the role which defeated me.

As soon as I graduated, I lit out for Boston because I'd heard it had stacks of young people living more cheaply than in New York. After a typing test I landed a job as receptionist at the very employment agency I'd first visited. When my father visited and saw my rented room in Roxbury, he declared the whole situation had "no future" and I should apply to college and acquire some future immediately. To pacify him, I did enroll for one semester of English and accounting at Boston University. Yet my hunger to see the world, test myself against it, before settling into anything as overstructured as college, marriage (to whom-ever), or "career" remains eagerly alive.

For the future planning part of his advice, I quit the employment agency and transferred my efforts into a job with a group of three busi-ness women, who sought a younger staff member. Their brochure had passed my desk at the agency. They organize job counseling and other courses, help, and advice for women returning to work or changing lifestyles. I handle practical details of setting up workshops, prelim-inary contacting of speakers, hotel arrangements, typing records, rent-ing film strips, meeting applicants, especially young ones, answering letters between weekend or evening seminars.

The trio of women who united in this organization are energetic and loyal. I can't imagine working anywhere else, at least for now. Rona was a dancer and actress who tired of starving while awaiting the "right part" (any part, I guess) in Manhattan. Short and vivacious, she has red hair like mine, which always comforts me at meetings. Her capital quality is an even temper that can take criticism and even cause some-thing good to flow from it.

Bobbie, the only one of us currently married, has a businessman husband who advises us and seems unthreatened at either Bobbie's association with us or at women's acquiring business skills (not to be equated with typing). His latest suggestion is adding a Women in Management course to our seminars as soon as we locate another teacher for it.

Vera Lynne describes herself as having changed her college field five times before she graduated with "a schizophrenic major in English, law, business, psychology, and dating practices of the Midwest." Peo-ple, including me, who remain fearful of that momentous task—choosing one's lifegoals—enjoy Vera Lynne. Besides majoring in college, she wears tailored clothes and has worked in real estate. She kids me about buying a house in Endfield, "for your golden years." "I nearly died their during my leaden ones," I try to joke, "but how about organizing a seminar there?"

I'm half-serious as I fantasize a Women's Enterprises seminar in Endfield with Eila and Jody as speakers. The fun of it energizes me. I no longer fear talking in a classroom group of women although micro-phones still unnerve me—trauma courtesy of that Endfield teach-in night. It's no doubt a veiled goal of mine to get reported into the *Endfield News* for something useful rather than a combination of juvenile delinquency, social deviance, and total collapse.

At other times I believe I must be mad to want to visit Endfield at all. I switch my aim to inviting Eila and Jody here to address our next group of twenty-five students.

Compared with me, of course, Rona, Bobbie, and Vera all possess scads of degrees in business administration, guidance counseling, psychology, and related impressive topics that sometimes make me feel a second-class citizen. Will I ever see the day when I don't wind up the juvenile on everybody's staff? However, both young and older women who take our courses consider me something of a prodigy when I do my specialty—my ten-minute talk on the rewards of owning or managing your own business, with the nursery as my personal witness. Besides my own ideas, I did wring a few from Eila and Jody by letter, which I rearranged into Money, Service, and Anecdote categories. I tell, for instance, how the nursery mailbox got bombed, and the culprits turned out to be? ''Two sons of the Chief of Police in a town not so far from here. So if you plan to go into business, make sure it's a community where law and order don't get outwitted by the sons of law and order.'' People like this joke; I wish it were funny.

Not the least of our attractions is organizing women into follow-up teams to help them attain the goals they've defined for themselves.

I'm attracted to some of the women, as I am to Russ. And one night at a college party before I joined Women's Enterprises, Anna and I made love. It was sweet and tender but, as with Russ, when she leaves me, I'm not sure how I feel. Mostly I need space and time, since Endfield was so overdetermined in these matters. Why leap when I'm still learning to walk?

40

Early last week a surprise summer letter from Eila arrived. Usually she writes in fall or January when business is slower. Flashes of memory brought by her blue carnation stationery made my heart yearn, although after that last day at the nursery with Nedda, I'd hated how easily Jody and Eila appeared to give me up. Jody's speech praising me to Nedda was all I had for weeks until I wrote a complaint letter. Paradoxically my mother was the only one who actively resisted my departure for school, I admit.

Anyway, here's Eila's letter:

August 15

Dear Tinker,

Every time the holidays, especially Memorial Day and July 4th!, roll around, Jody and I want to say hello or come see how you're doing. But spring is spring, hard to get away. We know that without the events you set in motion, we'd have gotten run out of town on a rail. Jody adds, "Tarred and feathered, too," but you know how she exaggerates. Once in a while we overhear a snide remark, but the community assault that produced all those newspaper letters is over—we hope forever. We have more tourist business now, too.

So may we make you an offer? Jody and I still fight about tax returns and expenditures, but *we have a job opening*. Naturally we wanted to give you first chance and choice. It's a partnership —not just a job—with a share of the profits (now that we've built them up again). It's the opportunity to manage the branch store we're opening before Christmas at the new shopping mall outside Endfield. Of course, we'd help you with everything.

Do you trust us?

It's retail sales of plants, corsages, arrangements, terrariums, and other items we'd continue to make up here in the greenhouses. We've just signed a three-year lease on a corner shop at the mall.

Please let us know by August 25 whether you are interested. So . . . partner? May I call you that? Jody complains it sounds like a tv Western. She still calls you "kid" now and then, but I promise to make her stop.

We'd enjoy being and working with you again.

> With love,
> Eila

By the time I hit the last paragraph of this letter, I began to cry, smearing Eila's strong black ink. I dropped the pages onto my bureau. After six tries over the next three hours, I finally managed this reply, not trusting myself to phone.

Dear Eila and Jody,

Hey, you're doing great! A branch yet. I'm impressed. I still work here with Women's Enterprises. As you know, we run something between an employment agency and a women's job skills retraining program. It's a new idea and most exciting. May I inform them about your opening? Let *our* fantastic staff locate the perfect new employee for *your* fantastic staff!

Seriously, I don't know how to say this, but I can't accept your offer. . . . *[If only you'd made it when I was twelve and dying. Mentally I scrapped that and began the sentence over:]* If only you'd made it earlier, I might have accepted. Of course, I want to join you but can't see how, six houses from "home," I'd ever manage a life of my own. You know how those people always wasted me with their gossip, illnesses, and interference. . . . I know I could live outside town, but that's still too close.

[What next? For the sequel was even harder to write.] I loved both of you knowing, as I still do, that you love each other. Can you see how this always forced me to the fringes of whatever you had left. . . *[Scratch those final four words]* . . . . What you could offer . . . after meeting each other's needs plus work needs? If I returned, Endfield would have nobody there for me and I very

much need right now to make my own way here.

About Endfield: Maybe you'd like to read something from my college English class written by a Russian author:

> *You must know that there is nothing higher and stronger and more wholesome and good for life than some memory, especially a memory of childhood. People talk to you a good deal about your education, but some good, sacred memory, preserved from childhood, is perhaps the best education. If a man carries many such memories with him into life, he is safe to the end of his days, and if one has only one good memory left in one's heart, even that may some time be the means of saving us.*

Well, you both are my "good memory," but even so—*[("We need you and appreciate you, Tinker, but"—always the "but"!) Scrapping the "but even so," I continued:]* as someday my family may be.

Perhaps as my father predicts, I'll fail if I don't graduate from college, but everybody attends college, and some fail there as well. At least if I mess up some problem or other, I'll make my own mistakes, not somebody else's. . . .

I just checked with Rona. We have a client named Diane Barker with a B.A. in something useful. She's free and can be just the woman you need. I enclose her resume. Wanna meet her? Please come some weekend and see how we operate. Rona and I have rented a lake cottage here for the summer. My rooming house in Roxbury burned down. I'll be living with Rona in the fall.

With much love,
Tinker

Dear Tinker,

Can do. Send travel info. See you soon. How's the weekend September 15–16?

Love,
Jody
Eila

P.S. I understand.

Did Eila "understand" also? Or just Jody?

Eila had added her signature plus something else that fell into my hands as I opened the envelope tonight. White discs, about an inch wide. At first I thought they were sea shells. Had Jody expanded in an unlikely direction—gifty trinkets?

As I fingered their satiny, opaque surfaces, Bridgewater's night of velvet and scent rushed back. Neither plastic nor shell, they were— they must be—pods with seeds from one of Eila's Chinese Honesty plants. She must have coaxed it to flower early this year.

Carole Spearin McCauley has written eight books. Some of her recent titles are **Computers and Creativity, Pregnancy After 35, Surviving Breast Cancer,** and **Happenthing In Travel On,** a frontier adventure novel of a women's commune. **The Honesty Tree** is her second novel.

Ms. McCauley's short work has appeared in more than 100 magazines, newspapers, or anthologies, including **Omni, Self, National Catholic Reporter, Gaysweek, Feminist Art Journal, Writer's Digest, Mystery Time, Personal Romances,** and **The New Fiction: Interviews with Innovative American Writers** (University of Illinois Press). Five of her short stories have won prizes in international contests, including Writers of the Future.

For five years Ms. McCauley was a coordinator of the Woman's Salon, a New York area writers' and artists' group. Currently she resides in Connecticut.